Other Titles By

Monique Lamont

DOUBLE TAKE

HEALING HEARTS

FREEDOM'S QUEST
(MERLICIOUS TALES ANTHOLOGY)

MERGER FOR LIFE

Fire and Desire

Monique Lamont

Parker Publishing, LLC

Noire Passion is an imprint of Parker Publishing, LLC.

Copyright © 2007 by Monique Lamont

Published by Parker Publishing, LLC
12523 Limonite Avenue, Suite #440-438
Mira Loma, California 91752
www.parker-publishing.com

ISBN 978-1-60043-015-2

First Edition

Manufactured in the United States of America

Dedication

To my husband and daughter, I thank you both for your love and patience. For every time we were headed somewhere and I said, "I'll be ready in a minute" and you waited...hours. I love you both with all my heart.

Acknowledgements

To my family, thanks for your support and understanding every time I brought a laptop to family functions. To my mini fan club La-Tonya, Julinda, Jackie, Pascha, Jeannie and Germany Ladies. To Andrea, Cheryl, Denise and Jasmine, a critique team who's straight forward and honest, as well as friends. You all are the best. Mark and the other men who reserve our table in a busy Starbucks every Tuesday night when we write, Cheers!

Lastly, but never least, Ms. B. Jenkins who told me, "Don't worry, it will all work out" and D. K-B., for your confidence.

Prologue

Five years since the "accident" and his life changed. Trevor still couldn't release the anger he'd harbored for so many years. Carrying it around with him became as natural as the air he breathed. Over the years, he learned that Manning men got everything handed to them on a silver platter, never struggling for anything. They had the world eating out of their hands because of a smile that could calm babies and woo women—never appearing to get what they so often deserved.

The Mannings of the world could ruin the lives of other people with a smile and an apology. They never knew what it was like to lose something and never fully get it back.

Trevor's thoughts rambled on, and sweat rolled into his eyes as he brutally attacked his punching bag. He did his best to wipe away the image of Manning from his mind. Just like he had done many times before, he began to repeat his mantra of five years, *One day, Christopher "Golden Boy" Manning, you'll lose something that you hold dear...I'll see to it personally.*

What would you do if you got caught in the
revenge you set for someone else?

One

The sounds of running water woke Tiffany. Her world was spinning, and she hadn't even opened her eyes yet. The emptiness of her stomach cramped with pain, along with the subtle aches in various places on her body. Her mouth was filmy and dry, as if she had been eating a mixture of cheese and cotton all night.

She dragged her body to a seated position, placed her head in her hands and took a few calming breaths before opening her eyes.

Excruciating minutes passed before the topsy-turvy room righted itself enough for her to look around. Her unfocused gaze traveled the room. A sinking feeling came over her. Things weren't quite right. Instead of being at the townhouse with her friends, she was in bed at a hotel. Her clothing was scattered in multiple places on the floor, leading her to believe she had been drunk when she'd undressed.

The warmth of the starched sheets against her skin made her very aware that her underclothing had met the same fate.

Tiffany leaned back against the headboard with a groan of disgust. Because she was so focused on trying to figure out how she'd gotten there, she didn't hear the shower turn off or the bathroom door open.

"Good morning, sunshine," came a silky baritone voice.

The voice caused heat to radiate up her spine. Tiffany lifted her head slowly, not wanting to believe her ears nor allow the dizziness to attack her again.

While dealing with the shock of her situation, the sight of the male standing in the bathroom doorway was undeniable. He was at least six-two with broad shoulders and skin the color of chocolate satin, which looked smooth and inviting. He stood leaning against the doorframe, his body still glistening from his shower. The only form of modesty he showed was the towel loosely tied and riding low on his hips. Tiffany knew he was the guy from the party.

The desire to kiss his chest assailed her. A quick deep breath helped to clear her mind. *Man, what is coming over me?*

Her gaze returned to the sex symbol now lounged against the bathroom door. He looked different without his mask. Especially to anyone who didn't know he had light brown eyes instead of the dark brown contacts he'd worn during the performance.

Hmm, perfect fit, his words echoed in her mind. Feeling her nipples tighten at the memory of the day before, she pulled the sheet to her chin and held it firmly to cover the evidence of her arousal. "What are you doing here?" she inquired.

He lifted his eyebrow.

Tiffany realized it was a stupid question. Since she never remembered booking a room, most likely she was the outsider.

"Let me rephrase that…Why am *I* here?"

"Where else would you be?"

Tiffany always hated when people answered a question with a question. Being hung over didn't make it any more likable. "I was supposed to be with my friends in Las Vegas."

"Well, one out of two isn't bad," he said in a voice that brought back vague memories of the previous evening, causing her pulse to accelerate.

"I'm probably going to regret asking this…but what happened last night?" Finding it hard to make eye contact, Tiffany stared down at her hands.

"You don't remember…*anything*?" The skepticism was evident in his voice.

Tiffany gazed toward him. "Nothing after midnight," she confessed. Glancing at her clothes again, she mumbled, "Can pretty much guess some of it…"

"Hmm…you think?" was all he said.

"It's not rocket science," Tiffany informed him. The best defense mechanism—sarcasm.

Tiffany had had enough. She needed to get out of *this* room. She had a plane to catch that evening, and she wanted to put all of the ugliness of the night before behind her. It took three attempts before she could negotiate her body off the bed without falling over, while keeping the sheet wrapped around her. Seated on the edge of the bed, something caught her eye on the nightstand. She turned and saw the bold writing across the top. *Marriage Certificate.*

One hand clutched the sheet behind her while she reached for the paper with the other hand and read the names across the bottom, just above the signature of the minister of Eternal Bliss Wedding Chapel.

She snapped her head around to face the person she could only assume was the name and signature below hers—Trevor Lewis. "Tell me this is some kind of joke." Anger catapulted through her body. It had been a long night, and she felt disgusted with herself. She was not in the mood for any more foolishness.

He looked straight into her eyes. "It's no joke."

Tiffany couldn't stop the tremor of rage that shook her hand. Throwing the paper down, she began to gather her clothes from the floor as if someone had just yelled fire.

When she located everything but her underwear, she held the bundle to her chest and headed toward the bathroom.

She stopped in front of Trevor, who was still blocking the door. Using the voice she used to put reporters in their place and keep them at bay, she bit out, "Move."

"It isn't necessary for you to dress in the bathroom." A lopsided smile adorned his lips.

Tiffany couldn't miss the slow roaming of his eyes down her body and the heat that radiated from his body as they stood in close proximity.

"Well, I think it is *very* necessary, *Trevor.*"

The calm shrug of his shoulders as he sauntered out of the way annoyed Tiffany.

She waited for him to clear the path, then rushed into the bathroom and stopped cold as she realized that her toga had slid off her body. She closed the door, but not before she caught a glimpse of Trevor with one corner of the sheet in his grasp and a dimple winking in his cheek, confirming he had gotten a full view of her backside.

"Even better than I imagined," she heard the echo of his voice rumble through the door.

Once inside, she immediately moved to the toilet and dropped to her knees with remorse over her alcohol consumption the night before. It was several minutes of dry heaves before she was able to get up. Sheer alarm apprehended her when she noticed her reflection in the mirror above the sink. Her hair was in disarray. Her eyes were blood shot and puffy. The biggest shocker was her nipples, which were swollen, red and tender to the touch. Only one explanation came to her mind for their state—thoroughly suckled.

Tiffany raised her hands to them. She was amazed when her breasts responded by puckering to pebbled points. She quickly dropped her hands. Operating on automatic, she dressed, refusing to ponder what had happened the previous night. After she combed her hair in a bun and splashed cold water on her face, she felt controlled enough to exit the bathroom.

She was relieved to see that Trevor was dressed. She ignored the small voice of disappointment inside of her at seeing his body clothed.

She figured him to be a reasonable man, so she decided to start with logic and a confident smile. "Listen, I don't know exactly what happened last night. A big part of me never wants to know. Unfortunately, we have to address one of the issues that can't be allowed to linger. But there's an easy solution to it."

Trevor sat on the edge of the bed with his elbows on the top of his knees. "What's that?"

"Well, evidently…" Tiffany tried not to look at the evidence of the rumpled bed, "an annulment is out of the question. We're just going to have to get a quickie divorce. It's Las Vegas. As easily as a wedding can be done, it can be undone."

"Only one problem with that. It's Sunday."

Tiffany hadn't thought about that. Even cereal-box license law offices in "Sin-City" had to take a day off. "Then you can stay here for a few days…I'll pay for the room through the week. Tomorrow you can go down to one of those pop-up courthouses they have for situations like this and get the form. Then FedEx it to me, and I'll sign it uncontested. Overnight it back, and we can be done with it," Tiffany finished, broadening her confident smile, praying he didn't realize it was for bravado's sake.

"Listen, I don't have time to kill sitting on my butt in some Godforsaken city waiting to do your bidding."

Her smile dropped, and her anger returned, evident in the trembling of her voice. "Look, I can pay you, if that's what's bothering you." Looking around until she found her small black Coach clutch, she picked it up and opened it. "How many shows do you normally do in a week?" She whipped out her checkbook, pen poised.

Tiffany could have sworn she heard a growl as he stood up, taking the few steps to bring them eye-to-eye. *He's even sexy when he's angry.*

"I'm not for sale."

Tiffany's nerves jumped with his nearness. For the first time that morning, she looked into his eyes and felt a little trepidation. *Oh my God. I would be the one to find myself married to a stripper with principles.*

Fear was not something she was used to feeling. "Maybe you're taking this the wrong way. I mean no offense, but you need to understand something…I'm Tiffany Hatcher."

"So?"

"*The* Tiffany Hatcher. I don't know if you follow politics in your line of work, but I'm the governor's daughter."

"Frankly, in my line of work, I wouldn't care if you were the Queen of Sheba. I'm not staying." His tone rose an octave.

"And *I can't* be married to a stripper." Her own pitch elevated to a screeching tone.

They both stood toe-to-toe, almost breathing in each other's breath.

"Too late." He punched out through clinched teeth.

"So, you'd stay married to someone you don't love because it isn't convenient for you?" Tiffany threw her hands up in frustration.

"You could always change your plans," he countered.

"Believe me, if I could, I would."

"Things probably are different in *your class*, but in mine, wedding vows are something you honor for life."

"What vows, we were drunk…God only knows if we even made any."

"That's right, but He's the only one who counts. Well, you do what you have to do," He said softly.

"Fine!" She turned to walk out of the hotel room.

"Tiffany."

She stopped her progress toward the door upon hearing her name. A glimmer of hope bubbled in her heart that maybe he'd changed his mind.

When she turned and saw what he held in his hand, the glimmer died.

"You don't want to forget these. If you got into an accident, you may have to explain how you lost them."

Marching over to him, she grabbed her panties out of his hand and shoved them in her purse. "It wouldn't be any worse than having to explain being married to you, if anyone ever found out."

She turned and stormed out of the room.

§

Trevor could have kicked himself a dozen times. *What have I gotten myself into?* He repeated the same question to himself after Tiffany left, as he began gathering up his few meager belongings into the overnight bag he'd brought with him when he flew in yesterday afternoon. His plane was due to leave in two hours, and he needed to get to the airport.

The last thing he grabbed before leaving out of the room was the piece of paper binding him to Tiffany Hatcher. *Leggy, sexy, caramel-brown skinned Tiffany Hatcher.*

He checked out of the casino hotel and took a taxi to the airport.

Once seated in the waiting area with forty-five minutes to spare, he allowed himself to think about the past week—back to when the plan started.

Leslie, his aunt and the owner of Elite Entertainment, had called him at home last weekend in dire need of a dancer. His aunt hadn't called him in over five years about doing a job for her, not since he'd told her he was focusing on his business and wouldn't be available to help her in that capacity any longer. *The* Tiffany Hatcher, the governor's daughter and party planner extraordinaire, had just called her about a bachelorette party. He had originally thought maybe it was her own and that she and Manning had decided to do a small secret wedding with family. But his aunt assured him it was for someone else.

Aunt Leslie was his favorite. They dined at least once a month with each other. Her business had been a tremendous help to him while he was in college. Dancing for her during holidays and summers had allowed him to pay the twenty-five percent of his Ivy League college tuition that his scholarship hadn't covered.

His aunt told him that providing the entertainment for a party thrown by Miss Hatcher was a definite opening for her business into another realm of the upper class. All of her other male dancers were already obligated over the weekend, so none of them would be able to perform.

He originally thought about turning her down, not wanting to jeopardize the contract he was bidding for until he discovered the party would not be held at the governor's family home in Northern Virginia nor the Governor's Mansion in Richmond, but in Las Vegas—over 2,400 miles away.

This was a golden opportunity to get even with Manning for what he had done to him years ago. He knew he would never be able to hurt Manning like he'd been hurt, but he figured he could at least wound Manning's pride. For men like Manning, sometimes that was the best place you could attack them.

He agreed, and within days, his plan was moving into action. When he met Tiffany Hatcher at the door of the town house, the first thing that struck him was her smile. Her face lit up in a way that the news camera's lens couldn't capture. As she gave him a tour, she was warm and friendly, but left no doubt a stripper party was not her type of entertainment. She told him it was something she did per her friend's request. In no way did she want to be involved in his act.

That was okay with him because the striptease was just how he planned to set the stage. He'd met women like Tiffany before, women who appeared to keep themselves aloof during the party, but after the show, they were the main ones trying to get him in their beds—a big no-no in his aunt's company. The reputation of her business was important to her.

He was willing to risk his aunt's wrath to get back at Manning. This was the last job.

"United Airlines flight number A320 from Las Vegas non-stop to Dulles International is now boarding."

The efficient voice of the airline's female ticket agent crackled across the overhead speaker and broke into Trevor's thoughts. He pulled out his first class ticket from the side pocket of his laptop case and got in line. He flowed with the line until he was able to hand the agent his pass, walked down the jet-bridge, nodded toward the flight attendant, located his seat on the plane, then stowed his laptop case and small overnight bag in the compartment above.

Snapping his seatbelt, his thoughts returned to the prior day's events. Everything had been going well until he'd come face to face with Tiffany Hatcher in the kitchen. He hadn't expected the strong attraction between them. He'd thought revenge was something he could do, and then walk away.

He remembered walking into the kitchen to retrieve the bowl of ice Tiffany was supposed to have prepared for his last act. He had stopped instantly at seeing her.

Tiffany stood in silence at the window, draining a glass of water as if it were a gift from God. Her eyes closed as she sipped the cool, clear liquid.

She was in rapture. As if she were being touched in deep and intimate places only a lover would know.

He remembered instantly yearning to be that lover, if only for a moment. Selfishly, he wanted to be the one to put that look on her face. That had been his goal that night…to set the stage, then make love to Tiffany Hatcher before the evening was through.

One of her friends had given him the perfect opportunity to fulfill his plan with Tiffany when she asked him to stay and party with them, but he couldn't do it. He had been fooling himself to think he could be cruel and heartless enough to sleep with a woman just to get back at Manning. He was not into casual sex. Sex was too intimate and intimacy was personal, so he'd left and returned to the casino hotel.

The squeak and rattle of the food cart in the coach section of the plane pulled him from his thoughts.

"Hello, Mr. Lewis, would you like to hear the meal choices?" The first-class attendant stood next to his leather captain-style seat with a bright smile.

Trevor felt nauseated. His queasy stomach reminded him how disgusted he had been with himself. "No, thank you. Just a ginger ale no ice, please."

"No problem, sir." She walked away, disappeared around the corner of the mini kitchen and returned with a tumbler glass of bubbling soda, matching her personality. "Here you go, sir. Please let me know if you'll need anything else."

Trevor gave her a nod of confirmation.

His mind drifted once again. Last night he'd arrived back at the hotel after his performance, showered, got dressed and went down to the casino. It was not in his nature to gamble or drink, but he'd given in to the urge and placed a few nickels into a slot machine. Trying to erase not only the disappointment he felt toward himself, but also attempting to drown away the realization that he would probably never get back at Manning. He had realized that, with all of his strategic planning, his conscience was not warped enough to play on his nemesis's level.

After he had finished his fifth drink and debated on whether he wanted a sixth, Tiffany came around the corner with her friends. They all were extremely drunk. He knew none of them recognized him, nor would they without his half mask.

He'd sat back and watched them in action. Tiffany sat next to him and began to chat and flirt with him. She became the epitome of a rambling drunk. She told him how constricted her life was and how, at times, she just wanted to be Tiffany without all of the responsibilities of being a governor's daughter. She desired the freedom to marry anyone she wanted without having to worry about what others thought. Everyone expected her to marry Christopher Manning, but marrying Christopher hadn't even made the last item on her "to do" list.

With that, a new plan had formed in his pickled brain—his opportunity had come back around even better than he had dreamed.

Sitting on the plane, it amazed him that, while drunk, an idea always appeared to be the most brilliant.

What better way to get back at Manning than to marry the girl he wanted before he had a chance. Acting on his drunken thought, he'd asked Tiffany to marry him right there by the nickel slot machines.

She'd thought about it for a minute, then turned to him with a big smile that lit up her alcohol-glazed eyes and said, "Why not?"

She'd found one of her friends and told her she would see her in the morning. She was going to get married.

Her friend, who was just as drunk as she was, had looked him over, laughed and said, "Whatever you say, Tiffy."

Then they'd left and stopped at the first chapel of love they had come upon. He hadn't even remembered the name of the place until he'd looked at the certificate while Tiffany dressed that morning. All of it had seemed like a dream when he awoke.

He barely remembered the quick kiss he had given her at the chapel, and he had a foggy memory of them arriving back at his hotel room. He vaguely recalled Tiffany giving *him* a striptease and his reaction to her body. He had a vivid recollection of being rock hard. Even now, his penis swelled in his pants with the thought.

The only thing that was clear to him was the fact he had stuck to his resolve not to have sex with her. He had touched, fondled, nibbled and played with her until she'd passed out on top of him. He had found it very difficult to keep them from taking the next step during those heated moments. He'd never professed that he was a monk, but after last night, he would probably have enough good deed points to qualify for his own robe.

No sex. No kissing. He had stuck to his personal rule. Even with Tiffany's lips looking appealing and full. She had a mouth made to kiss.

Nevertheless, kissing was personal and intimate. It was something he couldn't give without investing his heart.

In an attempt to ease the pressure in his jeans caused by his straining manhood, Trevor fidgeted in his seat.

That morning when he'd awakened and watched her while she slept, he had tossed around his options to the situation. Deciding that the only way to see his actions through and have the ultimate revenge was to stay married to Tiffany, just for a little while.

Just long enough for her to break the news to Manning. He knew there was a possibility of Manning coming after him, but as a soon to be congressman elect, there was only so much he could do without tarnishing his own reputation. The thought of Manning's character in question brought a smile to his lips.

However, it was what he didn't want to happen to Tiffany, a stained reputation. That's why he left it completely within her power to get an annulment on the grounds of an unconsummated marriage. He contemplated telling her this morning until he noticed the debased look in her eyes as she looked at the bed.

She seemed appalled at the thought of sleeping with someone in his class. Trevor thought she should have felt grateful. He'd given her an out to the possible marriage with Manning. In her own words *marrying Christopher hadn't even made the last item on her "to do" list.* He quickly put the thoughts aside and stuck to his decision.

Two

Tiffany was glad about the four and a half-hour flight back to the East Coast because she planned to put on her headphones and sleep the entire way. She and five friends sat in first class. Tiffany was exhausted, physically and emotionally. Josephine didn't say anything to her about last night when she entered their room. Josephine just wished her good morning, then walked out, leaving Tiffany to her own musing.

Tiffany didn't understand how she'd allowed herself to do three things she had never done before with little regard for propriety.

She hadn't even thought about marriage sober, even with the media and Christopher both hounding her. She never drank more than one or two glasses of Champagne or wine at any time. And the third…

As she reclined back in her seat, she knew why she had gone way beyond that limit. She'd tried to drink until she forgot what had taken place at the party—her first mistake.

Tiffany remembered standing on the outer fringes of her zealous group of friends, her body on fire as she watched the dancer. He had called himself The Fireman…*dressed in a black and yellow striped assault coat and pants, black boots, gloves and waving a bright yellow Pelican flashlight suggestively in his hand. His costume wouldn't have been complete without the red helmet with reflective patches and it's large black shield on the front that read* Engine Co. 69.

Her friends were in a frenzy as soon as he removed his first piece of clothing, the coat. Revealing his bare chest and red suspenders. The crescendo of screams in the house roared to an almost ear piercing level, by the time he teased and taunted them. He stood in front of one of her friends with the flashlight hovering before his crotch. He repeatedly prompted her to take it as he flicked it off and on, finally surrendering it to her. Then he began tossing his gloves out one at a time. Placing his helmet on top of another woman's head, revealing the smooth chocolate skin of his bald-head as he stepped back to the center of the room.

After a few more insinuating gyrations, he removed his assault pants with a snap, leaving himself in nothing but a mask, suspenders, boots and a leather bikini. She could hear moans and sighs slipping past the lips of her friends.

She was having a hard time stifling her own reactions. Thoughts of having his strong arms lifting her, pulling her tight against his chest as he carried her out of a flaming building made her burn with desire. Desire to know what it felt like to be pressed against the scorching heat of his body and—

Her fantasy was interrupted as her friend Karen yelled out, "He can drive his fire truck down my lane anytime."

The other women around the room hooted and hollered; Tiffany exhaled.

From where she stood, she had a full frontal view of him. The Fireman was magnificent, sculpted, every firm ridge and plain vivid and evident. God must have molded him by hand incredibly slow. The skin on his pecks seemed so tight that if his nipples became erect, the flesh around it would beg for mercy. With her twenty-twenty vision, she couldn't spot a single imperfection, except for the scar on the side of his knee.

At one point in the show, he'd filled the bride-to-be's hands with baby oil and told her to rub it across his chest. Diane didn't hesitate a moment before leaping out of her honored chair in the center of the room.

"Michelangelo had to be gay," Diane said as she rubbed his chest, "because the excitement I'm feeling would inspire someone to want to chisel a sculpture like David."

The atmosphere in the room vibrated with the envious laughter of the other ladies.

He pried Diane's hands off him. One of her friends yelled, "Now Diane, what would Todd think about your hands being all over that sexy male specimen?"

With a coy smile, Diane let go and returned to her seat.

He looked at Tiffany with cool black eyes and winked—his signal for her start the music.

Blaring music thumped through the speakers as he danced around Diane, contorting his entire body into one enticing move after another. The music continued to play with punctuated background vocals from a trio of friends. They seemed to fall in sync to the beat.

"Can he work it or can he work it!" Karen wiggled as a shiver ran down her spine.

Sonya sighed, "Oh my…" as if she couldn't quite think of the words to describe what she saw.

"Thank goodness life is a box of chocolates," Josephine shouted. "And I'm glad they come in king size treats."

At one point in the song, as he traveled around the ladies, Tiffany thought he would pass her. Instead, he stopped in front of her. His eyes issued a challenge, daring her to say something or bolt. Earlier when he'd arrived at the townhouse, she had informed him that she would handle anything he needed, but she was only there to make sure things went smoothly, not to be entertained by him.

As he stood before her, she couldn't move. Her feet felt as if they had been nailed to the floor.

He walked closer to her, reached out and placed his hands on both sides of her waist, then pulled her body into his until she was flush against him. His hands felt like fire, even through her clothes.

She looked down at his torso. The baby oil Diane had liberally bathed on him made the beads of sweat appear to glisten in the soft glow of the lights. She raised her head to peer into his eyes, wondering if he could feel her heart racing against his chest. A sly smile crossed his lips, letting her know he did.

He leaned forward until she could feel her breasts crushed against his upper body. He brought his lips just barely in contact with the shell of her ear, allowing the seductive heat of his hot breath to send a frisson down her spine as he spoke furtively, "Hmm…a perfect fit."

He left no doubt to his meaning as he snuggled his gloved organ between her thighs against her sex.

She had no time to stop the quick intake of air that rushed into her chest.

His dark eyes twinkled with mischief as he quickly let her go, then continued to the other ladies in attendance.

She wasted no time in her escape.

Exiting out of the side door, she stood on the porch, inhaling gulps of air from the cool night. Her ears still rumbled from the husky sound of his voice.

Through the open doors, she watched him entertain the other ladies. With her limited knowledge of his profession, she knew it was all just an act for him. It was his job to make women feel desired and sexually charged. He was very good at it.

She took a few more cleansing breaths, then returned to the living room just in time to see him heading toward her friend Charmagne, who sat as quiet as a mouse in a corner chair of the room.

Just as he had done before with Diane, he poured a generous amount of oil into her palm.

Tiffany watched as Charmagne plastered a fake smile on her face in an attempt to hide her nervousness. But everyone in the room, except the magnificent specimen of manhood, knew Charmagne was extremely shy; she had been that way ever since college. Tiffany was surprised her shaking hands didn't spill the baby oil all over the carpet.

"You want me to put this on your-r-r chest-t-t," Charmagne stammered.

"No." He used a rumbling timbre this time, as he turned and gave her his back, seeming to take pity on the poor girl.

The sigh that came through Charmagne's parted lips sounded like the whistle from a boiling teapot. She rubbed the oil into both of her hands.

"Here." He accentuated the words with a snap as he removed the fabric from around his waist, which at one time appeared to be the back to his bikinis. Leaving nothing but two firm cheeks separated by the thin black leather material of his thong. Final evidence of what the suspenders were connected to.

A unified gasp echoed in the room.

Fire and Desire

From her angle, Tiffany could see the two chocolate globes, and if she leaned the other way just enough, she would be able to see what held him in front.

She couldn't deny she was tempted. She took a step to the right and leaned over just enough to catch an eye full. Her breath caught in her throat as she observed the tight piece of leather that held the Fireman's genitals in its grasp. The fit of the material didn't leave much to the imagination.

She refused to believe the size of his sex her eyes observed. It was common knowledge, most underwear models stuffed for ads. No doubt, the dancer did, too.

He waited patiently for Charmagne to get up the nerve to massage the baby oil on his lower extremity.

Karen sat beside Charmagne. She must've lost her patience because she grabbed both of the shy friend's hands and placed them soundly on the man's rear end.

Charmagne swallowed noticeably and gingerly applied the oil in a circular motion. When she finally began to relax and smile, he flexed his buttock muscles and made them jiggle in Charmagne's hands. Her eyes and mouth rounded into perfect circles of shock.

As the music faded away, so did Charmagne in a dead faint, landing in Sonya's lap. He again winked at her to stop the tape, and then he exited the room to prepare for his last set.

She turned on some music while her friends snacked and mingled, conversing about the stripper's abilities. She needed something to drink. Something ice-cold.

She walked through the living room across the foyer, passed the dining room and the breakfast nook, to reach the kitchen. Today was one day she wished the kitchen wasn't located on the other side of the house. She resisted the urge to run.

Once she arrived in the kitchen, she immediately drained her first glass of ice water as if she had been stuck in the Sahara Desert for a month. She refilled it and sipped.

20

Since the moment she met him at the door and gave him a tour of the rooms he would be using, she had been experiencing tingling sensations all over her body. He had been dressed in a suit tailored to fit his body, and his mask covered over half of his face. Nothing showed but his haunting eyes and a set of lips women paid to have. There were no strings attached to the face piece, so she assumed it had to be stuck to his face somehow.

By the time he had finished stripping, her pulse rate had hit the ceiling. After the moment he'd pressed his body to hers, her temperature had risen to a fevered pitch. Breathing had stopped being a necessity when he removed the small piece of material over his buttocks.

The ice water cooled her throat, and she actually felt her body heat simmer down as she gazed out the window over the sink. Now grateful for the distance between the kitchen and the living room that allowed her the quiet solitude she needed to bring her nerves back under control.

She turned away from the window to head back to the living room and froze.

He stood two feet away from her, leaning nonchalantly against the island in the center of the kitchen. Now, he was dressed as The Dark Knight in black chaps, black leather underwear—another thong she presumed—with a matching vest, cape and the proverbial mask. She couldn't deny he made an appealing Fireman, but he was downright sexy to her as The Black Knight.

Just the sight of him caused her body to quiver.

"I'm sorry I startled you. I came to get some ice."

That voice again.

The sound of it brought to mind naked skin against silk sheets. Both textured and smooth—the kind of voice that came over the airways during late night radio for lovers. It made her want to close her eyes and moan.

Clearing her throat, she finally said, "The ice is in the freezer. I hope there's enough for your final act." *She hoped she did not sound like she was rambling.*

He made no move toward the refrigerator. "So what were you thinking about?"

She fought between wanting to drop the glass at his question and squeezing it until it shattered in her hand. How do you tell a man you were thinking about your body's reaction to him?

She opened her mouth, but no words came out.

"I know what you were thinking about." A self-assured smile decorated his mouth.

"Now, how would you know that? Are you a mind reader as well?" She was surprised she was able to keep her words on an even note.

"No."

How could one word be so seductive, *Tiffany questioned silently*.

"Maybe I was just hoping you were thinking about the same thing I can't get off my mind," he said, warm and inviting.

Mysterious eyes met curious ones.

"And what's that?" She felt breathless.

"How your body felt next to mine." His eyes issued a challenge to hers.

She opened her mouth to deny it.

His finger outlining her lips halted her words.

"God, you have the sexiest mouth." His finger traced her lips. "It blows my mind the things I can imagine you doing with it."

What? she thought.

As if he heard the question, he placed his lips next to her ear as before. "You taking me into it. I can almost feel it hot and wet around me."

At that moment, his words conjured up an image in her mind, and she could picture the same. It amazed her how she stood there allowing him to say such things to her. At any other time, she would've been insulted and pushed the guy away. Why not this man?

The plane glided past gray clouds of night, a small patch of darkness showed through the small portal window, shocking Tiffany out of her thoughts about yesterday's events. Taking a deep breath, she questioned herself again. *Why not?* She still had no answer. She pulled the shade down halfway, not wanting to see her reflection in the plexiglas.

Unable to stop her mind, she returned to her follies of the previous night. Nothing about that night had seemed real to her. Maybe because she couldn't see his face or know his name, but the passionate bites she witnessed in the mirror on her neck were real. Her mind flashed back to the kitchen scene...

His hands massaged her backside and held her firmly against his groin.

"So soft." Restrained passion was evident when he spoke.

She stifled a moan, took a deep breath in an attempt to clear the haze of lust, telling herself that she had to end it. She couldn't allow it to continue. With every intention of shoving him away, she placed her free hand against his chest. Too late, she realized it was the wrong move.

The feel of his hard body under her fingertips and the desire to rub him overwhelmed her. Her hands itched for the pleasure of knowing what he felt like.

"Touch me." He trembled with expectation.

Her breath caught as she struggled with warring needs.

What she needed to push her over the edge must have been evident because, with his words, she could deny herself no more. She explored the territory at her disposal, pressed her hand flat against his body.

He was solid as steel, smooth as butter and hot as a flame.

She heard her own sighs of enjoyment answered by his groans.

He became bolder with the confirmation. His hands stopped massaging her backside, moved down until they reached the hem of her skirt. His mouth continued to assault her neck, his fingers traced the edge of the material against her thigh, until they reached the inside. His hands trailed up past her thigh-highs to bare legs.

The little voice of reason inside her head hushed. Her legs, not waiting for a command, parted of their own accord, allowing him access.

He grabbed hold of her bottom once again, this time over her underwear.

"Tsk, tsk. A woman as sexy as you should be wearing thongs."

She never thought of herself as sexy before, but standing in his arms was doing a good job of changing her perception of herself.

"Take them off," he commanded.

She couldn't believe her ears. A practical stranger was asking her to take off her underwear. She couldn't do that—or could she?

Fire and Desire

Tiffany shook her head at the thought she'd had last night, jolting herself out of the memories. She'd been hesitant about removing her panties, but had easily put aside all of her personal convictions and married him. The perilous situation she now found herself in was ten times worse than if she'd followed her desires earlier in the night and removed her underwear.

Taking a loathsome breath, she returned to reminiscing about the erotic treat she couldn't resist.

No time to make a decision, there was a quick tug and the sound of something tearing. She felt cool air blowing past her heated most sensitive part, leaving no doubt of what he'd ripped.

It was going too far, she knew it was time for her to stop this little interlude. As the hand against him started to push him away, one of his fingers slid between her folds and circled the crest of her desire. It took only a moment before her hand on his chest began to flex and knead his flesh instead of pushing him away. Her eyelids closed. Her lips parted to permit her inhalation. A soft burst of cool air entered her mouth and danced across her mouth.

He growled, "Hmm, wet and stiff." The same finger persisted to explore. "You're so hot, I think you need cooling off."

Lost in a fog of pleasure. He sounded distant to her, and she couldn't comprehend his words.

There was a clinking sound, then the feel of something being inserted inside of her; it felt solid and cold—ice cold. The realization of what was happening made her eyes spring open widely.

"What are you…?"

She was unable to finish her words as he skillfully began to move the ice cube in and out of her woman's center—she'd shivered with need. She rested her hand and head on his shoulder fearing her legs would no longer support her. Her other hand, still held the glass of water and the remainder of ice—minus one—tightened around the cylinder as the tension began to mount in her body.

24

Tiffany's heart fluttered as she recalled how close they had come to being caught when Josephine called from somewhere on the other side of the kitchen door…

"Tiffany?"

She lifted her head up and looked into her mystery man's piercing eyes, with his constricted pupils—evidence he was as affected by watching her enjoyment.

The clicking of Josephine's shoes on the hardwood floor of the dinning room indicated she was within a few feet of the door.

As quick as a heartbeat, he gave her one last kiss on her neck and left with a flick of his cape. Gone in an instant the way he'd come.

"Hey, Tiff. Why are you still in here? The entertainment *should be beginning soon." Josephine burst into the kitchen.*

Tiffany clamped her thighs tightly together, feeling insecure because she was standing there with crotchless underwear.

"Water." Tiffany turned toward the counter and looked over at Josephine. She could still remember the strange look that had crossed her face.

As the fog lifted slowly from her mind, she realized how illiterate she sounded. She covered her error by tilting the glass up to her mouth for effect, giving herself a moment to put together at least an elementary sentence, she finally said, "I came to get some water."

"Well, come on, you don't want to miss the remainder of the show. No telling what he'll do next."

It was a good thing she hadn't been drinking any of the water for real; otherwise, she might have choked. She needed to get her friend out of the kitchen before she embarrassed herself anymore than she already had. "Jo, could you please take the ice out for me? It's in the freezer, and I'll be along in a moment."

"Sure thing."

It took forever for Josephine to remove the ice from the freezer and leave. As soon as the door swung shut behind her friend, Tiffany set the glass on the table and ran up the backstairs to her room. She prayed all the way that she wouldn't see the "Black Knight."

Fire and Desire

Tiffany remembered making a conscious decision to get drunk with her friends when they went out to the casinos. She was normally the one counted on to watch out for everyone else and be the designated driver. She was faithful, trustworthy and responsible. Tiffany Hatcher was guaranteed to do the right thing.

In one weekend, she'd put aside everything she believed in. Suddenly, she wanted to throw-up for the second time that morning.

The incident in the kitchen was something she had never done before, but she could blame that on the heat of the moment. She reassured herself, borrowing the excuse she'd heard her friends use on occasion. Even with the marriage she could at least say she'd made a drunken mistake in the wee hours.

The one thing she could not forgive herself for was the fact she had lost her virginity recklessly to a man she didn't even know—let alone love.

three

Six weeks later, Tiffany found herself, once again, in the middle of planning a wedding for a friend. Charmagne, the bride-to-be this time, was about to marry her college sweetheart, Charles, within a month.

"Now about the bachelorette party, what do you want to do, Charmagne? Go on a relaxing get away at a spa resort, the country club, a girl's night out..." Tiffany rattled off a few ideas.

"I want that fire fighting Black Knight," Charmagne said from the other end of the table.

Josephine, at her left, said, "You've got to be kidding."

"Nope," Charmagne responded.

"But you passed out at Diane's," added Sonya from her seat to the right. "I could just imagine what'd happened if you're center stage."

"I think it's a good idea. I'm with you, Charmagne, girl," said Karen, who sat between Josephine and Charmagne.

"Any reason to party and you jump right in, don't you, Karen?" Veronica commented from Charmagne's left.

"That's right, I sure do, Veronica. If you'd been at Diane's and seen that chocolate dream, you would, too." Karen reached for a napkin on the table and used it to fan herself.

"As long as there's something hanging between their legs, that's all you care about," Veronica said, her disgust clear.

"Well, what else is there, *Miss Thing*?" Karen looked across the table at Veronica.

Josephine stood up. "Ladies, please! We aren't getting anything accomplished. The wedding is in a few weeks, and I'm sure Tiffany didn't bring us here to argue about the stripper." She returned to her seat. "What are your thoughts on this, Tiffany?"

Still struck speechless by Charmagne's announcement, Tiffany had yet to render her opinion. Memories Tiffany still didn't want to face had been evoked. She also felt Josephine knew what had happened that weekend, even though her best friend never questioned her.

How do you tell your friends you don't want super sexy Fireman to come because you're married to him? She considered asking one of them if they knew how to get a quiet contested divorce.

"Tiff…?" Josephine's voice broke into her thoughts.

Looking down the table at Charmagne, Tiffany decided to ask the safer question, "Why do you want to have a stripper at your party?"

Charmagne glanced in Sonya's direction and said, "For one, I would like to redeem myself."

"We're all friends here, you don't have to do something that terrifies you to prove anything to us." Tiffany hoped to convince her against the idea.

"I know that, but there's another reason I want to do this," Charmagne said meekly.

"What other reason do you need, other than wanting to see a practically naked hunk of a man dancing for you?" Karen piped in.

"Sex, sex, sex…Is that all you all ever think about?" Veronica's face pinched with tension.

"Well, maybe if you gave it up sometimes, you'd talk about it too." Karen's chest puffed up, almost spilling her breasts out of her low cut blouse.

"You know what they say, 'those who talk about it all the time don't ever—'" Veronica began.

"I get plenty—" Karen interrupted.

"Can we please have one meeting without the two of you going at each other?" Tiffany shouted.

The room went quiet for the second time that afternoon. This time, six pairs of eyes aimed directly at her—obviously shocked to hear her uncharacteristic intonation.

She flushed with self-consciousness. She knew she was on edge, her nerves buzzing since the *mystery man* became the topic. "Sorry, but the bickering is getting us nowhere."

Her friends exchanged silent looks with one another. She chose to ignore the questioning eyes and got back to the topic at hand. "Now, what was your other reason, Charmagne?"

"The thing is, Charles is the only man I've ever been with." Flat open palms, Charmagne raised her hands boldly like two stop signs toward Karen, to forestall a comment. "And he's the only man I intend to be with. So I guess I like the thought of having a fantasy man doing things to please me." Charmagne cast her eyes down. "It's a once in a lifetime opportunity, and I don't want to miss it."

"Are you sure you want to do this?" Tiffany asked.

Charmagne raised her eyes toward Tiffany. "Yes."

"Okay, I'll call Leslie Janis tomorrow and reserve a stripper."

"Tiffany, I don't want just any stripper; I want our fireman," Charmagne said with a hint of stubbornness.

Tiffany exhaled a breath. *Man, this is the last thing I need right now.* "The Fireman it is." Tiffany pasted on a smile for her friends, concealing her inner struggle.

§

I want our fireman. Those words continued to repeat themselves in Tiffany's mind as she closed the door behind Josephine, the last of her friends to leave, and waved at Todd, the state trooper making his evening rounds. Tiffany didn't know how she had made it through the last hour while she silently struggled with the thoughts of the leather-clad mystery man, who was actually her husband yet still a mystery to her.

More than a month had passed since the last time she'd seen him. Her menstrual cycle had thankfully come and gone, letting her know a possible pregnancy was no longer an issue. Getting rid of a husband was one thing, but a child would have complicated things.

Fire and Desire

She attempted to put the torrid memories out of her mind. She told herself she must've added too much Bacardi to the punch, not to mention what she was drinking when they went out. It was the only possible reason Tiffany Hatcher, the daughter of Governor Donald W. Hatcher, would allow what had happened that night in the kitchen and the remainder of the night to take place.

Since her mother's death twelve years ago, she'd become the consummate hostess. By age twenty-one, society had dubbed her "Miss Hatcher, Hostess Extraordinaire."

At an early age, she'd learned how to handle affairs. Tiffany had been pushed into the position of being mistress of the manor because her father had needed someone to stand beside him at special engagements, accompany him around town, help host his parties and organize the volunteers for his campaign. Tiffany, the only child, had seemed to be the proper candidate, despite her youth.

Feeling drained, she walked up the stairs to her room. As always, the Virginia heat was oppressive, and it was only June. However, she knew the heat didn't account for most of her weariness. The battle of guilt she had experienced the last hour while sitting in the kitchen with her friends had taken a toll on her nerves.

When Veronica had asked for some ice out of the freezer, Tiffany's legs had involuntarily crossed in remembrance. She'd sat around the table with her friends, wondering if they would believe her if she told them what had happened.

Probably not.

She was the governor's daughter. It was completely out of character. *Maybe that was why I permitted it to happen.* Everyone always expected her to do the proper thing. Miss social butterfly…parties were her game and conservative was her name. She was disconcerted by the unexpected thought.

Charmagne's wedding was the fourth one she'd planned this year. Sometimes she felt as though one of her friends had put an advertisement in the yellow pages announcing she was available to coordinate for any occasion. Her friend Daphne was Jewish and had married two years ago.

She'd recently given birth to a son, Solomon. Tiffany wouldn't be surprised if Daphne and her husband Elijah expected her to orchestrate Solomon's Bar Mitzvah when he turned thirteen, regardless of the fact she didn't know much about the religion and customs.

Tiffany walked into her room and over to the closet to undress for bed. Normally, she waited until her father called, to make sure there weren't any changes for the next day's schedule of events, but tonight she was tired.

"How am I supposed to handle seeing him again?" Tiffany voiced to herself, as she stood before the full-length cheval mirror and stared at the woman in the reflection. Her hair was bound in an efficient bun, neutral, unassuming make-up graced her face, but it was the troubled look in her eyes that captured her attention. She turned away from the image, then hung up her powder blue slacks and cream shell. She removed and folded her bra and knee-highs, then placed them into their designated dirty clothes hampers. Her nightgown lay across the foot of her bed as always, the only symbol of disorder.

Sexy lingerie was one of her secret loves. She pulled the gown over her head—a sleeveless lace trimmed bodice with soft folds of silk that fell around her legs. She entered her private bathroom to moisturize her face. "Maybe I'll come down with the flu."

Her healthy reflection in the mirror told her it wasn't likely.

"Maybe he'll catch it." Using her middle and ring fingers, she applied the cool white cream to her face until it absorbed into her skin.

The final step in her night ritual was her satin cap.

She pulled back the blanket and crawled into bed. *Better yet, he'll surprise me and show up with divorce papers in hand.*

She'd been trying to get in touch with him since she'd gotten back with no luck. It would have been easier for him to get in touch with her. However, he'd been ominously silent. The only thing she knew about him was his name—no address and no telephone number. She had attempted to locate him through the white pages and even Googled him, but without knowing more about him, it was almost impossible. Attempting to use the process of elimination, Maryland and Virginia were out of the question. Both states were too large. Las Vegas would have been a nightmare.

Besides, she had paid extra for Elite Entertainment to fly one of their dancers out. So she narrowed her search to the D.C area. Amazingly, there were forty-seven listings for Trevor or T. Lewis. Deciding to call each one of them was also out of the question. She was determined to stay on the opposite side of neurotic.

She had considered calling Elite Entertainment when she first got back to try to get a message to him, but she could never come up with a reason for wanting to talk to him — with the exception of telling Leslie Janis that she was his *wife*.

She began to drift off to sleep. With her defenses relaxed, vivid dreams of her and Trevor invaded her mind. Every night since Las Vegas, she was haunted by similar images. She had begun to question whether they reflected what had truly happened in his hotel room that night, or if she was having erotic fantasies.

After tossing and turning, she rolled down the covers on her bed, telling herself it was the humidity, not the thoughts of Trevor causing her increase in temperature.

I have to remember to turn the air conditioner up higher tomorrow, she decided, unwilling to believe anything otherwise.

§

"Lewis here," Trevor said absently after he tapped the speakerphone button. He was currently involved in a computer project and, as usual, had become completely consumed. Ten virus-infected computers from the local library had kept Trevor buried in his lab all day. As he cleaned and repaired one bug after another, he wondered if the company who installed the PCs had ever heard of Norton or McAfee. Six unit hard drives could be repaired fully, the other four he would have to replace.

Trevor could just imagine how many home and office systems had downloaded information from the library's stations and been infected.

"Hello, Trev." A sultry female voice came through the line, interrupting his concentration. "How's my favorite nephew?"

"I'm your only nephew, Leslie." In jest, his aunt always told him she was too young to be someone's aunt.

But he knew it was really because most of their family didn't approve of Leslie's business, Elite Entertainment, even though it was very upscale. EE specialized in escorts, singing telegrams and dancers, cultural and erotic, for hire. The business catered to the upper echelon of society, mainly the tri-state area around D.C. It was based out of Maryland, close enough for easy access and far enough away for discretion.

She laughed. "You'd still be my favorite."

"How are you?" he asked as he stepped away from the terminal he had been working on and rubbed his tried eyes.

"I'm doing fine, sweetie. I hope you haven't been holed up in your lab all day," she said knowingly.

"No comment," Trevor said, humor evident in his voice. Leslie was always after him about wasting precious time, working too much. "How's EE?"

"Business is booming. As a matter fact, that's why I called." A hint of hesitation. "I have another favor."

Trevor knew that sound. It had been the same tone she had used when she'd called last month wanting him to do a show. He shook his head automatically, even though she couldn't see him. "The answer is no."

"Now, how are you going to turn down your dear old aunt before she even makes her request known?" Leslie said, syrupy sweet.

"Because I know what you're going to ask me, and it's still no," Trevor said with a firm tone, which never seemed to work on his aunt.

"Trevor, this will be the last time, Scout's promise."

"You were never a Girl Scout." Trevor laughed.

"I was a Brownie for a month; that's close enough."

"Not in this case."

"What if I sign a contract that says I'll never ask you again?"

"Not good enough."

"Trev, you know I wouldn't ask this of you unless it were really important."

Unmoved, he said, "You'll have to get one of your other guys to do it, or hire more staff. Or tell the customer that it's peak season and you don't have any available men."

"Having a man available is not the problem. I've hired six new guys over the last two weeks to make good on my promise I made to you last month."

"What's the problem then? Send one of them." Trevor went into the storage room to collect the parts he would need to replace one of the hard drives for the library's computers.

"Trev, this is a *very* important client."

He could tell by his aunt's insistent tone she wouldn't relent.

"Aren't they all?"

She didn't answer the question; instead she said, "There's one big problem with sending one of the other guys."

"Let me guess, they want Black and all you have is White and Hispanic left. No, I got it; they want bare chest, and all you have is hairy." Trevor didn't try to hide the sarcastic tone. He knew his aunt was aware of his thoughts toward her clients. He considered most of them to be extremely fastidious.

"No." She waited a moment. "They specifically asked for you."

Trevor paused. "They requested me?"

"Yes."

"I don't see why someone else can't do it. They don't even know who I am."

"They may not know your face, but they'll know if I send another. Remember, all Black men don't look a like — especially naked."

"Well, if the person only heard about my performance, then you could get away with it. Regardless of the situation, I'm not doing it." He hated to turn down his aunt because he knew she would do anything for him. Numerous times in college when he had gotten in a jam and couldn't ask his parents for help, his aunt was there and never judged him. Not to mention, her business was also responsible for paying a chunk of his college tuition.

But he just didn't have the time for it. The last show had put his career and life in a precarious situation. He didn't need another one.

"Tiffany Hatcher didn't hear about you from a friend, she hosted the party you did for me over a month ago," she said resolutely.

The vision of a conservative woman moaning in a kitchen did what nothing else his aunt said had done—piqued his interest.

"What type of party is it?"

"It's another bachelorette party, this time held at the Hatcher family home. So you wouldn't even have to travel out of state."

Trevor tried to sound nonchalant. "So is it finally her wedding this time?"

He didn't know what Tiffany and Manning were up to, but maybe this was her way of trying to get in touch with him about the divorce.

He wouldn't fall for that trap. He wouldn't settle until Manning came to him personally, man to man. His old college bud, looking him in the eye, knowing that he'd finally one-upped him. Five years and now he held something precious of Manning's. And *he* was in control this time.

"Governor Hatcher's daughter? Not a chance. If she were to get married, it would be all over the society pages. Manning would definitely be using that as another angle for a seat in Congress," Leslie said. "Hosting is her claim to fame. The party is for Charmagne Spelling. You know, the daughter of the president of Hudson Morris University in Alexandria."

Trevor had never met the president of HMU. However, if he wasn't mistaken, Charmagne was the young lady at the last party who had fainted. He remembered the woman seated next to her, Sonya, calling her name as she fanned her awake.

"Because she did the last party and she knows basically what you look like, it's the only reason I'm asking you." His aunt paused again. "Will you please do this for me, for the last time? I know your business is on the rise, and I would never do anything to jeopardize your success."

"I'm sorry, but I can't for more reasons than I care to explain right now. But I'll call Miss Hatcher and explain that to her myself if you would like?"

His aunt sighed in resignation. "No, that's okay. I'll call. I knew it was a long shot, but I thought I'd ask anyway."

"Whoever you pick, tell them they can have the persona, I'm hanging up my mask, fire hose and cape. Also a bit of advice for whomever you pick. Tell him they're a wild bunch, so be careful."

"I will. You were always my most popular dancer."

Trevor laughed. "The answer is still no."

"Can't blame a girl for trying." She chuckled. "Are we still on for dinner Sunday night?"

"Haven't missed one yet."

"Well, my love…I'll see you soon." His aunt blew a kiss into the phone.

"Same here."

They ended the phone call.

His chair squeaked as he leaned back in it. Another idea began to form in his head. He figured it was time he paid his *dearly beloved wife* a visit.

He beamed with satisfaction of the possibilities of their next meeting. The memories of their Las Vegas encounter flooded back into his mind.

Tiffany had abandoned everything else around her but him. He had become the center of her world. Living for the pleasure that he was giving her.

He looked down at his hands; he could still feel the warmth of her skin. His ears still rang with the sweet sound of her voice in the throes of passion.

Trevor was the first to admit he had not been starved of intimate female companionship during college and a few years after. But even with his vast experience, he had never known a woman to lose herself so completely.

Truth of the matter was, he wanted to bring her to that point again while they were both sober and could enjoy it to the fullest.

He knew he was making things hard for himself—literally. He squirmed, trying to get more comfortable, letting out a soft curse for Miss Hatcher's continued effect on his body.

He told himself he was only going to see her to keep his plan in action. He was out for revenge—nothing more. And helping Tiffany in her quest not to marry Christopher was just a bonus.

Four

The imitation Fireman started his second set. Tiffany was thankful that her friends took the news so well that the *real* Fireman wasn't going to be able to make it. Disappointed murmurs had gone around the restaurant table when they had gotten together last weekend, but other than that, they took it in stride.

She kept telling herself it didn't bother her that Trevor wasn't there. That she was happy she wouldn't have to be bothered by him. That she had no reason to expect anything different from him since he hadn't called her.

The voice in her head kept saying…*liar*.

Quickly, she blew it off by telling herself she only wanted to see him to get the divorce taken care of and that it had nothing to do with what had happened in the kitchen of the town house—let alone what may or may not have happened at the hotel.

She was glad she had asked Josephine to handle everything this dancer needed. She wasn't leaving anything to chance.

As the music's seductive beat began an enticing tempo, the dancer entered the room through the sliding door of the family room. He came in slow and sexy, making every move count. Tiffany watched as the dancer's keen eyes focused on Charmagne sitting in the honored chair in the middle of the room holding a bowl of ice. She had done surprisingly well.

Tiffany had to admit to herself, she was fascinated to see what he would do with the ice. This was a requested performance by her friends who had seen Trevor perform this act during his last set at the other party. They may have taken the news calmly that Trevor wasn't going to perform, but they'd made sure Tiffany requested this routine.

Fire and Desire

Tiffany had missed that set in Las Vegas while she had been in her room changing her underwear and composing herself. By the time she returned downstairs, he had finished. When she questioned her friends, asking them what was so special about the ice, she remembered Lydia saying, "Girl, you just had to see it for yourself. No words can explain."

This stripper, who was now dressed like Batman, finally arrived at the designated place in front of Charmagne. For a few moments, he danced around her, grinding his hips in a suggestive way to the notes of the song. At one point, he'd turned his back fully to her, stood within inches of her face and jiggled his buttocks, similar to the way Trevor had done when Charmagne had fainted before.

Remarkably, Charmagne didn't pass out this time and boldly placed her hands on his shivering muscles.

"You don't have a shy bone left in your body now, do you Charmagne?" Sonya called out from where she sat perched on the edge of the couch.

Karen followed up with, "Who could be shy? A body like that could make a nun want to reach out and touch." She made a grabbing motion with her hand in the air toward the dancer.

With his back to them, Tiffany couldn't tell how he was feeling about all of the catcalls coming his way. When he turned around there was a serious, determined expression on his face, as if he were going to perform a science experiment.

He removed the bowl from Charmagne's lap and placed it on the floor beside her chair. Squatting on his hunches in front of her, he placed one hand on each of her ankles. Slowly, he moved his hand up the back of her calves until he reached her knee. At a leisurely pace he parted her khaki covered legs widely.

Grabbing Charmagne by the waist, he forcefully slid her to him. He wrapped her legs around his waist. Before rising, he leaned over and picked up a piece of crescent-shaped ice out of the bowl.

Tiffany was drawn into the scene and couldn't look away. Her curiosity was piqued. *What had Trevor done that had been so captivating to my friends?*

As he stood up fully and his muscular thigh muscles flexed to support the additional weight in his arms, the dancer commanded, "Open your mouth."

Being caught up in the show, Tiffany felt her own lips part slightly.

Batman held her friend firmly in place with one hand on her hip and placed the ice partially in Charmagne's mouth. "Now close your lips around it," he said.

When Charmagne's lips enclosed one end of the cube, the man closed his mouth around the other end. He turned himself and his weight to the side, so all of the ladies in the room could see clearly what he was doing and imagine it was being done to them.

Gradually, he began to suck on the ice while pulling it in his mouth slightly and pushing it back into Charmagne's, until she finally understood and picked up the rhythm with him. In and out the ice cube went. Slowly at first, until they almost ended in a tug of war with the cube.

Charmagne's eyes closed and a moan echoed throughout the room. Tiffany wasn't sure if the noise came from Batman's pleasured captive or the spectators.

The one thing she realized was, in Las Vegas, this scene was meant for her…even if she hadn't witnessed it.

As she watched the slick frozen water enter and leave the recess of the other woman's mouth, she knew what Trevor would have been implying.

Tiffany's thigh muscles tightened with euphoric recall. Her whole body began to quiver as she remembered the hot scene they'd shared in the kitchen. If she'd seen the actual live performance a month ago, she would have known Trevor was reliving it too.

"Hmm, not bad…not bad at all," Diane groaned.

Josephine leaned toward her and whispered, "This guy does do it well. I'm definitely hot, but the last time, I actually thought I would wet my pants on the spot just imagining what *that* man could do to me with an ice cube."

Tiffany couldn't respond. All of the air in her lungs became trapped. Her throat squeezed. In her mind, she saw herself and Trevor re-enacting the part. It had become so vivid and real—her panties were beyond wet. She didn't have to fantasize what Trevor could do; she knew the skills he possessed with crystallized water.

Mercifully, the music finally ended, and Tiffany knew escape was in sight.

The dancer placed the charmed Charmagne back in her seat and exited the room, leaving enraptured women in his wake.

"Wow," Josephine sighed. Josephine's articulation ability seemed to leave her, like the rest of the women in the room, who remained quiet and still.

Tiffany watched as Josephine left the room fanning herself. When she returned with the bowl of fruit for the next act, Tiffany had finally regained a minuscule amount of composure. She knew the same could not be said about her senses.

"I'm not feeling very well. My head is starting to throb. I think I'm going to sit the last show out and take something for it." For effect, Tiffany pressed her fingers against her temple and rubbed in a circular motion.

As she prepared to leave the room, relief settled over her. If Josephine thought it peculiar how she was acting, her friend kept her opinion to herself.

"I understand. You didn't eat much today. Why don't you take some of this fruit with you, so you won't take that medicine on an empty stomach? I'll come and get you when the show is over." Josephine gave her a small smile.

Tiffany used the excuse of grabbing a banana and an apple from the bowl as a reason not to meet her friend's eyes. "Thanks, Jo, I'm probably going to just take a Tylenol and look over the plans for next week's fundraiser."

"No problem."

"Tiff," Josephine called.

Tiffany turned and looked at her friend.

"You don't have to cover with me. I know this is not your thing. Las Vegas…" her words drifted for a moment. "I think it was too much for you." Josephine's eyes, clear and piercing, held awareness in them.

You have no idea. Without elaborating, Tiffany gave her friend a small smile, retrieved her briefcase from the coat closet and exited the room with a cloud of guilt hanging over her. She knew there was no way for her to watch the next act without making a fool of herself somehow.

After her reaction to the last set, she didn't trust herself.

Watching the dancer mimic Trevor's act just reaffirmed that everything that happened had between her and Trevor was just a game to him—all part of his show.

Something they probably learned in an erotic dance class. Tiffany entered the family room and closed the double doors behind her. The room was one of her favorites in the house, decorated with white plush carpet and rose and ivy print furniture. Even though her father lived and spent most of his time at the Governor's Mansion in Richmond, it was the one room she and her father used for family holiday gatherings. Tiffany divided her time between both, but lately, she'd found herself staying at the family home more often. She liked to keep herself separated from the intricate political aspects of her father's career. Politics had never truly interested her. Coordination was her passion in life.

After her mother's passing, Tiffany and her father promised each other they would still keep the traditions her mother had set at this house.

Tiffany placed everything on the table with the exception of the banana and walked over to the fireplace. She needed time to get her thoughts together. Josephine was right; she hadn't eaten anything all day. Pins and needles. Her senses had been going haywire even though she knew Trevor was not coming.

She removed the yellow peel from the fruit. As she placed her mouth around the slender, curved fruit, her imagination conjured up an image of something long, warm, sleek and hard. Little tremors of heat ran through her body at the thought.

Quickly, she pitched the deceptive food into the trash, chastising herself for the vision and praying it wasn't a memory of an alcohol induced night.

Tiffany hated to admit it, but she was hiding out. Earlier that day while she and Josephine had been setting up for the party, she had asked her friend to act as hostess for the entertainment part. She fabricated a lie about having too many other things on her mind to attend to the needs of another stripper. Josephine believed she was uncomfortable with the subject of stripping in general.

She let the conversation drop, deciding not to enlighten Josephine. It would have taken too much explaining to tell her friend how far it had really gone out of her comfort zone. Besides, she was hoping that soon it would be all over, just a distant memory.

She'd barely come to grips with her behavior, let alone having to explain her actions to someone else, even if that someone was her best friend.

"Who am I fooling?" She stared into the empty grate.

She could pretend with her friends, but she couldn't make her own conscience believe the lie. The truth of the matter was she couldn't even rely on all the training she'd been given in charm school around Trevor.

Tiffany heard someone enter the room. Assuming it was Josephine, or one of her friends coming to check up on her, she didn't turn around. Not really wanting to be bothered, she hoped they would think she was mulling over fundraiser plans and leave the room as quietly as they came in.

After a few moments passed, she realized she would have no such luck.

"So, how's the stripper?" she asked, still facing the fireplace, wondering if he had started his final act.

"I don't know. You tell me?" The voice came out smooth, thick and rich like a Bavarian creamed éclair.

Tiffany's eyes closed automatically with the sound of the silky deep tone. She didn't have to turn to know who it was. All of her senses came alive in remembrance of their last meeting.

Staring into the fire, she asked, "How did you get in here?"

"The back door was open and your friends were too occupied talking about the stripper to notice me. I saw you head this way when I came in."

"I'll have to remember that," she commented as she walked back toward the couch.

She took a slow breath with every step, hoping to calm her nerves before she raised her eyes to look at the man who called himself her husband. Regaining her composure, she sat down on the couch and met his eyes.

Rich, sparkling, light nut-brown irises met hers. It was the smile that could seduce Aphrodite that made Tiffany quickly look away.

"I hope I'm not disturbing you," he said without moving further into the room.

"My prodigal husband returns. Why should that be disturbing to me?" She leaned toward the papers on the table as if his unexpected presence in the room and in her life was not disconcerting for her.

She wondered if one of her friends had spotted him or recognized him. If someone did, she knew she would be in for a lot of questions later. "Unless you have come here to talk about our divorce, I have nothing to say to you. I have work to do. However, you can leave your contact information for me so my lawyer can get a hold of you."

"Would it bother you if I decide to stick around for a few minutes?"

She noticed he had ignored her statement about a divorce. "I usually become so focused on my work it would take an earthquake to distract me. So why don't you just tell me what you've come to say and be gone?"

She didn't realize he had moved toward her until he sat down next to her.

"Well, since it's unlikely we'll have a noticeable one on the East Coast, I guess it wouldn't vex you greatly to have me here with you?"

"Not at all," she said nonchalantly.

Damn. Her heart was already beginning to race at the sight of him. There he sat, in a pair of snug fitting black jeans and a button down navy blue shirt, with the top three buttons open and the cuffs folded back, showing off his sinewy forearms, looking like a woman's bedtime fantasy. It was a torturous way to leave a woman before she headed to bed.

Trevor leaned forward. "What are you working on so intently? A proposal to Congress?"

Tiffany couldn't help but smile. "No, just a fundraiser." She made the mistake of looking his way. There was barely any space between them. If either of them wiggled their noses, they would likely touch.

As if he'd read her mind, Trevor reached his hand up and grazed the tip of her nose. "What would you say, Mrs. Hatcher-Lewis, if I told you I haven't been able to get you off my mind?"

"I would say you either haven't put that into action by filing for divorce, or you just don't have enough things to occupy your time."

"Would you?" Trevor slid his fingers across her cheek. "I don't think it's a matter of things to occupy my time. Just none are as challenging."

Tiffany could feel goose bumps rising on her flesh as Trevor's thumb stroked her bottom lip.

It took all her will power not to succumb to temptation and slowly drag her tongue against the pad of his thumb.

Turning her head, Tiffany said, "Look, Trevor, I think you got the wrong impression of me after what happened the last time."

A frown wrinkled his brow. "The only impression I have of you is that you're a woman with very deep passions. Which I'd love the opportunity to tap into further."

"I don't want to be tapped." She crossed her arms over her chest.

"I think you do." His lips tilted in a lopsided smile.

"I hope you're not a betting man."

"Why is that?"

"Because you'd lose." Tiffany unfolded her arms, dropping them back in her lap, her palms slapping against her thighs.

Trevor smiled. "You think so?" He waited until she gave an affirmative nod. "What if we put your little dare to the test?"

"I wasn't issuing a challenge." Butterflies danced in Tiffany's stomach as she leaned back and gave herself some needed space. She didn't know if it was from nervousness or anticipation of what Trevor would suggest.

He lifted a shoulder as if to say it didn't matter. "I propose you allow me to kiss you. If you don't become affected by it, then you win, but if you respond . . ." He let the statement hang in the air between them for a time before he said, "we both win."

"Deal," Tiffany said, not quite sure why she agreed. She told herself it was because she wanted to prove to him she was not in the least attracted or affected by him. Also to prove to herself that everything that occurred the last time was the result of a full moon or some freak of nature with the combination of way too much alcohol.

"Then let's seal it with a kiss."

His words brushed against her lips like a soft caress as he leaned forward, closing the tiny gap between them.

Suddenly, Tiffany knew she was in trouble. The contact of his lips on hers sent an electric shock through her system. She jumped back slightly from the sensation.

"Too late to back out now," Trevor said as he placed a firm hand behind her head to keep her mouth in contact with his.

She squeezed her lips tightly together, in hopes Trevor would tire of the game before she eventually gave in.

But he didn't give up. He became creative with his assault. Trevor used his tongue, teeth, and lips to persuade her to allow him passage into the warm recesses of her mouth.

Her resolve wore down, and she gave in completely, opening her mouth to the kiss.

Their mouths fused together as their tongues dueled against each other for rite of passage.

Her hands wrapped around the strong cords of his neck as Trevor's hands moved to her waist.

The kiss was intense. Tiffany lost focus of everything except how Trevor's mouth manipulated hers. She wasn't aware his hands had lifted her blouse until she felt the cool air against her skin moments before his hands covered her breasts.

Utterly captivated by everything Trevor was doing, Tiffany only registered sensual pleasure. She found herself leaning against the arm of the couch as one of his strong hands began stroking her breasts through her bra. He pushed up the lacy cups until the weight of her breasts was in his hand. He continued to massage her as his thumb awakened her nipples, both of them puckered into distinct points, begging to be adored.

Trevor's lips left hers as he trailed kisses down her neck. "The thing I like most about kissing is there's more than one place to kiss a woman." His breath brushed against her skin.

"Like here," he said as he kissed her collarbone. "And here." He brought his hot, moist, open mouth in contact with one sable nipple.

You need to stop this, her mind shouted, refusing to give up control.

A moan escaped Tiffany's mouth at the initial contact. As the weight of Trevor's body rested on hers and his mouth's suction became more intense, the sounds became soft cries of pleasure.

Tiffany's hips began to move of their own accord, bringing themselves in connection with Trevor's. She felt his groaned responses against her body where his mouth continued to feast.

Trevor used his other hand to bring her hips closer to his, allowing her to feel exactly how involved he was in their little foreplay.

The grinding pressure of his firm manhood against her cleft left no doubt that he was being just as affected as she was. Trevor's lips left her breasts and recaptured hers, allowing direct contact to answer the request of their gyrating lower bodies.

Tiffany had never felt so ravished. Trevor consumed her as he licked his way back down her body. Fierce heat overwhelmed her as he honored her breasts again with more vigor than before. Flicking, sucking and rolling his tongue around her nipples, then giving them small nips with his teeth.

"Trevor. Trevor," she began to chant. The pitch of her cries heightened. Suddenly, she found herself biting into something firm and sweet. Her mind registered the taste of an apple, as her teeth sank into the firm fruit Trevor had placed in her mouth to muffle her cries.

"You're going to bring the house down." Humor laced his voice. His hands continued to fondle her breasts, while his mouth journeyed on. He gave a few playful licks to her bellybutton as he passed, and then proceeded to another destination.

One hand left her breasts and began to undo her pants. The hook holding her pants together became free as Trevor's tongue slid across her lower abdomen.

Her body began trembling as each tooth of her zipper opened. She knew what was coming; it was something that she had heard her friends talk about more than once. With her limited sexual experience, to include the night in the hotel she didn't remember, it was an area she had yet to enter as far as she could remember.

Trevor's tongue slipped underneath the top edge of her panties as both his hands hooked on the side of her slacks to remove them from her. One of his thumbs slid over the panty-covered mound, then began to make slow and gentle brush strokes.

"God, Tiffany, I can't get enough of you," he said, words strained and heated.

Tiffany couldn't control her hips from arching toward his wandering thumb.

She knew what was coming next. She anticipated the feel of air against her thighs as Trevor removed her pants. In the distance, as she waited with expectation, her mind registered the opening tunes of the Rhythm and Blues artist Maxwell's sultry ballad "Until the Cops Come Knockin'."

"Damn," Trevor growled, took a deep breath, then quickly pushed away from her and the couch. "Not how I meant for this to go."

Shock hit her like ice water. *Oh, God, what am I doing?* Tiffany didn't look at him as she sat up, removed the apple from her mouth, flexed the tightness out of her jaw and righted her clothes. She could hear him taking what sounded like deep, cleansing breaths.

He headed for, and then opened the back door. "I guess we both win." Then he was gone once again, still without leaving any type of contact information.

Fire and Desire

Tiffany laid her face in her hands, wanting to scream at how far she had let things go again.

"Tiff, are you okay?"

Hearing Josephine, Tiffany looked up.

"Wow, Tiffany. You must be coming down with something. Your face is all flushed."

"I'm not feeling like myself. Do you mind making my excuses to everyone? I'm going to lie down for a bit." It was not a complete lie. She was becoming sick at the thought of not being able to control her response to Trevor.

"You know I don't mind. I'll get a few of the girls to help me straighten up, then I'll lock the door when I leave. You just get some rest."

"Make sure you check the side doors for me, Jo." The thought of Trevor coming back sent shivers down her spine.

After her friend responded and exited the room, Tiffany gathered her papers and escaped through the same door Trevor had entered moments before.

Five

S o, Dad, what's on the agenda for this month? On my calendar at the moment, I have a few meetings I need to attend for the local Breast Cancer Society's fall fundraiser. Also, I told Jo I would spend a couple of days this month with her to plan for next quarter's scheduling. Other than those things, I'm all yours."

Sitting in the dining room at the Governor's Mansion, Tiffany looked across the dinner table at her father, who sat intently listening to her as he sliced his roast into small edible bits.

Tiffany smiled as she observed him because she realized she modeled his meticulous nature. Rarely a break in their routines, it was her predictable gene.

Tonight was no exception. It was the first Sunday of the month. She and her father were having dinner as usual. Throughout the dinner, they discussed what functions she would need to attend with him and what engagements he was hosting that needed planning.

At times, Tiffany secretly wished she were more like her mother, spontaneous and adventurous. Her mother had loved trying new things all the time; she'd liked living on the edge. It made her wonder what had even brought her parents together since they were so different in their approaches to life. However, she knew as free spirited as her mother had been, nothing had surpassed her loyalty and devotion to her family.

Her mother had passed away due to breast cancer, and that was one of the reasons she gave so much time to the local chapter of the Breast Cancer Society.

When she was not working with her father, she worked with her best friend, Josephine, in the consulting business they had opened two years ago. The company's business had steadily climbed since its beginning, but she knew, if she had more time to put into it, the business could go a lot further. Because of her social responsibilities in assisting her father in his term as governor, it made it hard to give it her complete focus. She was thankful for her business partner. Often, Tiffany thought, if it were not for Josephine, the company would have sunk by now.

"Well, turtledove," the governor began, using the nickname he had called her since she was a little girl, "this month is rather hectic. I'll be out of town for most of it, but there are still four or five dinner parties where I'm expected to show face. On this Saturday evening, sorry for the short notice, but Tracie, the senator's daughter, is getting married, and it's her engagement party."

Tiffany looked up from her plate. "Oh, so Robert Sterling finally proposed to her?"

"Evidently."

"Why wasn't it in the papers?"

"Manning Senior told me they just wanted it to be a small private affair, with family and close friends. The shorter amount of time people had to prepare, the better chance they hoped the press wouldn't show up."

"I understand. It's amazing she has been dating him since high school. It makes you wonder what took him so long."

"One never knows. Marriage is a big responsibility, never to be entered into lightly."

Something she loved most about her father was he didn't rush her to the altar just because society still held the idea women should be married and raising a family by the time they left their twenties.

She was twenty-seven and couldn't see herself getting married in the next three years.

The words played in her mind, reminding her she had already married Trevor and not only by paper. She pushed the thought aside—it didn't count. It was a mistake she was in the process of correcting.

"Christopher asked me to tell you he would be expecting a dance from you that night," her dad said, breaking into her thoughts.

Christopher Manning, the senator's son, was a different matter entirely. They'd dated three years ago. It'd only lasted six months. She'd promptly broken off the relationship, realizing she didn't have the time or energy to play hostess for both her father and Christopher's career. Not to mention, she was in the mist of trying to get her own business off the ground. Christopher considered himself a senator hopeful and never missed an opportunity to be seen at the right function, by the right people, at the right time and expected Tiffany to be right on his arm at every event. That was before he was running for congressional representative; she could only imagine what he would expect from her now.

Since then, Christopher was under the assumption she would one day be Mrs. Christopher Kevin Manning, III. Tiffany had no problem with Christopher personally, except he was selfish. The prospect of marrying into a political family was not appealing, one of the main reasons she avoided a relationship with Christopher.

It was her responsibility as her father's daughter to accompany and host for him, but it was not something she wanted for the rest of her life. Besides, she'd always been left wanting, making it easy for her to keep all of her morals and values intact. Never having a desire to take their relationship to the next step.

Jo told her that was not a good thing, particularly in a husband.

Tiffany quickly refocused herself back on the conversation with her father before thoughts of Trevor and how *he* made her feel took over her thought process.

"What did you say to Christopher?" Tiffany sliced off a small piece of roast and ate it.

"I told him to speak with you directly." The governor took a bite of his roast, chewed slowly, then swallowed. "He said it was what he planned to do."

Thank God for Dad. It was classic of Christopher to attempt to press this issue with her father, but the governor always stood his ground.

"You wouldn't be able to take Martha to this would you?" Tiffany fought the urge to push her food around her plate. The thought of fighting off Christopher all night consumed her appetite.

The governor gave his daughter a look, which said it wasn't likely.

Martha Sanders was one of her father's female friends. She was one of the women who occasionally accompanied him to the opera, theater or dinner. Her father was very sporadic in his dating, not trying to give the press fuel for fire. He always told her, personal life was private, and he liked it that way.

Through their many talks, she knew the prospect of him remarrying was not a possibility. He had often said her mother was his one true love and he wouldn't settle for second best.

Tiffany wondered if she would ever feel that way about someone. Without warning, thoughts of Trevor entered her mind, his smoldering, secretive eyes and wicked smile. She pushed the thoughts aside before they went further. It didn't take much.

Getting back to business, Tiffany jotted down notes and dates in her planner as she listened to her father list his upcoming events. She was glad she wouldn't have to reschedule any of her appointments to accommodate his.

"Well, sweetheart, I must return my shoulder to the grind." Her father gave her a loving smile before he stood.

Tiffany stood as well and rounded the table to his side.

"I love you, Daddy."

Immediately, her father's arms swallowed her up into a bear hug. "I love you, too."

Leaning back, her father looked at her. "What's wrong, sweetheart?" her father asked, voice full of concern.

Weighed with guilt, Tiffany took a step back, removing herself from her father's protective arms.

"What do you mean? I always tell you I love you." Tiffany passed what she hoped was a convincing smile on her face that said, *all is well.*

"Of course you do. You just haven't seemed yourself lately. Your smiles even seem weighed down."

Tiffany returned to her side of the table and gathered her things. "Dad, you worry too much." Giving him that smile again, she said, "I'm fine."

Wallace Parker, his aide and right-hand man, stepped into the room. "Excuse me, Governor. Senator Jackson is on the phone. He says it's urgent."

Wallace had been with her father since he first started running for office. He was practically a part of the family with the exception that he kept himself separate. He never took a meal with them and never shared any holiday time—regardless of the fact he had no family. Wallace was a very smart, loyal and quiet man who valued his solitude. He was an attractive man, appearing to be in his early forties. Tall with thick broad shoulders, his presence was always formidable. When most people met Wallace, they mistook him for a bodyguard instead of the political intellectual who held a doctorate in political science. He knew his job and he did it well.

She had no doubt that Wallace would lend physical support whenever the need arose.

Wallace exited the room as quietly as he had entered.

"We are not done with this conversation, sweetheart," the governor said, as he walked to the door.

"Of course we are. You just worry about me too much when you have enough people in this state to look after." Tiffany walked over to her father, who was standing at the threshold of the dining room.

Leaning forward, her father kissed her on her forehead. "But none of them will ever mean more to me than you and your happiness."

Simultaneously, they both spotted Wallace coming from the direction of the office.

"I have to take this call."

Her father looked torn. A spark of fear entered her heart. The last thing she needed was her father telling Senator Jackson he would have to call him back, deciding now was the time for a father-daughter sit down.

"You go. Honestly, I'm fine."

Her father kissed her again, then finally left.

Tiffany closed her eyes and released the pent up breath she had been holding.

As she opened her eyes and started up the stairs, she noticed Wallace watching her. He gave her a silent nod, then entered her father's office behind him.

Tiffany retired to the room designated for her use while her father was in office. Sitting before her computer monitor, she logged in her password and began to pull up the program that would merge her and her father's schedule. Then she emailed the changes to herself. She rarely spent much time using this office, preferring her family home to the mansion. The Governor's Mansion had housed so many different families over the years, it always seemed so impersonal to her. As if so many people had lived there, no one could claim its heart. It lacked the warmth of their home in Alexandria. If her father became senator next year, he would return home. She was thankful they didn't give senators houses. Heaven only knew how she would get used to another.

Ring. Ring.

"Hello, Tiffany Hatcher," she answered on its second ring.

"Tiffy, sweetie, it's so good to hear your voice. I've been missing it."

She hated the name Tiffy. No one called her that but Christopher, and Josephine jokingly.

"Christopher, how are you?" she asked, controlling the exasperation the nickname always caused.

"Great. I don't have to ask how you are. I can hear you're hard at work."

She stopped typing, which she knew was his true reason for making the comment. He hated to feel as if he didn't have her full attention. "So to what do I owe the reason for this unexpected call?" she asked, not wanting to prolong the conversation.

"Well, I'm sure your father told you about Tracie's wedding this weekend."

He paused for her response.

"He did."

"Well, I'd like you to be my date," he dropped his voice an octave.

Christopher's low-pitched tone did nothing for her, yet the deep inflections of Trevor's voice sent sensual shivers down her spine. This amazed her.

"I thought you would be in the wedding."

"I will, but that's only significant for the ceremony and the dinner. After dinner, I'd be all yours."

"I'm sorry, Christopher, but I already told my dad I'd escort him."

"That's too bad. Maybe we could skip out early…you know, Tiffy, it's been a long time since we spent any quality time together." Amazingly, he dropped to an even lower tone.

"That's usually what couples do, Christopher. *Not friends*," she emphasized, reminding him that the latter was their status.

"Tiffy, how about letting me come pick you up tonight? We can drive around the city and talk."

He is relentless.

"Is everything okay?" she asked because, although she had no feelings at all toward him as a boyfriend or a husband, she did care about him as a friend.

"If I said, no…would you agree to go with me?" he said sounding more like a little boy pouting instead of a grown man who was soon to become a Congressman.

She laughed. "I'm sorry, Christopher, but I've got a lot of work to do and not enough time to do it."

She could hear him exhale through the phone. "Tiffy, you've always worked too hard. If you were my wife, you wouldn't be bogged down with half of the things you do."

She knew that was right. Everything would be him and only him. She could see her life being *very* boring.

"I'm sure you're right, but we've always been much better friends."

"That's only because you never allowed us to give anything else a chance."

She didn't want to revisit that old argument, so she cut it off. "Good night, Christopher."

"Tiffy, I'm a man with needs, and I've been holding out for you for a long time. I don't know how much longer I can wait."

"Well, it may be in your best interest to look elsewhere for them to be fulfilled. I'm sure you could find one of your campaign groupies ready and willing."

"They're okay for a time, but I'm at a critical point in my life where I have to make wiser choices than just a warm body."

"Your public relations man must be getting to you." There was never any factual evidence to make her doubt Christopher's fidelity in their relationship. But if part of what she heard about his over active libido since the break was true, his PR man, Roderick Blunt, had every right to caution him—repeatedly.

"You have no idea."

Christopher was big about things concerning image and status, and he would never allow anything as meaningless as a one-night stand with the wrong person to jeopardize his chance for Congress or even the Senate.

She was sure Christopher having to be discreet and conservative was the reason for his sudden reawakening need for them to continue their relationship and possible marriage. He was trying to get a steady bedmate.

"Okay, Tiffy, I'll table this conversation for now, but I'm not letting it go."

She wondered how easily he would let it go if she told him she was already married. He probably wouldn't believe her—especially if she told him it was to a stripper. He would've gotten a good laugh from that one.

"I'm sure that's true. Bye," she said, then hung up the phone.

Tiffany exited from the powder room. Out of habit, she looked at her diamond-encrusted watch. Her father had given the watch to her on her seventeenth birthday, telling her, if she were going to attend social engagements with him, she would need to keep him on schedule. He claimed it was easier for her to look down at her watch without notice, but for him, it would seem rude and impatient.

The time was now nine P.M. In about thirty minutes, her father would have to make his excuses and depart. He had an early meeting in Norfolk.

Tiffany smiled and chatted briefly with the people as she made her way back to her father. Most of the evening's attendees were members of

S.T.O.P = Gun laws, which stood for Safety to Our People, a committee that lobbied for more gun control laws. They were extremely active since the D.C. Sniper incident a few summers ago.

Her father usually attended banquets of both sides of an issue, with the attempt to appear impartial until he had made his decision. He stood firm on certain things he held strong beliefs about, but for most, he was willing to look at different ways of doing things.

His fair attitude was what most of the residents of the state liked about him. But there were others, particularly some journalists who were for the other party, who sat and waited in the wings, looking for any mistake her father made so they could bring it to light.

"...so I said to Wallace, call up my financial advisors for a meeting tonight. I want money for more child development centers, recreational centers, after school facilities and parks. Wallace said to me, but sir it's two o'clock in the morning; they're all asleep."

Tiffany watched her father pause for effect and look around at his captive audience circled around him.

"And I said, wake them up...it's for the children!"

Everyone laughed as her father finished waving his arms in the air enthusiastically, looking like a king prepared to lead his troops into battle.

"What can I say, every now and then I feel like Kris Kringle," her father said jovially.

When Tiffany reached his side, she took hold of his arm briefly and firmly brushed her thumb down the underside, their signal that it was time to leave.

Her father covertly signaled to Wallace, who was standing by the door, letting him know he was ready to go. Tiffany didn't have to turn to see if her father's right-hand man got the signal—she knew from years of experience Wallace missed nothing. She would be surprised if he hadn't caught the signal she had given her father.

As people moved away from them, Tiffany's father turned and reached toward a man whose back was turned. Evidently, it was someone he had been speaking with earlier. From her angle behind them, Tiffany didn't recognize the man.

"Well, I must be going. I'm sure our paths will cross again."

"I'm sure they will," the man said, his speech distinct.

Confounded by the tingling sensation running down her spine, Tiffany tried to place the voice. It seemed so familiar to her for some reason. As she pondered, she could hear her father saying, "Before I go, I would like you to meet my daughter."

She pasted on one of her social smiles as both men turned toward her.

"Tiffany, this is Trevor Lewis," her father said.

"It's a…" Tiffany's eyes made contact with her husband's light brown ones, eyes that sparkled with knowledge of her secret sins, "…pleasure to meet you."

It took every ounce of her dignity to stand with her father in front of the only other person who knew how wantonly and recklessly she'd behaved over the summer months—Trevor.

"My sentiments exactly."

She could see the subtle twinkle in his eyes.

She prayed fervently he wouldn't say anything.

His hand moved out and grasped hers gently, consuming her by the warmth of his touch. She had visions of hands that made her body sing, caused her to beg for the pleasure they could give her. At that moment, she could feel heat flood her sex, making it clench in response. A woman could never forget hands like that—no matter how bad she wanted to break the ties that bound them.

Wow! The man really knew how to wear a suit. She took a moment to take in the fully clothed package. She'd had so many sleepless nights from visions of him in a thong and snug fitting jeans; she'd never considered how good he could look dressed any other way.

The material fit his body perfectly. His broad shoulders drew her eyes; they were the type a woman would love to lay her head against for support.

If someone didn't know better, they would be convinced he belonged in this type of setting. Too bad she did.

She sighed. Telling herself it was indifference, not disappointment.

Before anything else could be said, Sherri Matrix, a woman who had rivaled her through college, walked over to them and slipped her arm through Trevor's, snuggling close. Tiffany had been wondering what he was doing here, but the claim the other woman placed on him answered it.

For an instant, Tiffany considered telling Sherri to get her hands off her husband, but she restrained herself.

If he and Sherri are dating, perhaps he will file for divorce soon.

"Governor Hatcher, it's so nice to see you again, looking handsome as usual." Sherri held her hand out so her father could bestow a kiss upon it, which he did.

Sherri oozed with false flattery.

"And you're looking lovely as always." Her father was always the consummate gentleman.

"You're too kind." Sherri viperously turned her eyes toward Tiffany. "Well, Tiffany dear. Every time I see you it seems as if you haven't changed at all."

To an outsider, that would have sounded like a compliment, but she knew differently. "I can also say the same for you." She looked down at her watch for effect. "I must apologize for having to leave our reunion, but the governor has an early day tomorrow, and we must be going. I'm *sure* you understand Sherri, your father's a city councilman."

She smiled as she and her father exited, knowing Sherri caught the jab she had thrown. Tiffany never considered herself better than anyone because her father was governor, but at times when she came face to face with Sherri, the woman who had made herself available to all the guys who were interested in her since college, she didn't bat an eye in offending her. Sherri had even flaunted the fact she had been with Christopher shortly after they had broken up, which was a big reason why she would never renew her and Christopher's past relationship.

It was almost humorous to Tiffany that the femme fatale was so down on her luck that she had to stoop to hiring a male escort to take her to functions—someone else's husband at that.

Fire and Desire

It was almost worth the humiliation to see the embarrassed look on Sherri's face if she'd told her that Trevor was her husband.

§

As Tiffany walked away, Trevor watched the gentle sway of her hips and thought, *Now, there's a jealous woman.*

He had seen how clearly and efficiently she'd tried to act nonchalant about Sherri linking herself so tight to him. He could easily feel the imprint of the other woman's breast on his arm, and he was sure Tiffany hadn't missed seeing it.

He had seen a quick twinkle in her eye and had almost overlooked the subtle lift of her eyebrow.

Neither could he disregard the tension between the two women. There was some bad blood there. It almost seemed as if their history was as harsh as his and Manning's. However, nothing could touch the spiteful feelings he carried toward the soon to be congressman.

"I do believe I'm ready to end this part of the evening. Would you be a dear and take me home?" Sherri said to him. About an hour ago, she had spotted him and had linked herself to him the rest of the evening.

"I don't mind, but are you sure your date won't mind?"

"He won't mind. I came with my brother tonight. His wife was sick. She's having her *third* child and couldn't accompany him." Her voice was laced with disgust.

He was quite positive that, if she were ever to become pregnant, it would be by accident, and it would probably only happen once.

Trevor loved kids. He didn't get a chance to be around his sister's four children as much as he would have liked, but he knew one day he would have a few of his own.

"Do you need to tell him you're leaving?"

"Nope, I waved good-bye to him about thirty minutes ago."

"Oh," was all he could say. He knew that meant he was stuck. He was too much of a gentleman to leave a woman stranded. He had no doubt that Miss Matrix was very resourceful and would easily find a willing guy to give her a *lift*.

He escorted her to his BMW and assisted her into the car.

She babbled on about a party she was invited to the following weekend and how everyone who was anyone would be there. Attendees consisted of politicians, musicians, actors and, most importantly, people whose pockets were laced with old money.

As she continued without pause, except when she was giving him directions, it gave him a chance to think about Tiffany and their situation.

Only a week since the last time he saw her, tonight was a welcomed surprise. His being there was strictly for business, to network. The tickets had been a gift from one of his clients. Hours ago he had decided to attend.

He was glad he did. He'd made some good contacts and expected several opportunities to open up.

When he saw Tiffany, his body had responded instantly. Just like Saturday when he'd shown up unannounced. Since the day they had met, he was drawn to her, and he wanted to get to know her better. But it seemed like his hormones kept getting in the way. He knew there was a lot more to Tiffany Hatcher-Lewis than what the world knew and much more than she wanted to admit.

From everything he'd learned about her, she was a woman who needed to let herself go and stop living for everyone else, always in the camera's eye, standing proud and faithful by her father's side. Even tonight he caught the subtle touch she gave her father, making sure the governor stayed on task. Tiffany was so immersed in her father's career, he wondered if she even knew where her life began.

If he did nothing else, before they divorced, he would make it his personal mission to ensure Tiffany learned what it was like to let go and live.

Six

Hi, Marti. Is there a table available for a hungry man to have lunch?"

"Mr. Lewis, there is always a table available for you." Marti was the headwaiter at Gilligan's, a small seafood restaurant in D.C.

Trevor had enjoyed lunch at the place at least once a week for the past five years, when he could pull himself away from one project or another. He and his staff frequently worked through lunch while sitting in front of a sick computer.

Marti escorted Trevor to a small table located in the back next to the kitchen. "How is this, Mr. Lewis? We're a bit busy today; otherwise, I'd have found you one by the window so you could have a better view."

"It's perfect. As hungry as I am, I need to be as close to the kitchen as possible." He smiled, hoping to ease Marti's mind.

"Great, I'll tell Cliff to come quickly to take your order."

Without another word, Marti weaved through the tables toward Cliff. When Marti reached the other man, he leaned forward and whispered in his ear, then was off to greet more waiting guests.

Cliff crossed the room moments later. "Good afternoon, Mr. Lewis. Do you know what you're having or would you like to see the menu?" Cliff stood poised to write on his little tablet.

"No menu, Cliff, what's the special for today?" Trevor was too hungry to peruse a menu. Last night's dinner was the last meal he remembered eating. If they were serving nails covered in a light peppercorn sauce, he would have eaten it.

"Crab cakes, rice pilaf, your choice of vegetable and a tossed salad."

"That sounds good to me. I'll take it...green beans and the house dressing please."

Cliff scribbled on his pad. "What beverage would you like, sir?"

"Ice tea with lemon, please, Cliff."

"Coming right up, Mr. Lewis." Cliff made a one-eighty and headed into the kitchen.

Trevor wisely used the waiting time to go wash his hands. On his way back, he heard someone call his name. When he turned around, he saw Marsha Leigh waving at him from a table in front of the restaurant. As he zigzagged through the tables in her direction, he could see she was not alone. There was another lady with her, whose back was to him, so he couldn't identify her.

"Well, hello, Ms. Leigh."

"You know better than to be so formal, Trevor. As many times as you've rendered your services to me, you should call me Marsha."

A choking sound came from Marsha's lunch companion. Trevor still couldn't see her face from his position behind her.

"Are you alright?" Marsha asked, her expression etched with concern.

The other woman attempted to clear her throat; raspily she said, "Yes, some water just went down wrong."

"It happens to the best of us." Marsha gave the woman a reassuring smile. "I am so rude. Trevor Lewis this is…"

Trevor made his way around the table and finally saw the mystery woman—his wife.

"…the governor's daughter."

"You two have met?" Marsha asked curiously.

Trevor gave a slight pause. "Last week at a banquet. It's good to see you again, Miss *Hatcher*."

"And you." Tiffany mumbled, leaving him with no opening for further conversation.

"Well, Marsha, I must be getting back to my table before my lunch gets cold." Trevor turned and left.

§

Tiffany's client turned to her. "That man has talent written all over him. He did a job for me; it amazed me how his mind and fingers performed sheer magic. I've never experienced another problem since. If I did, Trevor is the man I would go to."

Tiffany could see the light radiating out of the other woman's eyes. She could understand how the other woman felt. She was fully aware of Trevor's talents.

She wondered how many other women in the Tri-state area had experienced his skills. She was amazed the other lady spoke so openly about having hired Trevor's services.

"Well, Ms. Leigh, about the Children's Christmas gala you want to have for the orphanage." Tiffany changed the subject and brought the focus back to the reason for their lunch appointment.

"Yes, I was thinking about the second Saturday in December. I've already contacted some toy stores to see what they would be willing to donate."

"That's a good start. We'll need clothing store participation, grocers and volunteers, both for the event and ones who will give of their time year around."

"Goodness, I didn't even think about all of those other things. I can see why you come so highly recommended."

Tiffany and Marsha created a rough outline of the plans for the gala and arranged to meet in a week.

The meeting concluded and Marsha left. Tiffany pulled out her cell phone and dialed her office. While she waited for someone to answer, she opened up her laptop.

"Occasionally Yours, this is Jaunice. How may I help you?" Jaunice was one of three college students who worked for her and Josephine part-time.

"Jaunice, this is Tiffany. Is Josephine available?"

"Hello, Miss Hatcher. Miss Dailey is in a meeting with Mrs. Collins, the woman from the Breast Cancer Society. Would you like me to interrupt her?"

"No, it's nothing that can't wait. Open a file for Marsha Leigh and have a carrier take a copy of the standardized contract papers by her office. Tell Josephine I'll place the outline sketch on the office drive and meet with her tomorrow about it."

There was a brief pause. Tiffany knew Jaunice was writing all of the information down.

"Anything else, Miss Hatcher?"

"No, that'll be all."

"Have a nice day, ma'am."

"You, too." Tiffany snapped her phone closed and began to power up her laptop.

It took Tiffany only a few moments to transcribe the notes from her tablet onto the office drive. She even added in some spur of the moment ideas she had while inputting the information. Tiffany knew if she didn't write the ideas down right then and there, she would have forgotten them later on.

She smiled as she reviewed the contents of the electronic folder. Tiffany made a few corrections, and then saved the file.

The screen went black.

Tiffany's eyes became round as saucers as she looked down at the mechanical device, wondering what had gone wrong. Afraid to breathe, she held her breath, knowing if she couldn't figure out what happened soon, she would lose all of her information.

Tiffany tried not to create a scene while she banged on various keys in hopes that one of the combinations would cause the computer to start again.

"Looks like you're having a problem. Can I be of assistance?"

Tiffany could feel the wisps of heat circulating from the person's mouth. She didn't have to turn around to know it was Trevor who spoke.

"I don't think so." Tiffany tried to sound annoyed, so he would get the hint and leave. She was already frustrated by the possible loss of her document and didn't feel like battling her emotions for him.

"What seems to be the trouble?"

The heat moved to her neck.

Tiffany swallowed several times to combat the sudden dryness of her mouth.

"If you must know, my laptop seems to have decided now would be a good time for a nap, and I can't get it to wake up."

Not seeming to be put off by her tone, Trevor asked, "Have you tried plugging it up?"

"It has a charger." Tiffany shook her head at the man's ignorance.

"Maybe it needs to be recharged. Every now and then, all of our juices need recharging. If it only happened once in a lifetime, think how boring it would be."

"It's new," Tiffany spoke through clenched teeth.

"Then it's defective and you need another that won't quit until the job is complete." Trevor moved to stand beside her chair. "At any rate, do you have your cord with you?"

Tiffany considered what Trevor was saying and believed it was entirely possible he might have been right about the *computer*, but she refused to ponder the underlying points he made. Tiffany reached down in her case and produced the cable.

"May I?" Without awaiting a response, Trevor took the cord and laptop, then walked over to the headwaiter's stand.

Left with no other choice, Tiffany followed.

She watched as Trevor plugged the computer into the socket and the equipment came to life.

A smug look crossed Trevor's face.

"So it's on. I've still lost my document since it wasn't saved."

Trevor turned back toward the mini computer and began punching in a series of commands. Moments later, he asked, "Is this what you were working on?"

Tiffany stared at the screen in amazement. "How did you find it?"

"I guess it's a gift I have with computers. What would you like to call it?"

"Marsha Leigh."

Trevor executed the command to name and save the document, then he shut it down and unplugged it.

"You just saved me a lot of time in re-writes. Thanks." Tiffany took her laptop back from Trevor.

"No, problem. People usually pay me for my time."

Tiffany could feel the change in the atmosphere, something that happened too often when she was around Trevor.

"Will you take a check?"

"No. Dinner."

"Dinner?" Tiffany tried to stifle the laugh that began to bubble up. There was no way she could be seen out in public with him, especially since recently she was becoming aware of how many people hired him for his talents.

"Yeah, it comes after lunch, but before a night cap invitation." Trevor smiled beguilingly.

The urge to trace his lips with her tongue overwhelmed her. "I don't think dinner would be appropriate."

"And why not? Don't you think it's time we got to know each other...wife?"

"No, Trevor, I don't. And stop calling me that," she whispered. "Too many people know you and me. It would be in the papers before we could order dessert." Tiffany could imagine the headlines: Stripper Dates Governor's Daughter.

"We'll go out of town. The Harbor is nice this time of year, and I don't think your face is that well known in Baltimore."

Tiffany could tell he wouldn't give up. "*Fine*. When?"

"What are you doing this Friday at six?"

"Friday at six is fine. Where do you want to meet, the courthouse?" Tiffany made sure he understood he couldn't drive up to her house to pick her up for a date, nor had she forgotten they still needed to get the divorce taken care of and soon.

"Howard is having their homecoming," he said. "There'll be so many people around no one would be able to pick you out from the celebrators. I'll be in front of the Mordecai Wyatt Johnson, the admissions building."

Fire and Desire

"Friday at six, in front of Admissions," Tiffany reluctantly confirmed the place and time.

Tiffany gathered her things, paid her bill and left without another word, believing her agreement to have dinner with Trevor only confirmed she was past the verge of losing her mind.

Seven

"Hmmm," he moaned, eyes closed.

"Is it really that good?" she asked.

"Yes." Trevor could hear the hissing sound of the word as it exited.

"Honestly, Trevor, you sound like it's the best thing in life."

He opened his eyes and looked directly into Tiffany's. "Very few things can compare."

"I've had it before, and I don't remember it being that great," she said with disbelief.

"Maybe it was who did it. It takes time to learn how to get it just right." Trevor moved closer and set the speared meat before her. "Here, taste." Waiting patiently until she parted her lips, he slowly slid the delectable morsel into her mouth.

He watched Tiffany's eyes close instantly. "Hmmm."

The sound of Tiffany's enjoyment caused his heart to race. Everything within him wanted to reach out and brush his thumb across her juice glistened lips. "I told you it was good."

She opened her eyes. The candlelight flickered in her gaze as she smiled. "I have to admit you are right. That is the best piece of steak I've ever tasted."

Moving his seat back around the table, he gestured toward Tiffany's plate. "How do you come to a place called Hoof and Claw and get a chicken salad?"

"I try to eat healthy, my days are so busy most of the time I miss a lot of meals. It's my way of not doing any further harm to my body."

"That only counts at home. When you're out, you're supposed to indulge." He finished his steak and began on his lobster tail.

Fire and Desire

"Not when you're out as much as I am." Her forehead creased as she spoke, and he heard a trace of discontent in her voice. No matter the façade she put on, Tiffany wasn't completely happy with her life.

"If you don't enjoy what you're doing, do something else."

"I enjoy working with my father. It just gets taxing juggling time between him and my own business." Tiffany began picking through her salad.

"What's your business?"

She propped her fork against the salad bowl. "Consulting. I plan and coordinate parties and events."

Trevor didn't miss the gleam of excitement that lit her eyes as she spoke.

"You're a busy lady."

She leaned back in her chair and rotated her shoulders to maintain her posture.

Years of etiquette school, Trevor thought, watching her settle herself in the seat.

"The consulting business is run heavily by my business partner, Josephine. You may remember her from the party. Sometimes I feel guilty because I do a lot of the preliminary, but she does all of the hard work. I guess it's more important that in the end we're both always there to get the praise." Tiffany bowed her head and reclaimed her fork again.

"Did you want dessert?" he asked as he watched her sift through the remainder of her salad.

"No, thank you. I'm afraid I may make the same poor choice as I did with dinner." She raised her head with a humorous smile on her lips. "Or worse, I'd have to listen to you do an encore."

He laughed and signaled the waiter. "We could always make it a two part harmony. Your small part wasn't so bad. It needs a little fine tuning, but it's all right for starters."

"I'll work on it."

Trevor watched the playful rolling of her eyes.

You'd better watch yourself, man. She could easily get under your skin.

Clearing his throat and his thoughts, he asked, "How about a nice walk to digest some of this food?"

"Sounds good to me."

§

"When was the last time you rode a merry-go-round?" he asked as they came upon the ride in the park at the end of the harbor.

"I can't even remember. I think I was twelve." Excitement danced in her eyes.

Trevor liked the whimsical smile that graced her lips. He silently admitted to himself there were many things about Tiffany Hatcher he liked. Trevor felt a slight twinge of delight as Tiffany genuinely smiled. The smile he frequently witnessed her using for the press was so plastic.

"Would you like to ride it?"

She hesitated, her features encumbered by indecision. "I think I would." She turned to him with a radiant smile.

He walked over to the attendant who appeared to be around sixteen years old. "How much for two tickets on the carousel?"

"Actually, I was about to close up for the night." The kid flipped the OPEN sign over on his ticket stand to CLOSED.

Trevor leaned toward the teen conspiratorially. "Listen," he whispered, "I have a beautiful woman with me, and it would totally make her night if I could get her a ride on this." He took a twenty out of his pocket and handed it to the kid.

The teen snatched the twenty and slid it into his front jeans pocket. "Look, I have to catch up with my ride home, but I'll start it and you can ride until I come back." The teen shook his head. "My boss will fire me if he finds out I left it unattended and something happened."

Trevor raised his right hand toward the kid. "I give you my word I will look out for it."

The teen still looked unsure as he held the entrance rope for them, but he nodded his head and let them on.

"Your chariot awaits." Trevor assisted Tiffany onto the ride with all the flare of a seventeenth century prince.

They chose to sit in a carriage type seat with two benches facing each other inside. Their knees brushed as they got comfortable in the small cart.

It was clear to Trevor the builder probably hadn't intended it to fit two adults, but they both adjusted to the accommodations of the secluded seat. Covered from any viewing eyes, he and Tiffany looked out at the park as the ride began to twirl.

"I should be back in a few minutes," the kid yelled as he jogged away.

Neither one of them responded to the teen.

Trevor watched as Tiffany leaned her head back against the wall on her side of the seat, closed her eyes and looked at peace.

Unwilling to disturb her solitude, he took pleasure in the sight.

He remembered that her golden brown skin was smooth as cream. A perfect match to her honey speckled eyes. He fantasized about holding and touching her skin, how she tasted and what it was like to align his body with hers for a brief moment. The subtle sent of raspberry she wore was driving him crazy. He would be lying to himself if he said he didn't want that again, but for a longer period of time.

With Tiffany's head tilted as she relaxed, the expansion of her neck appeared available for a lover's kiss. His eyes continued to travel down her body. Today, she wore a pale orange sundress, which fell in soft folds around her legs, stopping just below her knees. A slight breeze from the moving carousel ruffled her dress. It allowed him to get glimpses of her inner thighs. He noticed the smoothness of her legs.

"Tiffany, would I be out of line in saying that I find you very sexy?"

Her eyes fluttered, then opened. "Yes, you would." Something flickered in the depth of her eyes and disappeared.

He leaned in closer to her. "I mean no offense, but it's the truth."

"Trevor…"

"What…Tiffany?" He loved saying her name and watching the quick leap of her pulse at the base of her neck. "You can say whatever you want to me. I don't pull any punches. I just give it as I see it."

Tiffany bowed her head briefly, raised her head again and looked at him. "Look, Trevor...I *know* it's part of your job to flatter women and make them feel special while they're with you."

He ignored the anger that wanted to rise. "Tiffany, you didn't hire me, and I'm not on a job. Regardless of what I may or may not do professionally, when I'm on a date—"

"Trevor, this is not a date. I don't want you to get the wrong idea of what is happening here."

Trevor refused to move back and give her space. "So what is happening here, Tiffany? You tell me."

She averted her gaze away from him and looked out over the moving view of the park and exhaled. "It's dinner, Trevor. Just dinner."

He reached out with a gentle finger under her chin and brought her face back around to look at him, eliminating any confusion. He was attracted to her. More than he had ever been to anyone.

"Tiffany, is dinner truly the only thing that is happening here?" Trevor's finger slowly moved down her neck.

"Yes..." she uttered.

"Are you sure?" His finger continued past the modest V-neck of her collar.

"Trevor, I can't get caught up in a situation with you." A pleading tone danced in the texture of her voice.

He could hear what she was saying and would have been easily convinced, but the trembling he felt from her body told the truth.

"Too late." He placed both of his hands lightly on her knees and leaned in until their lips almost connected, his fingers flexed against the silky texture of her skin.

"Why?"

"Because you're already there..." He brought their lips together.

The first few moments of the kiss continued without much participation from Tiffany.

"Tiffany, I won't force you to do anything you don't want." Trevor's hands began to make seductive circles on her knees where his hands rested. "All you have to do is tell me to stop."

Looking her deeply in the eyes as his hands journeyed up her legs. "Say it, Tiffany," he whispered, then dragged his tongue slowly across her bottom lip. "Tell me to stop…" His hands slid under the edge of her skirt on the side of her thighs.

Trevor's memory served him well. Warm satin were the words that came to mind.

"Trevor…" Tiffany's hips squirmed on the mini bench seat.

Their words seemed to entwine themselves in the minute space between their lips.

"Yes." His hands ventured around the tops of her thighs, "Want me to stop…" then shifted between her legs and tenderly pushed them apart.

"Trevor…"

Leaning away from her mouth, he murmured, "Tiffany, let yourself go…if only for tonight."

In the quivering of her voice, her internal battle was evident. He knew he wasn't playing fair, but he was willing to pull out all the stops to get what he wanted…Tiffany.

"I can't." Shutting her eyes, she leaned her head back against the wall.

Her lids were squeezed tight, her eyebrows pinched together, making her feelings of defeat clear. Trevor refused to allow her to walk away from their evening together with it.

"Should I stop then?" He slid a finger beyond the lacy edges of her panties.

"Trevor…" Shocked, she snapped her legs together and trapped his hand in the middle of them.

Her wetness bathed his fingers as he caressed the stiffening bud of her desire that yearned to be touched.

Tiffany's head rolled along the partition. "Ohhh…"

"Stop?" he threw out the question one more time, waiting to hear her verbally acknowledge her decision to let go. Trevor slid the same finger inside her moist heat while his thumb made pressured circles on her clitoris.

Helplessly, Tiffany spread her legs open wider. "Don't stop, Trevor, please don't stop."

"With pleasure."

He observed the play of emotion across her face in the dim light of the chariot. He briefly thought about all the other times. "No interruptions this time, baby."

As if she needed that small amount of encouragement, Tiffany's hips began to meet his hand play. She bit down on her lip as if to keep the vocal sounds of her enjoyment down, even though her moans permeated the air. Trevor couldn't be sure, but a big part of him sensed what she experienced was a first for her. It was somehow connected to the complete unguarded rapturous expression on her face. As if she hadn't learned over the years of experience how to school her features and control her response.

He glanced down, the high rise of the hem of Tiffany's dress around her waist gave him an unobstructed view of her wide spread legs and the recreational activity of his hands. In another place and time, he would've been buried deep inside of her to feel her body quake around his shaft when she reached completion.

When he noticed the tremors of her body begin to intensify, he knew the end would be near for her. He adjusted the pressure and rate of his hands and led her toward her peak.

When the climax finally overtook her, he kissed her. Tiffany's hands firmly held his head in place, which he assumed was more for support of the shock waves than anything else.

"Sorry, sir, but I have to lock up now." The kid yelled from his ticket booth.

In the dimness of the carriage, they broke apart and Trevor readjusted Tiffany's clothes and legs as the carousel slowed. Moments later, it came to a stop.

Assisting an unsteady Tiffany from the ride, he thanked the teenager and they left.

§

Fire and Desire

On the ride home, she sat in the passenger seat of Trevor's BMW and felt like crying. Once again, Tiffany found herself caught up in the sensual game Trevor so easily played.

He seemed to respect the fact that she needed time by herself because he turned on the radio and didn't say anything.

Part of her wished he would say something, as "Thinking Of You" by the Rhythm and Blues artist Justin Guarini played softly in the background.

Staring out of the passenger side window, she wondered what it would be like to have no responsibilities but loving someone.

Shaking the thought off, she knew that fantasy wasn't for her. She was Tiffany Hatcher, the governor's daughter. Her fate was sealed.

"Tiffany, we need to talk."

The music faded as he turned down the volume.

She closed her eyes for a moment and took a deep breath before turning toward the front of the vehicle.

"No, we don't. This whole thing was a mistake from the beginning, and this date just topped it off," she said in a quiet tone.

"I don't agree."

"I don't care. Trevor, why won't you just end this farce of a marriage? Then we can both go our separate ways."

His jaw clenched, but he remained silent.

"Trevor, you can't believe this *relationship* has potential?"

"Why, would I think of something like you honoring your vows and staying with someone ridiculous?"

She could see his anger plainly in the way he stared intently out of the front window and tapped his thumb against the steering wheel.

"*Vows*? Trevor, I'm not going there again with you." Tiffany tried to remain calm.

The returned silence in the car seemed to stretch on forever.

Trevor exhaled a slow breath. "Look, Tiffany, I'm sorry for getting upset. I know you don't know me and I don't know you that well, and you're probably right. Regardless of what my feelings may be about marriage, this one started off in a way neither of us would have planned.

You're also probably right; a divorce is most likely inevitable. However, we've been attracted to one another since the moment we met.

She snapped, "So what do you suggest, Trevor, that the two of us get together for casual sex every now and then to relieve a little stress and tension?" She rolled her eyes toward the ceiling of the car.

This is just great, she thought. *Men are all the same, no matter what their social class or occupation. It is all about sex.*

Taking his eyes off the road, he briefly looked at her. "In spite of what you may think about me, sex has not been casual for me since I was in my early twenties."

"Then why even bring it up?"

"Because it's a fact that *neither* of us can honestly deny."

"I may not be able to deny it, but I plan to disregard it." In an abrupt motion, Tiffany crossed her legs and folded her arms over her chest.

Trevor merged into the off ramp traffic, taking the exit back to the college. "Tiffany, I'll give you your divorce."

Shocked, she turned toward him. "Are you serious?"

Trevor held up his hand, curbing her enthusiasm. "On one condition."

She observed his profile through squinted eyes and asked cautiously, "What's that?"

"The moment you begin living for yourself, I'll let you go."

"What kind of garbage is that?"

Trevor turned the corner to the college. "I know you're not only totally consumed by your father's career, but your friends are sucking the rest of the life out of you."

"You don't know anything about me *or* my life." Tiffany slid her hips back, her posture ramrod straight in the seat.

As he pulled into a parking spot, he turned toward her. "I know enough to know you are suffocating. You're stifling your own passion and life to fulfill your father's dreams."

Tiffany inhaled a sharp breath, then forced it out. "As you can see, Mr. Trevor Lewis, I can breathe just fine. I don't need your amateur medical advice to tell me what's best for me."

"Maybe not, but one thing I do know for sure is you're in dire need of a good lay."

The silence in the car almost crackled with the tension ignited between them.

"Where do you get off—"

Trevor cut her off, saying, "As you may have noticed tonight, I didn't."

Mad enough to spit needles, she grabbed the door handle and attempted to exit the car.

Trevor grabbed her by the shoulders and turned her toward him. "Look, Tiffany, you need to learn to live your own life before you get smothered under the pile of people wanting a piece of you." He looked into her eyes, his gaze intent and strong. "You may be Governor Donald W. Hatcher's daughter, but you're not his wife. It's way past time for you to step out of his lime light."

She pushed away from him, gripped the door handle, opened it and faced him one last time. "Listen up, Trevor, and listen well. I never asked you to be my guardian angel. I don't know why you *think* you have a right to dictate to me about *my* life."

"I'm your husband," he said, his tone austere and quiet, like a vault door sealing her fate.

§

He watched Tiffany walk to her car, get in, start it up and pull off. The sound of spitting gravel assured him she was still very angry. He pulled out of the parking spot and headed toward his apartment.

He didn't know why it was so important to him that Tiffany got a life. Maybe it was because he'd noticed the minute signs of strain and fatigue around her eyes. Even when they were at the party a few weeks ago and she smiled her fake smile for the public, he could see how exhausted she appeared. The hints were so subtle that, if someone weren't paying close attention to her, he would miss them.

He steered his car down the deserted dark streets. "That woman's going to start living, even if I have to drag her kicking and screaming."

Eight

Tiffany exited the kitchen. She was happy that everything was going well. The Breast Cancer Society's annual fundraiser benefit and ball promised to be a resounding success.

She and Josephine had worked on this non-stop over the last month. It was an issue she and her partner held dear. Standing by the kitchen door, she observed all of the attendees. The ballroom at the Marriott was packed. The BCS committee had sold over three hundred tickets at three hundred dollars a plate.

People arrived at the cocktail hour and took the time before dinner to mingle with each other as the live band played.

She observed everyone. A bald, tall, brown-skinned man with broad shoulders and what appeared to be a nice build under his suit caught her attention. Her heart paused; for a moment she'd thought the man was Trevor.

Her mind instantly drifted to two weeks ago when she had last seen Trevor. She recalled how angry she had been. No one had ever made her lose control in so many ways as Trevor did. She denied herself the memory of the carousel ride. It took everything in her power not to think back to the interlude. When she slept, her dreams were filled with heated reflections. The morning after it happened, she awakened with a strong desire for sex.

She had to hurry up and divorce him before things went too far or, worse, her feelings began to get involved.

Maybe it is too late.

Tiffany refused to believe that. She wouldn't allow herself to become entangled in this *relationship* with him—anymore than she already had.

When the man turned to speak to some woman on his right, she realized her mistake. She berated herself for her wayward thoughts about Trevor.

There were three twenty-minute speakers set up during dinner, besides the remarks and comments made by Lavonia Demhart, the president of the local chapter of BCS. Two of them were personal testimonials, and the other one was a family member who had lost a loved one to breast cancer.

Four years ago, Tiffany had been one of the speakers. The testimonials were always an emotional time of the evening for her—as well as for other attendees.

Tiffany heard Josephine through the speakers as she directed everyone to take their seats.

Tiffany and Josephine's seats were reserved in the back, closest to the kitchen. If anything happened, they could leave without disturbing the function.

"How was everything in the kitchen?" Josephine asked her when she took the seat beside Tiffany's.

Josephine wore a black chiffon dress with a scooped neck that left the crown of her shoulders bare. It clung nicely to her body, stopping modestly above her knee. Sheer black stockings and a pair of black chiffon covered heels topped off the outfit. The only color to her ensemble was the honey color highlights in her bone-straight, jet-black, short, tapered haircut. Her best friend's eyes were so dark brown even they appeared black.

Tonight, Tiffany wore a black tuxedo dress with a white lapel collar. The dress was sleeveless, tapered in the front at her waist and ended at the tips of her shoes. The back of it was the part that made her a little self-conscious because the dress wasn't as conservative as those she normally wore. It left the full expansion of her back bare.

She'd received some curious looks from people. More than once, she'd wished she'd just worn her sequin suit, or had left her hair down to cover up part of her back instead of deciding on the French roll.

"Great, no problems, Jo. Any concerns or worries from Lavonia?" Tiffany sat next to Josephine.

"Not a one. Things are going smoothly." Josephine smiled.

"Good evening, ladies and gentlemen. On behalf of the Breast Cancer Society, we would like to welcome you to the Virginia Chapter's Sixteenth Annual Benefit dinner." The emcee Bridget Kruse, the vice president of the chapter, began the opening remarks as the servers collected the dessert plates.

§

"Wow, Tiffy, you look fabulous. I almost didn't recognize you," Christopher said in a soft whisper as he came up behind her. She stood on the outskirts of the dance floor, watching people move to the beat of the live band.

Tiffany drew in a slow breath, then turned around with a smile. "Christopher, I didn't expect to see you here. Things like this aren't usually your thing."

Looking at her with a conspirator's smile, he said, "You know me so well, Tiffy. Another reason why we'd made a great team. Anyway, now that I'm running for congressman, it's important for me to show face in the right places. People in the BCS are heavy voters."

"That's true and they're pretty smart also."

"Humm," he grumbled. "So what do you say about allowing me a few moves with you on the dance floor?"

The first thing that came to mind was to turn him down, telling him she was working wouldn't work. With the main part of the program concluded and a few people having already left, it was a weak excuse. The truth of the matter, she liked to dance, and even though Christopher was a very persistent friend, she knew he would be safe.

"Sure, that would be nice."

Tiffany allowed him to escort her to the dance floor and even disregarded the cocky look on his face as he led her to an empty spot.

She and Christopher danced to one fast song, then the band switched to a slower ballad. She allowed Christopher to pull her in close and hold her. She admitted to herself for a moment that it felt good to be in a man's arms, even if only for a moment.

§

Trevor stood holding a Sprite in his hand. As the carbonated bubbles rose to the top, so did his anger as he watched Manning hold Tiffany in his arms.

He was supposed to be listening to Matthew Benedict, an alderman and congressman hopeful from Texas, talk about the benefits of health care for migrant workers in border States. It was known that Benedict's wife was at one time an illegal alien who had been trying to escape the border patrol in Del Rio, Texas, when she jumped in his car at a gas station. Rumor had it he had waited weeks before turning her in to the officials—only to marry her a month after she was deported. That didn't stop Benedict from lobbying to whomever would listen. It was easy to tune him out.

Trevor glanced around the room while he gave Benedict an occasional, "Hmm, interesting…" or a "You may have a point there," when he spotted the couple on the dance floor.

He had seen Josephine earlier that night but didn't realize Tiffany was there also. After their "date" two weeks ago, he'd learned about their business Occasionally Yours and knew they managed functions such as this one but assumed they alternated who showed up for the engagements.

Tiffany looked sexy tonight. Her hair was in some type of up do. Different from the normal conservative bun she wore, making him desire to reach up and remove every pin and clip until it cascaded unencumbered down her bare back. Trevor's eyes followed the curve of her spine. Her skin made him think of caramel or toffee. He'd always had a sweet tooth for both. In the weeks since he'd smelled her scent on the carousel, sweet musk, he'd continued craving her, desiring to know what she tasted like. While in Vegas, the perfect opportunity had been within his grasp, to spread her legs wide and sample until his lust was slacked. Even if only temporarily.

Tiffany was someone whom, if he ever had her, there would never be an end to his wanting her. He would never get enough.

Even at that moment, he recalled the sound of her voice begging him to touch her. *Trevor, I want your hands on me. I need them inside,* she had cried. He had given in to her request and touched her. Felt her slick wet heat surround his finger as it slid inside. Felt her walls tighten and quiver around it. However, the alcohol-induced memory was nothing compared to the memory of seeing and feeling her in Baltimore. The memory of watching the freedom of her sexuality. That had been a remarkable sight.

Trevor felt the response of his body—rapid heart beat, beads of sweat rolling down his spine and the rush of blood in his ears as it left his head and moved south. He felt his shaft begin to pulse with the increased blood flow.

A dish clattered somewhere in the kitchen and brought Trevor's mind out of the fog. *Pull yourself together, man.* He cleared his throat and refocused on Tiffany.

He would have been pleased to see her under any other circumstance, but she looked too cozy with Manning for his comfort. Manning held one of her hands while his other hand lay on the *bare* flesh of her back. Tiffany in a skin revealing dress had shocked him enough without adding her dance partner into the mix.

It took all of his will power to keep his hand relaxed and not squeeze the glass until it shattered.

A bead of sweat trickled down his spine; his temperature rose and he saw red. He'd never felt blind rage like what he experienced at that moment.

It was one thing to see Manning and know how he had gotten away with murder five years ago, but seeing him standing so close to Tiffany pushed him beyond his breaking point.

Turning, he headed to the bathroom for a moment to get himself together. The urge to walk across the room and plant his fist in Manning's face was a temptation too hard to resist if he continued to watch them. In the end, he would have made a spectacle and embarrassed Tiffany publicly. After he entered the men's room, he made his way to the sink and splashed water on his face. The anger burned so hot inside of him, he thought for a moment he saw steam when he looked into the mirror. He blinked and the illusion was gone.

Short of him telling Manning explicitly to take his hands off his wife, there was little he could do to rectify the situation right now. Grabbing several paper towels, he dried his face. He couldn't do what he wanted to do, but he could take care of what he needed to do. Remove Tiffany from his clutches.

§

"Tiffy…"

God, I really dislike that name.

"Look how people are watching us."

Must I.

"You can practically hear them whispering about how good we look together."

Tiffany looked at him. They stood eye to eye with her heels on. He was tall, at least six one, and slender in his build, in an athletic runner sort of way. He was fair skinned with curly hair he kept cut low, no facial hair and hazel eyes. He was a "pretty boy," never lacking for female companionship. One reporter had described him as captivating to the camera's lens.

"Christopher, you could never understand how that doesn't matter to me."

He looked at her as if she had just begun to sprout warts on her nose.

Voice laced with disgust, he questioned, *"Tiffany,* how could it not matter to you? You're a governor's daughter for crying out loud."

Tiffany stopped dancing for a moment. "And that's enough lime light for me."

Christopher gave her a slight tug to start her feet moving again. He glanced around them quickly to make sure no one had noticed her moment of *insurrection*.

"What do you want me to do," he whispered, "turn down the congressman seat? Is that what you want, for us to live some quiet no name life?"

"Christopher, I wouldn't dream of asking you to give up anything on account of me—except me."

He gave her one of his camera flashing smiles. "Tiffy, you'll give in to me eventually. We were too good together for you not to want us again. I don't know why you're playing hard to get."

He is truly unbelievable. How could he be that self-absorbed with his own desires and discount mine.

Thankfully, the song ended, and she broke contact with him. "Thank you, Christopher, but I must get back and check on some things."

Tiffany intended to leave the dance floor. She turned around as the next slow song began and walked straight into Trevor.

For a brief moment, she stared into his eyes and felt like a fox in the sight of a hound. However, without saying a word or doing anything, he completely consumed her, once again, making her oblivious to everything around them.

"Trevor Lewis...I haven't seen you in years and wouldn't have expected to see you here. I wouldn't have thought this was your forte." Christopher's voice did what she would have never been able to accomplish on her own—break the spell.

Trevor looked past her to Christopher. "Then you never really knew anything about me."

Christopher smiled broadly, but there was an unreadable look in his eyes that didn't carry the same happy glow.

Immediately, Tiffany knew there was friction between the two men.

"You're probably correct. Considering I was a year ahead of you."

"I did have the *pleasure* of crossing paths with you on a *significant* occasion," Trevor said.

"Hmm." Christopher paused slightly. "Aah, yes, now that you mention it, I do remember an *encounter*. I must say that, over all of these years, it must have slipped my mind."

Tiffany saw Trevor's chest expand.

"Well, if you don't mind, I'd like to dance with *Miss Hatcher*."

Oh, no, Tiffany thought.

"I didn't realize you even knew Tiffany."

Please, Trevor, don't say anything, Tiffany pleaded with him silently.

Trevor looked at her briefly as if hearing her, then back at Christopher. "Her father introduced us almost two months ago."

Voice raised, Christopher said, "Well, then by all means I don't mind you dancing with her. Just don't get too friendly. You're a little out of your league with this one…besides she and I are practically married."

Trevor lifted an eyebrow.

"Oh, *really?*" The steel tone of Trevor's statement almost sounded like a threat.

Tiffany fervently prayed to God that Trevor would not let the truth out.

Tiffany's gaze shot daggers of fury at Trevor and Christopher, but neither paid any attention to her as they let the level of testosterone build in the atmosphere.

Tiffany took a quick breath and fought the urge to grind her teeth. "Excuse me, but neither of you have even asked me what I want."

Christopher placed a hand on her bare shoulder. "Come on, Tiffy…this is a benefit. I'm sure you can find it in your heart to be charitable." He finished his statement by leaning down and kissing her on the corner of her mouth before she could turn her face away from him.

Christopher walked away, leaving her and Trevor standing in the middle of the dance floor.

"Well, *Tiffy,* let's dance." Trevor wrapped an arm around her waist and pulled her forward.

She tried to disregard the tingling sensation she experienced when his warm hand made contact with the lower part of her back. She placed her hand in the one Trevor held out to her and the other hand around his neck, bringing her body lightly against his. "Please don't call me that...I *detest* that name."

"Why do you allow him to call you that?"

"Like I have a choice. Christopher does what Christopher wants to do."

"So is that how it's going to be when the two of you marry? You're just going to allow him to delegate your very existence."

Tiffany looked into his light brown eyes. "I think that's a bit much. Besides, as I've told you before, my life is not up for discussion by you."

"Then it's a good thing I just came over here to dance with you," he said with a slight lift of one corner of his mouth.

Her gaze rested on his mouth, and the urge to lean closer was strong.

Shaking herself, she remembered they were in a room with three hundred other people.

In the arms of her long time friend, she felt nothing, so it amazed her that with Trevor, a virtual stranger, her senses sang and her thoughts fled.

She would never admit it to Trevor, but she liked the feel of his arms around her. She felt safe and secure. She stood on an even eye level with Trevor—light hazelnut colored eyes, to match his smooth mahogany skin.

Trevor was muscular and well built. She remembered quite vividly his chiseled body. Something she'd thought for years would never attract her. *Boy, had I been wrong.*

Attraction was not everything; otherwise, she would have said yes to Christopher a long time ago.

The music faded as Trevor's thumb softly grazed the skin of her lower back. His breath fluttered across her earlobe as he turned his head and whispered, "Your skin always feels like velvet, soft, warm and inviting." His thumb brushed against her spine.

Tiffany's steps faltered.

He pulled her tighter. "I remember so much of our night together. Do you?"

Tiffany felt the heated weight of desire as it moved from her lower belly and headed toward her sex. "No."

Trevor made a soft chuckle in her ear. "It was hot. We were all over each other. Touching. Grinding."

Trevor's feet never missed a beat as he continued to lead Tiffany on the dance floor. Just for a moment, she allowed herself to enjoy the feeling of being snuggled firmly against him. Even though she knew she should stop this. Not allow the flow of words that was evidence of her reckless behavior.

Her pulse rate picked up as every nerve became alive to the feel of his body moving against hers. Her breath quivered. "Trevor, what are we doing?"

"Dancing, sweetie, just dancing." He fused her body to his and continued in a tone that was as smooth as silk. "Aww, Tiffany honey, you had me on fire. I would have gone up in flames if not for your wetness. I still imagine your creamy, lush scent, like my very own spice treat." He placed his mouth directly on the shell of her ear. "Tiffany, baby, just thinking about it makes me want to eat until I'm full."

She couldn't breathe. Trevor's words were making her head spin. "Trevor, you shouldn't say these things to me. You have no right."

"Oh, sweetheart, I haven't even begun to take my rights." Trevor's hand moved up to the center of her back, then returned to the small of her back.

She felt her nipples tighten and press against the fabric of her dress. Tiffany knew she was in dangerous waters. "Trevor—"

"I feel your nipples coming alive." He moved his chest and brushed the sensitive tips concealed in her gown.

The air caught in her throat. She had to swallow to force down the sigh trying to escape.

"I could write poems about your breasts, baby. Poems about how full, soft and responsive they are. How I suckled them for hours and you begged—"

"Tiffany, I'm sorry to interrupt, but I need to see you."

The sound of Josephine's voice startled Tiffany out of the cocoon Trevor had so eloquently weaved around them. Tiffany opened her eyes, not realizing she had closed them and looked at the other woman.

She couldn't miss the look of concern in her friend's eyes.

Tiffany stopped dancing and immediately stepped out of Trevor's arms as if she'd been burned. "Thank you." She bowed her head slightly. She appreciated him letting her go without a scene.

"It was my *pleasure*." He leaned forwarded and placed a firm kiss on her cheek, lingering slightly longer than appropriate. "Miss Dailey, I believe it is. It's nice to meet you." His words accompanied a nod of his head toward Josephine.

Remembering her manners late, Tiffany made introductions. "Yes, you're correct. Josephine Dailey, this is Trevor Lewis, an associate of the governor's."

"I hope you're enjoying the evening, Mr. Lewis," Josephine said.

He pierced Tiffany with a lust-filled gaze, and then to Josephine said, "I am."

He gave them both a smile and turned to leave.

Sherri stopped in front of them briefly, saying, "Tiffy, I was beginning to get worried that you weren't going to let him go so some of us single women could have at him. You're virtually married already, and you were hogging Trevor all to yourself." Sherri tapped her arm lightly as if she were disciplining a child. "Shame on you."

Tiffany refused to look at Trevor.

"Well, don't let me stop you." She pasted on a fake smile.

Sherri led Trevor away. "Oh rats, it's a fast song coming up."

Tiffany was truly seething inside but refused to allow either one of them to see her anger.

Besides, what reason do I have to be angry? I don't want Trevor, right?

"So what was it you ne—" Tiffany began to ask, when she turned around and saw the questioning look on Josephine's face.

"It would be better if we discussed it in private." Josephine led the way through the crowd.

Tiffany followed her into the ladies room.

"What's up?" she questioned, anxiously.

Josephine checked each stall for vacancy. When she was assured they were alone, she turned to face Tiffany. "Tiff, what's going on?"

"I don't know, Jo. I thought you were going to tell me. Isn't that why I followed *you*?"

"You and Trevor Lewis?"

Tiffany's heart skipped a beat. "What about us? We're just...just nothing."

One of Josephine's eyebrows arched toward the ceiling. It was the second time someone had given Tiffany that expression.

"It's not what it looked like to me when you two were on the dance floor."

Were we that obvious? Or was it because Josephine is my best friend that she noticed?

"So we're acquaintances." For a brief moment, the image of him and Sherri on the dance floor flashed across her mind, and she said quietly, "And as you can see, he's acquainted with a lot of women."

"Well, I'm not concerned with lots of women...only you. For that matter, you need to be thanking me for keeping the reporters tied up with interviewing Lavonia. Otherwise, there would've been pictures of you and this Lewis fellow plastered all over tomorrow's society page."

How stupid could I have been? Tiffany berated herself.

"There's nothing to worry about." Tiffany was trying to convince herself.

"If you had seen the two of you embracing out there and the expression on your face...you'd be worried."

"Hey, Jo, what can I say...?" In an attempt to laugh away the situation, she finished by saying, "I was completely zoning while I was out there. I just needed a break. I'm human."

"Contrary to popular belief...Tiffany Hatcher has always been human. But Tiff, you've been acting strangely for a while now. If you would like to talk—"

A woman entering the bathroom saved Tiffany from having to respond. She smiled at her friend, hoping to reassure her that everything was all right. "I'm fine. I've had a lot on my mind."

Josephine didn't respond, but her eyebrow lifted in question. Tiffany was beginning to dislike that gesture.

Tiffany linked arms with her friend as they exited the confines of the restroom. "I should be back to my old self soon; trust me."

Josephine said, "I'm always here if you need to talk. I hope I don't have to tell you that you can always *trust* me."

Tiffany nodded to her friend as they re-entered the large room where the remainder of the guests gathered. She was going through a lot, and she would have loved to open up—particularly with her best friend. Mostly, she was hoping the situation would go away soon.

She couldn't have stopped herself if she wanted to from noticing that neither Trevor nor Sherri was among the lingering guests. *I don't have to guess where they've gone off to, knowing Sherri.*

She also noticed Christopher had departed, too. She already knew he and Sherri had history together.

Now which one was the un-lucky one, Tiffany thought.

Looking around, and thankful Josephine had already walked away, Tiffany said aloud, "Well, none of them are my concern. And my marriage problem will be over soon enough."

Tiffany shook away the gray cloud that hovered over her at the thought of Trevor and Sherri together.

A divorce was what she wanted, after all…wasn't it?

Nine

Ms. Sanders, it's nice to meet you. If I'm not mistaken, your late husband was one of the main physicians at the Cancer Research Center," Trevor said to the older woman whom Governor Hatcher introduced to him outside of one of the luxury suites in the new FedEx Field.

It was the game of the season in Washington, and he'd had his tickets for months. Anyone and everyone who was a football fan was there—the place was packed to see the Redskins versus the Cowboys! He was on his way to his seat to watch the opening kick-off when he passed the governor and his guest.

"You have a very good memory, Mr. Lewis. My husband has been dead for three years now," the woman said with a soft smile and hint of sadness in her eyes.

"That's how we met," the governor added. "When we found out my wife had developed breast cancer, I personally invited them over to the house for dinner to see what could be done."

"I'm very familiar with the agony of the disease. My sister was diagnosed with it, and I'm very thankful she survived it. When the family is strained with worry, you look at all the options," Trevor said.

"Even if some are experimental…you're willing to try anything," Ms. Sanders commented.

The governor spoke, breaking the moment of silence between all of them. "Trevor, why don't you join us for the game."

As much as he would have liked to, Trevor couldn't. "Sir, I know you probably already have the seats reserved for your colleagues."

The governor nodded his head. "I do, but one of my comrades will not be able to make it. He had something unexpected come up at the last minute. So there's room."

Trevor looked toward the outdoor seats and thought about the hype of the game and the excitement of being in the active stands with the other Redskin's fanatics. He considered the joy of leaping to his feet excitedly with others at a touchdown and having someone spilling their coke on him, by accident. Having the opportunity to sit on a misplaced hotdog after he'd hovered above his seat in tension while following a quarterback down the yard line in anticipation that he'd reach the goal. That was most of the reason he came to the stadium—part of the game.

Trevor only deliberated for a moment, and then agreed. After the game, he still had a company to run and see succeed. Not to mention, this man was his father in-law. He wasn't sure for how much longer. Better to be in his good graces while he could.

The governor patted him heartily on the back and escorted him in along with Ms. Sanders.

Trevor smiled at his own good fortune as he stood up with the other people in the box in honor of the pledge of allegiance. The stands were divided in half, one side red and gold, the other silver and white.

Trevor *loved* football. Playing the sport had been his dream for as far back as he could remember—until it was snatched from him.

His heart raced with excitement as he watched the coin toss and the Redskin's team captain calling it in the air. Luck was with the home team as the quarter landed head side up—per the coach's request; they opted to receive the ball.

Trevor shook his head with many other fans. He was always an advocate for deferring the ball, to have the advantage in the second half. Despite the decision, Trevor could feel the vibrations of the fans' roars as the game began.

§

The Redskins were down by six when Ms. Sanders excused herself during half time to use the restroom.

"I guess your daughter doesn't like football." Trevor opened the discussion to the person who was never far from his mind.

"Actually, she doesn't mind it, but she's been keeping herself so busy with her business and my obligations. She's doing a great job of burning her energy candle at both ends." The concern for his daughter was evident on his face.

"I'm sure that doesn't leave much time for a personal life." Looking around, Trevor briefly observed others in the box. Few people sat watching the game like he and the governor, Douglas Hatcher. Most milled around the back end of the box, talking, eating and socializing like it was a party instead of a football game.

"Personal life?" The governor chuckled. "It's truly evident you don't know my daughter."

Trevor could imagine the governor would've been shocked to know how familiar he was with Tiffany and how close he'd come to knowing her in the biblical sense. He figured the governor would have been down right astonished to know he was actually sitting next to his son in-law.

"Tiffany finds it hard to see past her responsibilities. I'm to blame for a lot of that. I leaned on her at such a young age. She was so busy taking care of me, she never learned how to take care of herself."

The governor's voice was weighed with the heaviness of his burden, and Trevor was sure he didn't need any comments from him. Hearing Tiffany's father's words just reiterated to him that Tiffany wasn't doing a good job of taking care of herself, reaffirming he needed to.

§

Tiffany walked into her house after midnight, feeling as if she'd been dragged brutally behind a sixteen wheeler during the forty-minute drive home from her office. Earlier that evening, she and Josephine had worked out the arrangements for a few Christmas functions they were planning. Three hours ago, Josephine had left for a date with her boyfriend, Ruben. Tiffany had stayed on, taking the time to figure out a balance between both of her itinerary schedules—her father's and her business.

While they'd worked, Tiffany's mind wandered. She was having an internal conflict about whether or not to open up to Josephine. She really wanted to talk to someone about everything but could not bring herself to do it. Ever since the BCS dinner, she'd felt ashamed she was not being forthright, but for now it was best to keep things quiet.

She decided tonight it would be best for her to file for divorce and soon. She resigned herself to the fact that Trevor was not going to do it. The question of why continued to plague her. Every time she brought it up to him, he changed the subject. Fear that he would contest it had kept her from filing in the months since the Vegas trip, but no more. She had to take a stand and fast. She knew the real reason. After the erotic words Trevor had whispered in her ear while they were dancing, vivid images haunted her no matter if she were asleep or awake.

She couldn't deny she was more than a little sexually attracted to Trevor. Every time he was within touching distance of her, her hormones went wild. She yearned to have his hands on her, fondling her breasts and using his magnificent talented hands between her legs. Tiffany wanted to be pleased, touched by him. She wanted Trevor to make her beg. *Now where did that thought come from?* Then she recalled the carousel and how she had acted impetuously and as if starved for affection.

She had never had sex with anyone else. Not even Christopher, who had attempted to cajole her into it several times during their brief dating period. It had been easy to say no to Christopher. He had never made her feel like Trevor did. Never made her body even come close to shaking and trembling the way Trevor did.

Before the divorce was said and done, she would have loved to feel what it was like to have him between her legs, deep inside. And remember it.

It was just sex, right? she thought.

But she knew her feelings were beginning to grow for Trevor. Every time he showed up, she learned more about him that she liked. On the way to the harbor and at dinner, they had talked and opened up to each other about their families. Not to mention, every time she needed rescuing, he was there. First with her computer, and then rescuing her from Christopher on the dance floor.

However, if she didn't cut the strings soon with Trevor, it would be too late.

Already too late.

She felt no need for light as she walked through the dark house and mentally shook herself to regain control of her thoughts. *Maybe I should have driven to the mansion.* It was only twenty-minutes from her job. She could have stayed with her father tonight. The football game was over hours ago. She could've ridden in with him tomorrow afternoon to the family home, her home, where she was now. She didn't want to be alone tonight, nor did she feel like company.

She exhaled forcefully, making her cheeks puff out.

Her father would be home tomorrow for the annual Labor Day party. That meant there would be security personnel and state troopers everywhere when he arrived. Socially, she already felt drained.

Worse yet, she was emotionally exhausted.

Over the past month, she'd tried not to think about Trevor and Sherri possibly being together since the night of the BCS banquet. As much as she tried to fight it and tell herself otherwise, she desired Trevor. Her body yearned to know what she had missed the night she drank herself into a black-out when they'd gotten married—what Sherri had most likely enjoyed.

Tiffany took a deep breath to clear her mind.

Something must be totally wrong with my life. She reached the top of the second level and entered her bedroom. *I should have better things to do than worry about who Trevor is doing.*

"I truly need a life," she said aloud. "Anything to keep my mind off him."

Tiffany walked through the blackness and headed toward her bathroom, placed her hand out and located the doorjamb. She reached around it and found the light switch.

"I can only hope you're talking about me?"

She froze; could that voice have materialized audibly out of her thoughts? Yet her body went on automatic alert—fight or flight. Instantly, her mind registered the distance between herself, the voice and the door.

"How should I take your silence? Is it a yes or no?" he asked, reaching out to her across the darkness.

Her heart began to race, she knew without turning around who was there. Only one person could stir her senses so erotically. One person could cause her body to begin to pulse. One person caused the lips of her sex to swell instantly. "How'd you get in here?"

"Your balcony window was open, not to mention a perfectly solid table underneath it on the patio. Even though your room is on the second floor, you should really be more careful."

"Only lately have I had a problem with unwelcome guests strolling around the property. A bit medieval, don't you think? What are you doing here?" she asked, becoming keenly aware of the heat of his body, directly behind her.

She was astounded that she hadn't heard him moving toward her.

"Would you believe me if I said I wanted to see you?" He placed his hands on her shoulder, causing her skin to tingle.

"Why?" she asked, trying to keep her mind focused.

"Because I'm concerned about you, and I can't get you off my mind." He lightly squeezed her shoulders.

Tiffany stepped out of his arms, turned on the light and faced Trevor. His face appeared a bronze color in the glow of the light.

"Don't play with me, Trevor. I don't have the patience for it tonight."

Unable to respond quick enough to stop him, Trevor grasped her hips and propelled her body forward, closing the gap between them.

Holding her firmly against him, he asked, "Does this feel like I'm playing?"

Tiffany couldn't have mistaken the look in his eyes, nor the significant feel of his hardening sex pressing intimately against her. Her body responded instantly. The sensation of heat building in the center wasn't something that was foreign to her. This was a feeling she fought in the middle of her nights when she awakened with dreams of him.

"We can't," she said breathlessly, placing her hands on his chest between their bodies; she pushed herself away. Turning away from him, she said, "This has already gone far enough."

He walked up behind her. "That's where you're wrong, Tiffany...I don't think it's gone far enough."

Trevor leaned forward and began to place light kisses in the curve between her neck and shoulder above the scooped collar of her blouse. Her body promptly acted in response: her eyes closed, heat ran down her spine and her heart skipped a beat.

"Tell me you want this just as much as I do." His lips progressed around to the back of her neck, and his tongue joined in, making lazy circles over her skin while his hands advanced to her breasts and began to squeeze simultaneously.

"Hmm..." the soft moan slipped past her lips as her head descended forward. She could feel the tightening of her nipples as Trevor mastered them in his hands.

Tiffany could feel his breath whisper against her skin as he said, "Tiffany, I've needed you for so long."

Tiffany felt like screaming that she wanted him too, that she was tired of fighting her feelings. "Make love to me, Trevor." She placed her hands over his as the ministration continued. "I want to wake up tomorrow and remember what it was like to be totally consumed by you."

§

Trevor turned her around and lowered his mouth to her lips. Her confession had given him permission to proceed to the next level. They'd never kissed before, so it was like an electric shock for him.

Drawing her closer, he deepened the kiss. Her lips opened to his. He placed both his hands on the side of her face, and he delved into the hot recesses of her mouth.

Tiffany surrendered completely to him and wrapped her arms around his neck.

Trevor was only vaguely aware of moving deeper in the darkness of the room and backwards toward the bed until he felt the mattress against the back of his legs.

Heavy breathing filled the room as he detached his mouth from hers, saying, "Turn on the lights…I want you to know who's making love to you."

"I know who you are." Tiffany leaned over to the lamp on the nightstand without moving out of his arms. The lamp filled the room with a soft amber glow.

He pulled her blouse out of her pants and over her head. "Then say my name."

"Trevor." She reached out and assisted him in removing his Redskins sweatshirt.

He liked the quirky lift of the corner of her mouth as she looked at his shirt logo.

"Would you stop if I told you I was a Dallas fan?" she asked.

Sitting down on the bed, he proceeded to unfasten her slacks. "Not on your life. Especially since your team just lost."

"I heard on the radio…" her words faded in and out as he began to rain kisses across her abdomen, "…one poi—" she stopped talking completely when he dipped his tongue into her navel.

Trevor slid her pants down her hips. After she stepped free of them, he ran his hands along the inside of her thighs and felt the tremors in her legs.

He paused for a moment to enjoy the view. Tiffany wore a sheer black bra and the sexiest pair of matching boy-legged cropped panties with lace trimming. If the translucent material of her bra didn't take him over the edge, the transparent underwear almost did the trick.

He had to take a few deep breaths to keep his body under control.

He admired her body with his hands. "If I had known this was what you wore under all of your business apparel…hmm," he moaned, unable to complete the sentence.

"As I recall, when you first met me you told me I should only wear thongs."

Trevor remembered that and knew he'd been misguided in his assumption. Leaning onto the bed, he held her and brought her body on top of his. "I was wrong. You're perfect just the way you are."

§

Tiffany's heart was warmed and overjoyed. No man—especially not Christopher—had ever *truly* looked at her and appreciated her for who she was. It amazed her that someone in Trevor's profession could.

Her body sang as Trevor's hands roamed her back and moved down to cup her backside, aligning her body to his. She lost herself in the feel of his hands on her body. Responsively, her thighs tightened as she felt the bulge in his jeans pressing against her.

It amazed her how easily she had forgotten his touch. Forgot what it felt like to be with him. "In someway, I know I've always been meant to be with you like this because I don't feel scared, afraid or shy. The first time we were together, it had to be wonderful."

Trevor began to extract the pins from her hair. "Tiffany, we need to talk about that night."

"No, we don't…" She placed a finger over his mouth. "All I want to think about is us being here and now."

As he sifted his fingers through her hair, it cascaded like a curtain around them.

Looking intently into her eyes, he asked, "Are you sure?"

She answered by leaning down and kissing him.

Taking hold of her hips, he pressed her body to him. Between kisses, he said, "Then I want you to start saying my name…"

"Trevor," she began in a sultry voice as he removed her bra.

Rolling her onto her back, he began to move down her body. Cupping her breasts, he placed a kiss in the center of them. "I want you to keep saying it," he said huskily.

A frisson of warmth filled her woman's center as he circled the puckered tip of one of her breasts with his tongue.

"Tre-*vor*," she said as her voice began to quiver.

"Until I'm buried so deep inside of you...you can no longer speak." He took her breasts into the searing wet heat of his mouth.

§

Trevor suckled her breasts until her chocolate nipples stood out full and engorged. Two begging points. He smiled with pleasure, then descended to the lips located between her legs and began intimately kissing her. She was consumed with feelings and emotions she could have never imagined as his tongue thoroughly adored the very essence of her core.

"*Trevor*," Tiffany shouted, as her back arched off the bed and an orgasm launched her into a shuddering mass and overtook her.

Body calming, she became aware of the rustling sound of Trevor removing the remainder of his clothing.

He lightly kissed his way back up her body, until they lay face to face. She recognized the tense look in his eye as he centered himself at the apex of her thighs.

Tiffany pulled his mouth down to hers for a hungry kiss. The heady aroma of her own scent enveloped her.

As her tongue lifted up into his mouth, Trevor thrust his hips forward—fusing their mouths and bodies together simultaneously.

§

He swallowed Tiffany's scream as he tore through the barrier of her innocence.

Her snug, moist heat engulfed Trevor and took him to the brink of rapture. If his life depended on it, he could not have implored his member to remove itself from the haven. He could feel the bite of her nails in his back.

He was as shocked and astounded as Tiffany appeared to be as he looked into her tear filled eyes. "I'm sorry, sweetheart," he whispered. "I didn't know."

He brushed his thumbs across the corners of her eyes, removing the tears. He waited, biting on his bottom lip to be patient. Giving Tiffany's body a chance to relax and accept him. She was tight, hot and wet. Squeezing him like a fist. Her spicy musk scent was driving him wild. Every fiber of his being wanted to slide his shaft in and out of her. Feel her body quiver around him.

When Trevor felt her hips begin a tentative rise, seating him deeper in her warmth, he groaned. Then buried his face in her neck and began to move. Cautious at first, aware her body was tender and the act was unique to her.

Grasping her hips, he instructed her to follow his lead, meet each of his thrusts and swivel her body against him. Allowing her clitoris to be stimulated and heightening her pleasure. As her body became accustomed to the rhythm, Trevor rotated his hips until her moans began to echo around the room.

Trevor's manhood swelled more, making him aware of the growing tension in his body. His sack pulled up tight at the base and begged for release.

As the pressure mounted toward his own release, he pulled her legs up higher toward his shoulders, allowing himself deeper access. Increasing his tempo, Trevor gave himself over to his need.

Finally, reaching his peak, his thunderous groans reverberated throughout the room—joined by Tiffany's second cry of release that night.

Trevor got more than even he predicted at the beginning of the heated session. The unexpected issue between them had rendered them both speechless.

Ten

We need to talk," Tiffany said as she came out of the restroom, her naked form now covered by the nightgown she'd grabbed from the foot of the bed.

Trevor stood at the window, staring out into the night. He had put his jeans back on, which rode low on his hips. While they were in the heat of the moment, she hadn't taken the time to reacquaint herself with his well-sculpted physique. *He really is beautiful.*

The simple sight of his back made her envision running her tongue along his spine. She could see the small half-moon shapes her nails had made.

"Yeah, we do." His voice sounded as thick and smooth as molasses pouring out of a Mason jar.

The tender muscles of her sex flexed in response. It made her very aware of the difference in the soreness her body was experiencing now compared to when she'd awakened in Las Vegas.

He turned around, and she noticed the top button of his jeans undone. She berated herself for the quick skip of her pulse. *Get yourself together, girl. You need some answers.*

An internal war raged between her body and mind. She had every right to be angry at him for the ruse he had been playing with her…at the same time, her body was reveling in the life altering experience that had just taken place between them.

Tiffany folded her arms over her chest to keep herself composed. "I want you to tell me the truth about Las Vegas."

"Sit." He directed as he sauntered toward her.

The only reason Tiffany sat on the edge of her bed was because she didn't know how long her trembling legs would hold her up. *All he did was move toward me.* She took a deep steadying breath.

Grabbing the stool from her vanity, he sat down in front of her. "What do you want to know?"

"Everything."

§

Trevor knew he couldn't tell her everything. Over the past months, Tiffany had begun to mean too much to him. If he revealed everything about the precarious situation, it would all be over—he would lose her forever.

He wasn't willing to jeopardize it. After tonight, he was assured his feelings for her ran deeper than even he imagined.

"I'll start off with what you know. We didn't have sex that night."

"*Nooo*, you don't say," she responded sarcastically. "Let's just cut to the chase and tell me something I don't know."

"If I'd known that you were a virgin—"

"What else would I have been, Trevor?" Tiffany said through clenched teeth. "I wasn't married before our little…" She waved her hands around in the air, unable to come up with a word to describe their relationship. "Do you think you're the only person who can have morals?"

"It's just not common."

"Nothing about how we got into this mess is *common*," she yelled.

"Look, if I'd known, I never would have—" he cut himself off. "Damn." Trevor got up from the chair and began to pace. "I can't lie to you or myself, Tiffany. I've been attracted to you since the moment you opened the door in Las Vegas. This was inevitable, and we both know it."

She stood up and faced him. "Since we're finally talking *truths* here, what I know is this: If I had realized before now…that I *was* still a virgin. *This*," she said pointing to the bed, "would have *never* happened."

Trevor could see her chest rising and falling with anger. His pulse began to pick up in response.

"How can you be so sure?" he asked her calmly, keeping a lid on the rage inside of him. "Because I'm not *good* enough for you? Heaven forbid your fiancé would have discovered that the governor's daughter had been soiled. Especially if he wasn't the one to do it."

She looked at him through squinted eyes. "My relationship with Christopher is *none* of your business."

Trevor's struggle to keep his anger under control wore thin. He leaned toward her until they almost stood nose to nose. "Want to bet?"

"*Ooh…*" Tiffany shrieked. "Sometimes you make me so mad I could scream."

"Well, sweetheart, you did enough screaming tonight that you should be good for a month."

"You boorish jerk," she shrieked.

"You could've ended this as easily as I could have," he bellowed back.

"Trust me, if I'd known I was still a virgin, I would've filed for an annulment immediately."

The room vibrated with the crackling energy between them.

"Why didn't you just file for divorce even though you thought we had slept together?"

Tiffany turned away from him. "Because I didn't want it to get out. If I had filed for a divorce, then people would have found out." She pivoted back to him. "Especially since you insinuated that you'd contest the divorce."

Trevor had to give her that. At the onset of this predicament he had set out to seduce her and let Manning know he'd done it. But he couldn't go through with it. Marrying her hadn't been part of that plan, no matter how he'd tried to fool her and himself. Tying himself to Tiffany had been instinctual, something he didn't understand then and was still trying to sort through now.

Now, revenge against Christopher Manning was no longer important to him, and he wasn't sure when things had begun to change.

"So you think a divorce would've made our attraction for each other go away?" he asked, crossing his arms across his chest.

"It would be irrelevant," she said quietly.

Trevor arched an eyebrow at her.

She dropped her gaze away from his. "Regardless of what has happened now. You still should have told me we didn't have sex."

Trevor took a breath and asked calmly, "What if I tell you I want more?"

She looked up at him with shock in her eyes. "More of what?"

"Of us..." he declared.

"Trevor, you can't be serious." She shook her head. "It would *never* work."

Trevor could hear the fear as she spoke. He walked up to her and took hold of her shoulders, looking her directly in the eyes. "Tiffany, for a moment, put aside what or who you think I am. Pretend for a moment that I was just some regular guy with a job and you had a normal life...what then?"

§

Tiffany looked at the man who had just made love to her. The man who was supposed to be her husband—the stripper.

Everything inside of her yelled for her to trust him, to let go of her fear and concerns. Surrender to him. She wasn't sure when her feelings had changed—but they had.

Can I risk it? Tiffany asked herself. *No*, her mind answered, *there is too much at stake*.

"Trevor, there's no reason to fantasize. We are who we are, and we can't change that."

She took a breath to steady herself, but all of a sudden, she felt like crying.

"Tiffany, I'm falling hard for you, and that can't be changed." He used one of his hands and lifted her chin up. "Can you tell me you don't feel the same?"

The moment her tears spilled over, Tiffany pulled her face out of his hands and turned away from him.

Her heart seemed to swell with the news of Trevor's feelings.

"It doesn't matter, Trevor. In the morning when the sun comes up, I'll still be the governor's daughter."

She could feel his presence behind her. Her nipples tightened in spite of her internal war.

"So you're willing to sacrifice—"

"I made that choice a long time ago." Tiffany faced him. "No matter what I may feel, I can't hurt my father's career. I won't allow myself to be the reason behind him losing the Senate seat." Tiffany stepped around him and moved to stand in front of her window. "It wouldn't be fair. It's not right."

She didn't even hear Trevor advance. The next thing she knew, he was spinning her around with lightening speed to face him.

"Not *right*?" he spewed. "Control be damned," he muttered between gritted teeth. "What you want me to believe is that you're willing to deny your feelings for me because…it's 'politically incorrect?'" His hands made quotation marks in the air.

"Yes…" she said weakly with tears rolling unchecked down her face.

"That's a bunch of bull!" He seized her by the hips and brought her body in full contact with his. "Tell me this isn't right…"

A whimper passed her lips when she felt his body swell from their flushed contact. She could feel his elongated shaft pressing against her throbbing core. She was amazed how she hungered for him again. She yearned to have him thrusting between her legs, even though her body was still tender from their last session.

"What about this, Tiffany?" Placing his hand over her breast, he began to knead her until her nipples tightened and stood out begging for attention. He took it into his hot, wet mouth and suckled through her silk gown. "Is it right?" His tongue flicked rapidly across the tip.

Tiffany moaned as the vibrations of his speech fluttered across her skin.

Trevor kissed his way to her neck and began to nibble up past her chin until he reached her mouth. Once he arrived, he began to give her soft kisses until her tongue joined him in the dance and the kiss became demanding.

Her mind was in a fog as his mouth mastered and manipulated hers.

They parted for a brief moment. The kiss stopped as he pulled her gown over her head, revealing her naked body. The chill of the wall welcomed her butt cheeks as Trevor held her hard-pressed against it with his hands on the round flesh of her hips. She didn't have time to ponder what would come next as he dropped to his knees before her, then delved his tongue between her thighs. His expert tongue parted her needy, slick, plump lips and circled her clit. Tiffany's legs began to tremble, part and tilt toward the feasting, small, firm pink member. She was being tortured into absolute pleasure.

His tongue moved down further and entered her body, reaching and flicking inside her heated center. He alternated between sliding his tongue into her, then back out to circle the begging seat of her desire, causing her hips to rotate and dip, meeting each adventurous stroke until her hands grasped his head, and she found herself launched into quaking oblivion.

When she came down from her sexual high, Trevor was lifting her up, and she could feel the cool, hardened texture of the wall against the heated skin of her shoulders as she slid down it to find herself fully impaled upon his thick, swollen, rigid shaft he had freed from his jeans.

The initial thrust that entered her tight, moist center stole her breath. She could feel herself stretching and conforming to his welcomed intrusion.

More than willing to ride the furies tempest, she wrapped her arms and legs around him and clung to his body.

Trevor's gyrating hips moved deep inside of her, while his heated breath teased her ear. "When I'm inside of you, Tiffany, does this feel right?"

Before she could respond, he reached down between their bodies and fondled the slippery, distended nub of her passion.

"Yesss," she moaned as her body began to quake with release.

Tiffany disregarded the instant chill of the surface against the small of her back, as Trevor pressed her body against the wall from shoulder to hip. They were compressed, chest-to-chest as he drove powerfully inside of her until he followed suit with his own fulfillment.

§

"I want to wake up with you like this every morning," Trevor whispered softly against the shell of Tiffany's ear. He had been awake for the last hour, staring at her and wondering when he'd given his heart to Tiffany.

His feelings for Tiffany had begun to blossom into something that made him think about permanency. About what life would be like with her by his side.

His conscience urged him to tell her the truth, to be honest with her. He brushed it off, kissed her on the crest of her shoulder and pulled her body closer to his like two snug fitting spoons.

Feeling her snuggle her derriere toward his hips, he said, "Good morning, sunshine."

Tiffany looked over her shoulder and smiled. "Good morning."

Amazingly, his body began to react to the wiggling closeness of her hips and her smile. Last night they had made love three times, and he still couldn't get enough of her.

"If you don't be still, you're going to start something I'll be enticed to finish," he warned, rolling her onto her back.

Tiffany's eyes rounded as she lifted up her hands in front of him as a sign of surrender. "I'll behave. I will not be able to move from this bed anytime soon as it is."

He ran an index finger down the side of her face, looked into her eyes with sincerity. "I meant what I said last night, Tiffany. I want this marriage to be real."

Trevor watched as Tiffany cast her eyes downward, shielding them from his view. Her body was relaxed in his arms, and he couldn't determine what was going on inside of her, or how she would respond.

Tiffany clutched the sheet to her breasts as she sat up with her knees drawn to her chest. "I can't deny what I feel for you, Trevor. But I'm going to need some time. I'm not sure if I'm ready to announce our marriage to the world."

Sitting up behind her, he pulled her into the circle of his arms until she relaxed and leaned back against him. "Tiffany, we're going to do this one small step at a time. Let's decide to spend some time together and get to know one another better, then when the moment is right, we can make the choice on how to present it. So take all the time you need. Just try not to make it too long."

Turning her medium brown eyes toward him, she said, "I'll try not to. I do care for you also, Trevor. As hard as I tried to fight it…I couldn't. But I had a lot of decisions to make—even before last night happened."

"Believe it or not, I do understand. My life is not as uncomplicated as it may seem."

Trevor saw the glimmer of curiosity flicker in Tiffany's eyes, but before she could begin to question him, he said, "Well, beautiful, I need to go. I have a million and one things to handle today."

He placed a kiss on her temple, got up from the bed and pulled on his clothes.

"You wouldn't happen to have an extra toothbrush would you?" Trevor asked her after pulling his shirt over his head.

§

At the front door, Tiffany initiated their parting kiss, and then watched Trevor walk across the street to his car. She laughed at the evidence of how troubled her mind must have been last night that she didn't notice Trevor's car parked across the street.

Waving good-bye as he drove away, Tiffany made a mental note to call her doctor today for a prescription for birth control pills. If she and Trevor were going to be in a physical relationship, she had to protect herself. The fewer complications in this relationship, the better.

While she strolled onto the front lawn to retrieve the morning paper, she gave Trevor a final wave as he pulled away.

"Good morning, Miss Hatcher."

Startled, Tiffany turned to see a man coming around the side of the house. He was dressed casually in navy blue slacks and a light blue, short-sleeved crew neck shirt. He could have been any executive with the exception of the gun holstered to his side held up by the black leather straps around his shoulders.

With her father being in politics for most of her life, Tiffany often saw bodyguards and state troopers around her house. However, this morning she felt apprehensive.

"Sorry to have startled you, Miss Hatcher. I'm here with Todd, the state trooper. I'm Dan."

She clutched the paper to her chest. "Why the extra help? Am I unaware of something that happened?" For a brief moment, Tiffany wondered if one of her neighbors might have witnessed Trevor climbing into her bedroom window and reported the incident to the police.

The guard gave her a strange look. Before he could answer, Todd came around the other side of the house.

"Miss Hatcher, I see you've met Dan." Todd stopped in front of her and gave Tiffany a warm smile. "There are also six other guards showing up in an hour or so. Only two of the guys are new. I'll bring them up to the house for introductions. The rest of them you'll remember from other functions."

Functions?

Before her mind could fully process what Todd said, Dan jumped in. "Yeah, I was just telling Miss Hatcher that we were here to check out things before the governor's annual barbeque."

Oh my, God. I forgot about my father coming today. Not to include the house full of guests. That would've been the last thing I needed.

Hurriedly, Tiffany said, "Well, as always, Todd, I'm sure you have everything under control." Smiling at both of the men, Tiffany pivoted back to the house, but she didn't miss the slight gleam in the new guy's eyes as she turned around.

For a brief moment, her mind questioned whether he had seen Trevor leaving or not. She didn't have time to ponder that. She had to shower and change before her father arrived in an hour.

Eleven

Tiffany stood in the kitchen, gazing out of the window. She could see the guests milling around outside in the backyard, enjoying her father's annual barbecue, but her mind wasn't on them. She couldn't help reminiscing about last night with Trevor. Her body still tingled, and every muscle screamed from exertion. She remembered the way he'd touched her and how he'd made her feel.

She knew it wasn't just about the sex. It was more than that…much more. She had begun to feel things for him even though she'd tried to fight it. He made her laugh and smile. Pushed her to live her own life. Trevor made her want to be Tiffany, just Tiffany. Without all of her father's political image. She didn't know exactly when it had happened and wasn't concerned about processing it at this moment. She just knew she was overdue for a little enjoyment in her life.

"That glorious smile on your face must be for me."

Tiffany whipped around and saw Christopher leaning against the doorjamb. Unwilling to rehash the fact that she wasn't interested in more than friendship with him, she took the cautious route and ignored his comment. "Christopher, I was lost in thought. I didn't hear you come in."

Christopher needed no encouragement. He pushed away from the door and sauntered into the room. "That's because you work too hard. I told you once you agree to marry me, you'll never have to work again."

I wonder what he would say if he knew I was already married. "I love working too much to give it up."

"Humph." He chuckled as his eyes made a quick roll toward the ceiling.

Christopher never understood why women chose to work if there was a man willing to take care of them. He wasn't old-fashioned. He was archaic.

She turned away, ignored the sound effects coming from Christopher and walked to the refrigerator to get herself something to drink. Hoping he would once again get the message that she had no intentions to debate this issue with him.

"Tiffy, when are you going to stop fighting it and come to terms with the fact it's best for both of us if we marry?"

Taking her time, Tiffany got herself a bottle of apple juice, closed the refrigerator door and turned around to face Christopher. He now stood five feet away from her. She could smell his cologne, some expensive brand that didn't affect her senses at all. No goose-bumps. No shivers of heat. Nothing.

"How do you figure that, Christopher?" Tiffany bit on the inside of her lip, working hard at keeping her face void of expression.

"We have the same political views…" He leaned his backside against the island in the middle of the kitchen, crossing one foot over the other, hands crossed over his chest.

Tiffany rotated her free hand at the wrist, giving him the gesture to continue.

"We know each other very well."

Tiffany lifted an eyebrow.

"Our parents know each other and get along famously." One of his cheeks raised in a side smile.

Tiffany nodded slightly in agreement. Senator Manning and her father had been friends for years, and the voters loved it.

"The public would eat it up." Christopher righted his body, standing away from the counter.

Ahh-haa, there was the plug I was waiting for. She leaned her back against the refrigerator and waited for him to finish his pitch.

"To top it off, we would be great together."

She watched Christopher advance and stop in front of her—too close for comfort.

Fire and Desire

She clutched the bottle of juice to her chest as a protection from him, a pseudo shield, prohibiting Christopher from moving any closer to her.

It amazed Tiffany that Trevor could say similar words and send chills of multiple possibilities down her spine. Yet whenever Christopher utters words of commitment, all she could think about is running from the room.

Christopher must have noticed the hold she kept on the bottle. He reached out and wrestled with her slightly until she released the bottle from her clutches, then he placed it on the countertop.

"Christopher—" she began, prepared to break away from the little isolated area.

"Tiffy…" he cut her off, saying her name in a slow seductive manner that probably made other woman melt. Christopher placed both of his hands against the refrigerator—boxing her in. "You know you want me."

She felt uncomfortable with him being this close. When they were dating for a short while, he'd attempted to cross her moral and personal boundary lines several times. They would be married soon, always his excuse. Since she'd ended the relationship, he'd always respected her space. Even though at times he bordered on the edge of her patience.

"Christopher, I feel fondness for you in a brotherly fashion. Over the years, I've tried to explain that to you."

Christopher leaned down, until he was an even eyelevel with her. "Tiffy, I have sisters, and I can guarantee my feelings for you are quite different. Let me prove it to you…"

His pitch dropped an octave as he slowly leaned in. Anticipating his course of action, she turned her head.

His kiss missed its intended mark, her mouth, and landed below her ear.

Not one to be detoured from his objective, Christopher began to kiss and lick her neck.

Her stomach turned, flip-flopped and lurched. She wanted to throw up. She'd reached her limit, and her last nerve snapped. She was done.

No more pandering to him. "Listen, Christopher." She placed her hands flatly against his chest and shoved him.

Christopher, caught off guard by her action, stumbled backward a few steps before stopping.

He started to advance toward her again.

With perfect timing, Josephine opened the kitchen door saying, "Hey, Tiff, your father is looking for you, and Senator Hutchinson is here. She has some questions about a fundraiser gala her staff is currently organizing. She asked to meet with both of us."

The atmosphere in the room was tainted. It was evident Josephine felt it in the obvious tilt of her head and significant lift of her eyebrow.

She almost felt guilty herself, as if *she* had been caught doing something wrong.

"Thanks, Jo, I'll be right out."

Josephine nodded and left, eyebrow still raised.

"You know, Christopher, I don't know why you can't seem to understand that I have no feelings at all for you, except of friendship, which at this point is waning. For some reason, you seem to believe it would be best if we marry, but we are truly not alike. I beg you to understand this. You want a wife that is at your disposal and lives to be by your side, forsaking her own thoughts or dreams. That's—not—me."

For the first time in a long while, Christopher really looked at her. Tiffany saw the comprehension slowly dawning on him. The sparkle of interest in his eyes began to dull.

"Well, Tiffany, I guess you're not the person I thought you were. I don't see why I'm so surprised, with the company you've been keeping lately."

Instant panic caused her heart to slam against her ribs, wondering if he knew about Trevor leaving the house less than a few hours ago. Tiffany licked her lips and cleared her throat. "What company would that be?"

"Trevor Lewis."

No! Tiffany screamed inside. "What about him?" she inquired, taking a deep breath in an attempt to keep her nervousness in check. "I hardly know him."

"That's what I thought. But apparently he knows you well enough to have the gumption to walk up and ask you to dance at the B.C. affair."

Phew. He doesn't know. "He's an acquaintance."

Christopher placed his hands on his hips, and dropped his head, casting his gaze toward the floor. "Where would one meet someone who doesn't even move in our circle...let alone our class?" he asked, voice dripping with sarcasm.

Tiffany never heard him speak with such narrow-minded views. Her brows pinched together in consternation as she began to see a glimmer of Christopher's true character. *And he calls himself a Democrat, yeah right.* "Well, evidently he does, Christopher. For your information, I know him from a previous function I attended with my father. Besides, it was an innocent dance."

His head jerked up and his eyes nailed her. "If that dance was innocent, then I'm running for the position of Pope."

She walked over to the counter and retrieved her apple juice, refusing to feel guilty. Josephine had told her the same thing. After last night with Trevor, she knew what Christopher said was true. She stopped trying to fool herself about the chemistry between herself and Trevor. For a long time, it had been igniting when they were within mere feet of each other. Until this moment, she could no longer deceive herself into thinking it was not apparent to everyone who looked, not just her best friend.

Christopher spoke to her back. "You know, Tiffany, the girl I grew up with cared about not only how she represented herself in public, but more importantly, how that image would reflect and impact her father's career—"

Tiffany swung away from the counter and faced him. "Christopher, how can you begin to try and tell me how I should act—"

He continued, as if her objection had not interrupted him. "But apparently, your feelings have changed dramatically. So it will be my pleasure to grant your request and give you your space."

She stopped. The words she was about to speak sat thick in her throat, rendering her speechless for a moment. Amazed. The disappointed look in his eyes stabbed at her as he turned and began to head toward the door. Her chest squeezed tight and her heart felt heavy, then released as she exhaled. She would not allow herself to feel guilty about the situation. It was becoming evident to her that Christopher never truly wanted or cared about her friendship. She was just a pawn in his political climbing game, and she wasn't having it. Their "friendship" would most likely end for good, but maybe it was long overdue. She stuck firm to her resolve.

Tiffany paused. She was shocked, but relieved. Nothing more needed to be said. "Thank you, Christopher."

He stopped in his tracks as if her words arrested him in mid-stride. In slow motion, he turned back around to face her.

There was a sadistic smile on his face as his empty laugh echoed across the room. "Don't thank me, Tiff*any*, because you're going to regret this in the end."

Stunned. Tiffany's heart vaulted from her chest to the base of her throat. "Are you, *serious*?"

"As a sinner with a heart attack making a death bed confession." His face shifted into a relaxed smile. His politician smile. Saying nothing else, Christopher exited the kitchen.

Tiffany was paralyzed. She couldn't believe her ex-boyfriend and childhood friend had turned on her right in front of her eyes. She'd never wanted to make an enemy of Christopher. But if she had the last twenty minutes to do over again, she wouldn't change anything.

Nothing. Besides, there weren't any circumstances in which she would have agreed to marry him. Her feelings toward him would never change. Not to mention, she was already legally married. Now in every sense of the word.

In a million years, she would've never thought she'd not only lose Christopher's friendship but incur his wrath as well. Tiffany dropped her face into her hands, battling between wanting to scream and cry at the same time. She refused to do either. If he was going to be petty and try to demand all or nothing from her, that's just what she would give him. Nothing.

She wouldn't allow this to overshadow the blissful night she'd had with Trevor. She was determined to bask in that glow for as long as possible. Tiffany took a deep, cleansing breath to relax and walked out of the kitchen in search of Senator Hutchinson.

Work is just what I need to keep my mind occupied.

§

"Well, to what do I owe the pleasure of this visit?"

Trevor leaned down and gave Leslie a hug. "Would you believe me if I said I had a taste for your peach cobbler?"

His aunt wore a pair of three-inch heels, allowing her to stand at an even five-five. She kept her hair designed in a long, jet-black, straight hip length style. She was petite with almond shaped eyes, skin the color of molasses and a smile just as sweet. "You know I don't bake."

"Oh, well, must be my other aunt." Trevor gave her a brazen smile.

Leslie led the way into her living room. "Then you better zip on out of here because I'm expecting my favorite nephew."

"I'm the one and only." He waited until his aunt was seated on the couch, then he choose a chair across from her.

"Tell me, dear boy, what's wrong and don't give me any fluff."

Trevor took his time looking around the room. He had been there many times since college, and it was still the same. Oriental décor, which suited his aunt perfectly. Everything in it was compliments of an Air Force colonel who used to be stationed at the Pentagon. His aunt's one and only love. When the military relocated the colonel to Japan, he had proposed to his aunt, but she'd said no, not wanting her life and chosen career to affect his advancement in the military. Six months after he had left, the furniture had arrived with a letter from his lawyer. Enclosed with it an obituary notice, a letter from the colonel and a ring—which his aunt had always worn since then.

At the moment, Trevor could see the emotional parallel between Tiffany and his aunt. Tiffany loved her father and was willing to sacrifice her own career and dreams to protect him. Trevor couldn't let that happen. He loved her and part of that love was seeing her happy. Watching her at the Breast Cancer banquet managing and controlling her environment, he knew that put the sparkle of life in her eyes—not standing proud and silent by her father before a camera.

"Whatever is going on with you must be really big..." Leslie commented, watching him as he gazed around the room.

Trevor looked at his aunt. "Do you have any regrets?"

She didn't bat an eyelash, nor did she question what he was talking about before she began, "Yes. However, it doesn't do me any good to dwell on what might've been. None of us are born with the power to change the past."

Trevor pondered what his aunt had said. She didn't know how close her comments were to the emotions moving through him.

"So who is she?" his aunt asked.

He gave her a half smile. "I can't tell you that because I'm not in a position right now to say."

"Hmm, a little intrigue." Leslie smiled, wiggling her eyebrows at him.

He laughed. His aunt could always find a way to lighten his mood.

After his laughter subsided, he said, "I'll tell you, I never anticipated my feelings becoming engaged the way they have."

"Which I can assume is causing you some problems."

"In a big way." He lifted his head and stared blankly at the ceiling.

"What are you afraid of?"

He refocused on his aunt. "Losing her in the end."

"Well, they say that it is better to have loved and lost, than not to have loved at all."

Trevor made a grumbling sound in his throat. The same pain he had seen back when she told of her lost love returned to his aunt's eyes and weighted down her voice. "But having been in that position before, I would say...do whatever you can *not* to lose *it* at all."

"What makes you think I'm in love with her?" Trevor questioned.

His aunt's soft laughter fluttered through the air, easing the heavy atmosphere. "*Pah-leeese*, sweetie...only a smitten man sits with his *youthful* aunt and contemplates life decisions."

"Maybe," Trevor smiled and rose to his feet. "Well, *Leslie*, I need to get going."

His aunt got to her feet, linked her arm through his and escorted him back toward the front of her condo.

Once at the door, Trevor turned to his aunt. "Thanks for listening." Leaning in, he kissed her cheek.

"You're welcome, even though you didn't say much." Leslie reached up and touched the side of his face, her gaze full of compassion and understanding.

"I will in due time." Trevor opened the door.

"Trevor, you have to be the gentlest man I know," she said, stopping him, "with the softest heart you attempt to hide from the world. Watch out you don't get hurt in the end."

Trevor looked back at her, paused and left without commenting.

§

Tiffany stood next to the table in the conference room with the Children's Christmas Gala project spread over the top. A large diagram of the Four Seasons' Garden Terrace Lounge covered almost half the table. The paper replica was speckled with mini tables, chairs and trees with little color squares underneath. It always helped Tiffany to set up the event, so she could visualize how she wanted things situated. She leaned over the table, her hand busy arranging the pieces, organizing the room in correspondence to her notes.

"Now, that's a position every man wants to see his wife in. Spine dipped low, hips arched high and thighs parted."

The tingling sensation sliding up her spine was the telltale sign of who it was that spoke behind her. It reminded her of how she felt listening to her favorite jazz artist. Her eyes slid shut and all of her senses became focused on Trevor.

"I'm surprised my secretary didn't notify me I had a visitor." Tiffany didn't turn or rectify her position, even though she'd ceased what she was doing.

Heat caressed her back as his masculine presence moved up behind her, but not touching. "If she's a college age platinum blond with a small natural, I caught a glimpse of her before she exited through the fire escape."

She inhaled the rich smell that was only Trevor. No cologne, he always held a clean, robust male scent. "Jaunice likes to take the stairs. It's all about fitness she says."

"Where's your partner?" he asked huskily.

Tiffany could almost hear the room crackle with sexual tension. "She took a contract over to a client, which just leaves the two of us." Body straightened, she attempted to turn around and face him.

Firm hands touched her waist, halting her movement. Intense seduction pulsed throughout the room as he said, "Don't move."

"What are you up to?" She couldn't stop the butterflies of excitement from moving with zeal in the lower part of her stomach.

"Lasciviousness," he rumbled deep, as his hands made their way around the front of her shirt and began unfastening her buttons.

Tiffany's breasts felt full and heavy, and her nipples tightened in expectation of his touch. She couldn't stop the giggle of anticipation. "Oh really, I do believe I was taught against such acts in my Sunday school class."

"Well, in mine, I was told the marriage bed is undefiled."

One hand slid inside her open blouse. Her skin tingled from the warm contact as her heart picked up its tempo and her breathing became strenuous. "Trevor, my darling, if you will notice there isn't a bed around."

"We're married, honey, which means wherever we lay, or stand, is our bed."

Tiffany glanced over her shoulder. "Glad to know I won't need to repent tomorrow."

He leaned forward and kissed her soundly on the mouth. "If you knew what I had in mind, you wouldn't be so quick to say that."

All thoughts of conversation left her mind. Trevor began to run his hands up her torso, under her bra and cupped her breasts. "It never ceases to amaze me when I feel your heartbeat against my fingertips…" Emotions hindered his speech. One hand began to massage her breasts, as the other moved away to unbind her hair from its clip. "I feel like an addict when I'm away from you. I can't get you out of my system, and I can't stay away." He kissed her on the back of her neck.

Oh, my. He's as entangled in this as I am. Her pulse quickened from his words and the feel of his fingers massaging her scalp and her breasts. Flustered, Tiffany didn't know whether she wanted to lean back into one hand or forward to the other. She solved her internal struggle by arching her back, allowing her to meet both needs and more. Her hips brushed his groin, making the level of his desire very evident.

Trevor squeezed and lightly tugged on her protruding nipples through their thin covering. "Ohh, Trevor. I know. I feel like I'm turning inside out." Tiffany's hips began to undulate against his groin, attempting to prolong and enhance every sensation. *I'm definitely an addict.*

The intimate masseuse technique halted and Trevor groaned. "Baby, are you trying to drive me mad?" He gripped her hips and fused them against his.

Tiffany's senses were alive. She trembled inside. She could feel the forceful breath he exhaled across the side of her neck, the occasional flexing of his fingers on her hips and the distinct imprint of his groin against her buttocks. The desire to have him buried deep overwhelmed her.

Memories of their previous night were vivid in her mind, and she knew she played with fire as she boldly asked, "If I'm trying to drive you mad, what do I get as my reward?"

As if all the restraints he held on himself snapped, Trevor became the audacious lover in response. He reached up without instructions or pausing to release the front clasp of her bra, baring her breasts to his seeking hand. Simultaneously, he hauled her skirt up around her waist.

A month ago, Tiffany would have been shocked with the thought of a man displaying such sexual aggression. For her first time, she was glad he had been sensitive, gentle, tender and caring, but not tonight. Tonight, she wanted him to lose control. She wanted him to desire her beyond thought or reason…she wanted to feel his unbridled passion.

§

Trevor had no problem fulfilling her verbal taunts and unspoken requests. The desire to be inside of her was so strong, he felt animal-istic — like a beast whose mate was in heat.

He smelled her arousal. Her scent was thick and heady, sweet and musky at the same time. The aroma of her essence enveloped him while beckoning him closer. He answered the call, sliding his hand inside her underwear to discover the lips of her sex swollen, in full bloom and satu-rated with her wetness. His questing hand met with the same fate. She was more than ready. She was his for the taking.

Trevor wasted no time shoving her underwear down so she could step out of them, and then leaned her forward. "Brace yourself." He masterfully clutched her hips and thrust home.

He heard her gasp a quick breath, felt the tightness of her core adjust to his quick invasion and sheath him in wet acceptance. It was pure heaven in its most erotic form. *The connection between a husband and his wife*, the thought raced through his mind.

She was his, his alone, his woman, and he wanted to brand her so there would be no doubt in the coming weeks.

Fire and Desire

Pumping into her, his thrusts were deep and sure. He ran one hand up her back and around her side until he reached her full, silky smooth breast. He smiled at the feel of her erect nipples.

He rotated his hips and moved his other hand to the seat of her desire. As he began to play her body in the sensuous dance, she trembled, and he knew she was close to the edge.

"Please, Trevor…" Tiffany moaned as she tilted her head back, allowing breathy sounds of rapture past her lips.

Trevor, on the edge himself, knew what Tiffany was asking for. "Your wish is my command, honey."

He relinquished the hold he had on his passion and drove into her until she shattered with a scream. The walls of her center clenched him repeatedly as he buried himself to the hilt against her womb. His own release came out as a growl between his clenched teeth. He squeezed his eyes shut and threw his head back.

§

The afterglow of their passion permeated the atmosphere in the room.

Long moments passed before either spoke.

Respecting the silence in the room, Tiffany began softly by saying, "We need to talk, Trevor."

"I know. There are a lot of things that I wish to say to you, but I can't right now, Tiffany." Trevor responded in the same tone as he ran his hands gingerly along her spine.

Tiffany's curiosity was piqued as she turned her head to look at him. "Things like what?"

Trevor withdrew from her and cool air greeted her in his place. The sounds of him fastening his clothes echoed in the room. Seconds went by, before she felt his hands readjusting her skirt. Then she turned her body into the envelope of his arms.

She wasn't sure if he was going to answer her as his eyes ran slowly over her face.

124

He reached up and smoothed the wrinkle in her brow with his thumb. "Just trust me."

"My heart really wants to trust you, Trevor, but my mind is screaming out that I don't know you."

"You know me, Tiffany. Trust in what your heart is saying." He ran his finger down the cooling flesh of her arm.

His eyes held an intense look in them she could not grasp, as if he were trying to *lure* her to trust him.

"Is there something I should know?"

"Of course there is, but my darling, now is not the time." He kissed her softly on the lips, ending the conversation, and then disentangled himself from her.

"When will that be?" She closed the front of her blouse over her bare chest as she watched him walk backward toward the door.

"Soon."

"You claim you want us to have a normal relationship, but every time we're together, it starts with you arriving out of the blue and ending with me watching you walk away."

A sexy smile crossed his lips. "How about dinner tomorrow night at seven?"

"You're on." She returned his smile.

twelve

"Wow, Tiff, I just came from the conference room. The Gala set-up looks great, and you even tagged in the seating arrangement. What got you pumped up while I've been gone?" Josephine began as she walked into Tiffany's office.

Tiffany hoped the heat rising to her face wasn't evident to her friend. "I just got a burst of energy and couldn't stop."

"Well, that's great because that shaved an hour off our time tonight. We'll give the names one final look and make sure there aren't any 'do not place in close proximity together' people at the same table."

Silently, Tiffany grabbed the file off her desk and followed her friend to the conference room, where she had only left moments before Josephine showed up. She hadn't lied to her friend. She'd felt a burst of energy after Trevor left…guilt was always a great incentive. She threw herself full steam into the project in an attempt to compensate for the time used while she'd made hot, passionate love with Trevor instead of finalizing the gala plans.

Now, standing next to her business partner, they worked through the list of guests and seating arrangements. She couldn't help but feel buried under the lie of omission she had withheld from not only her best friend, but also her father.

"Perfect as always, Tiff, all I's and T's appear to be dotted and crossed."

"Thanks," Tiffany said, distracted by the weight of what she needed to do. She took a deep breath. "Jo, we need to talk."

"About Las Vegas?"

Tiffany wasn't shocked Josephine was right on target about what was on her mind. Her friend had a memory like an elephant and was very intuitive. "And more. It would probably be best if we went to your office because you're going to need to sit down…so am I."

When they were seated at Josephine's desk, Tiffany began, "Jo, I know you know I've been keeping something from you since we went to Las Vegas for the weekend? Also, knowing me as well as you do, you know nothing short of cowardliness has kept me from talking to you about it."

"I'm assuming this has to do with why you didn't get back to the townhouse until the following morning?"

"That's right. I could go the long way around this in explanations, but I won't. The fact is, I got married that night."

There was no mistaking the look of shock on her friend's face, but the look of hurt tore at Tiffany's heart.

"You've been married for almost three months and you never felt like you could tell me?"

"Honestly, Jo, I didn't want to tell anyone because I prayed I would be able to get a quiet divorce and no one would know. Besides, how do you tell someone that you got drunk and did the most cliché thing by getting married in Las Vegas?"

"Just like that," Josephine snapped.

Tiffany smiled at her friend's simple reaction. However, her father would see things differently.

Tiffany walked over to Josephine's office window, pausing for a moment to watch the night activities on the street.

"I'm the governor's daughter, Jo. Up until this point, I've tried to live my life above reproach." Tiffany sounded distant as her thoughts drifted to past memories. "I remember one day when we were in high school, I was in the kitchen reading a tabloid that someone had left on the counter. There was an article in it about some senator's daughter getting arrested for indecent exposure at some club, and it made references to some past indiscretions she had committed. I remember Wallace walking into the kitchen, seeing the article and saying how everything that I did would impact my father's career." She faced Josephine. "I got the message."

"Tiff, as long as I've known you, I've watched you restrict yourself to some invisible boundaries that stop you from existing. A lot of the boundaries that constrict your life have been erected by you and you alone."

"I wish you were right, Jo. But regardless of how they got there…they are there, and I have to deal with them."

"Or get rid of them. Maybe it's time you knock some of them down and live."

"Look at me, Jo, I've lived." Tiffany held out her arms in a gesture to remind Josephine where they were standing.

"Tiff, we opened this company two years ago, and up until these last few months, you've only spent one to two days a week here. You've lived alright, but when it's in someone else's shadow, it doesn't count."

Tiffany was silent for a moment as she turned back toward the night scenery. "Funny, you and Trevor could be clones. He tells me the same thing."

Josephine's eyes lit up with shock. "Trevor…wasn't that the guy you were dancing with?"

Tiffany nodded.

"Well, maybe you should start listening to one of us."

"I want to, but I love my father."

Tiffany felt the presence of her friend beside her.

"I know you do, but don't you think it's about time you love yourself a little, too?"

Tiffany dropped her chin to her chest. The urge to cry was so strong, she pinched her eyes tight to hold back the flow. She feared that, if she gave in to them, she wouldn't be able to stop.

"Tiffany, there's nothing wrong with wanting to have a life. Get married, have a family maybe. Your father had one…don't you think you deserve the same thing?"

Tiffany swung around toward her friend. "He's a stripper, Jo, a male dancer. I paid for his services through an escort or entertainment service…whatever they call them now." Her shoulders shrugged in a hopeless gesture, the dam broke and she began to cry.

"Oh, Tiff." Josephine exhaled loudly as she embraced Tiffany. "I wish I could tell you how to get around it. But even I know if that got out, the press would have a field day."

"So what am I supposed to do? Ruin my father's career?" Tiffany prayed she didn't sound as pitiful as she felt.

"If this was just a fling, I would say have your fun and walk away soon. But if you love him…" she trailed off.

Tiffany looked at Josephine. "I love him, Jo. Lord, knows I didn't want to…but I do. Who couldn't love a man who wants nothing more from you than to see you live your own life? To top it off, he's smart. Especially when it comes to computers. That project on the table would have been horrendous if he hadn't helped me retrieve the data."

"Then it'll work out, someway."

"You're a true romantic, Jo." Tiffany leaned her head against Josephine's shoulder, and her friend's auburn twists brushed her forehead.

"I know, but at times like this, I wish I were a magician."

Laughing, Tiffany said, "If you were, what would you do?"

"Make all of the reporters disappear, of course."

They embraced each other, laughing.

"So what are you going to do?" Josephine asked after they broke apart.

"I'm having dinner with Trevor tomorrow night; he'll be surprised when I tell him I'm ready to go public."

"So are you going to wait until after you talk with Trevor?"

"It probably would be best, but I've waited long enough to confess. I'll stop by Dad's office tomorrow, maybe I can catch him before lunch. Now that I've made up my mind to tell him, I don't think I would be able to keep silent while being around him. I'll tell Dad after the event. So don't expect me anytime soon after lunch." Tiffany sighed. Her father wouldn't take the news very well. She hated hurting him, but there wasn't anything she could change about the circumstances of how she'd gotten married. If there were, she surely would have figured it out by now.

"At least give Trevor a heads up."

Tiffany nodded her head in agreement. "Maybe I'll call him before I go see my father."

§

"Lewis," Trevor spoke into the phone as he rotated the kinks out of his neck. He had been sitting at computer terminals for the last two hours, and his muscles were screaming.

To him, all of the aches and pains just added to the thrill of the job. He was a computer geek and proud of it.

"This is Wallace, I'm calling on behalf of the governor." Bold and direct, the governor's right hand man spoke into the phone.

Trevor's heart instantly began to race, and his ears perked up like a dog that'd just heard the jingle of car keys. For a moment, he considered the possibility that Governor Hatcher might have discovered the full extent of his involvement with Tiffany. But he put that aside, knowing more than likely, if the governor found out about that, he would have showed up personally at his office to confront him.

"Hello, Wallace." Trevor prayed he didn't reveal any hint of his internal turmoil.

"The governor would like to meet with you. A messenger will be by your office tonight with the details."

Trevor was amazed how Wallace managed to take all of the inflections out of his voice, making it sound direct and matter-of-fact. No doubt, Wallace wouldn't be entertaining questions.

"I'll be waiting."

Trevor heard the sound of the dial tone.

Sitting the phone back in its cradle, he went into his office to complete his work and wait for the messenger.

When Tiffany arrived home that night, she picked up her phone to listen to her messages. There were three new messages. The first one she listened to half-heartedly, not caring about some new phone plan or purchasing magazines for a year, so that a small percentage of the profits could supposedly aid some fund.

The second call was from her friend Veronica who wanted to have lunch with her next week to plan a surprise birthday party for Karen.

Tiffany smiled. Her friends never ceased to amaze her. Veronica and Karen were like oil and water, on any and every issue, but they would still do anything for each other.

Tiffany reached over to her appointment book and jotted down a note to remind herself to call Veronica and confirm the lunch.

"Tiffany, sweetie."

Her pen stopped mid-stride as she heard the sound of Trevor's voice come through the mini speaker, deep and slow.

"I was calling to hear your voice, but you must still be hard at work. I hope I didn't throw off your time too bad."

Heat rose in her cheeks with the memory of just how she had become thrown off.

"Well, I have to work tonight and won't be near a phone for a few hours."

Tiffany briefly wondered what Trevor's night work consisted of, if he was doing a private show for another group of groping, screaming women. She pushed that thought away, knowing if she were going to have a relationship with him, she would have to be able to deal with his current occupation.

Tiffany knew on a temporary basis she might be able to handle it, but long term was out of the question. Tomorrow, she would ask her father about arranging a position for Trevor with some of his associates.

Trevor's sexy tone interrupted her thoughts once again. "I can't wait to see you tomorrow night for dinner. There should be some exciting news I'll be sharing with you."

Her mind speculated on what that news could be, but quickly she put it out of her mind. She was exhausted, not only from the vigorous time spent with Trevor, but also the emotional conversation with Josephine. She knew that the meeting with her father would be difficult. She would need to have all of her strength and wits about her.

Thirteen

G ood morning, this is WNIS, and we have smooth jazz to get your day started…"

Tiffany stretched to the sound of the disc jockey's greeting and slowly pulled herself out of bed. Today was D-day to her. The day she would talk to her father and reveal her relationship with Trevor.

She looked at the twisted and mangled covers on her bed. She had lost count of how many times she'd awakened during the night. Her mind refused to shut itself off. Plagued with thoughts of her pending meeting, she'd finally exhausted herself into some disturbed sleep.

Walking into the bathroom, she turned the shower on full blast. She left and headed toward her closet. Opening the doors, she walked in and scanned her wardrobe.

She needed something that would assure her father she knew what she was doing. Something that said *confident* and not, "Daddy, I'm scared and nervous about what I feel for this man."

Tiffany pulled out two of her "power suits," charcoal and burnt orange. Alternating them both against her chest in front of the mirror, she rejected and tossed them onto the bed. Neither of them would do. If she wore them, she would look like she was going for an interview with her own father. Re-entering the closet, she grabbed her periwinkle colored jacket and georgette dress, then faced her reflection again.

She smiled. The dress made her look sweet, like Daddy's grown up little girl. She counted on that impression. It wasn't so much that her father treated her as if she were a little girl. She'd never fallen for a guy the way she had for Trevor, and she was scared. Everything in her wanted to crawl into her father's lap like when she was a child so he could promise everything would be okay. That she was making the right choice.

Refocusing, she said, "Definitely a keeper." Tiffany grabbed her matching slingback sandals from the shoe rack and placed them on the carpet.

Thick gray mist swirled around the bathroom, coating the glass door of the shower and light fixtures with warm dew. Tiffany could feel her face moisten from the steam as she entered. Drawing the nightgown over her head, she dropped it into the hamper. Stepping in, she took a deep breath, allowing the heat to surround her and bolster her nerves for her coming meeting.

Even while she stood in the relaxing atmosphere, it did nothing to calm the summersaults her stomach was doing. *Breakfast is definitely out.* The butterflies fluttering around inside of her were confirmation of the decision.

This was the first time she'd ever kept a secret of this magnitude from him. She knew her father would be disappointed. All of her life she had done everything within her power not to give him those feelings.

However, she was an adult now and able to stand up for herself.

§

"Trevor, I must say, I've been thoroughly impressed with your company in many ways." Tim Patterson, the CEO of Heritage's voice came through the speakerphone on the governor's desk.

The letter that had arrived by messenger informed him of the time he was to be at the governor's office. It also let him know he would be having a phone conference with Tim Patterson.

Governor Hatcher sat silently behind his desk assessing Computer Bytes' proposal. Trevor assumed it was most likely the hundredth time in the last seven months the governor had reviewed it.

"Thank you, Mr. Patterson." Trevor felt like he was sitting on pins. He could feel a bead of sweat slide down his spine. If he ever made it through this meeting, he would be peeling off suit jacket and tie as soon as he left the building.

He tried not to get his hopes up, but he couldn't deny the optimistic feelings.

When he glanced away from the speaker toward Governor Hatcher, Trevor saw the governor's slight smile.

The gesture set Trevor at ease...a little.

"Well, Trevor, I really could prolong this..." Patterson trailed off for a moment, and the room fell silent with the exception of the mild humming of the speaker.

In that one moment, Trevor tried to recall everything he ever heard about stress management techniques and attempted to draw several calming breaths into his diaphragm past his constricted chest.

"But you're a very smart man, and I'm sure you have already figured out why we've brought you here." Patterson sounded as if he were holding back a chuckle.

Just give it to me straight. Trevor couldn't take much more of the suspense. He wanted to know whether he'd gotten the contract or not. So much rode on this meeting.

"Doug, you want to give this young man the news?" Patterson asked the governor.

A full smile slowly spread across Governor Hatcher's face. "Trevor, congratulations, it's my pleasure to inform you that Computer Bytes has been awarded the Heritage contract."

Trevor's mouth went dry and his heart skipped a beat. He was in shock. Even though he had been anticipating it, it felt damn good to hear it. Confirmation was better than an assumption any day.

"Congratulations, Trevor," Patterson said. "That's a fine company you're running, and you should be proud of yourself. You had some stiff competition, but everyone on the board agreed CB would be a great asset to Heritage's future endeavors. I'll see you next week at my office."

"Yes, sir." Trevor wanted to stand up in the chair and yell, "I did it" at the top of his lungs.

"I'll see you at dinner tomorrow night, Tim." The chair tilted and squeaked as the governor leaned back in it.

"See you then, Doug." Patterson said moments before the dial tone sounded.

"You may celebrate now, Trevor." The governor gave him a knowing smile.

That was all Trevor needed to hear before he stood to his feet, threw his fists up in the air and shouted, "Hallelujah!" He took a moment to thank God because it finally seemed like everything in his life was coming together.

"Governor, I don't know how to thank you for this. I know my company was probably one of the smaller ones bidding for this, but I appreciate Heritage's faith and the opportunity." Trevor stretched his right hand across the desk toward the governor.

"You're more than welcome. We've always tried to give the little guys a leg up when we can." Standing, the governor took a firm hold of Trevor's extended hand and shook it.

"I've seen that in the years you've represented this state."

"Tomorrow, you'll receive the contract from Tim; have your lawyer look at it. The next time you meet with Tim, you all can hammer out the issues."

"Yes, sir." Releasing the governor's hand, Trevor was amazed he could talk through the broad smile frozen on his face.

"You and Tim should get along great. Make no mistake, he's a tough cookie, but he always tries to nurture all the companies involved. Who knows, maybe you and I will get a chance to work together someday."

"I'd welcome the opportunity, Governor Hatcher." Trevor knew it wasn't unheard of for a politician to give advice on an unofficial basis.

The governor came around the desk. "I'm anxious to watch how this relationship develops."

§

Tiffany stepped off the elevator and headed down the hall. Helen, her father's secretary, wasn't at her desk. Glancing at the appointment book on the desk, she read teleconference with Patterson at ten. After that, lunch was circled.

Tiffany knew Tim Patterson. He used to be the vice president at Heritage, her father's engineering company. He then took the CEO position after her father stepped down and into the office of governor. He was a longtime family friend and pseudo uncle to her.

Tiffany glanced at her watch. "Eleven twenty. He should be done by now. If not, it will give me a chance to say hi to Tim."

Tiffany stepped away from the desk, and then lightly tapped on the door before entering. She came to a dead stop.

The two most important men in her life were beside each other shaking hands. Tiffany caught her father's last words, "…how this relationship will develop."

"What's going on here?" Tiffany squawked. Her throat tightened, causing her to swallow several times to relieve the pressure.

"Sweetheart, come in." Her father walked toward her, arms open as wide as his smile.

Tiffany's feet were cemented to the ground. If her father's arm wasn't around her shoulder propelling her forward, she didn't think she would have been able to move on her own.

"Tiffany, your timing is perfect…congratulations are in order." Her father went on.

Congratulations, Tiffany thought. *Please tell me you didn't tell my father*, she wanted to scream at Trevor.

She didn't want to look at Trevor. She didn't want to see the face of the man she loved, who had betrayed her, but her father stopped, and she was directly in front of him.

"Hello, *Miss* Hatcher."

The inflection Trevor placed on her title made her finally look at him. Eyes large and round, she tried to question him about his purpose for being in her father's office.

"Mr. Lewis, I assume the governor meant for me to congratulate you. What for?" Tiffany tensed. She prayed her father couldn't feel it in her shoulders where his hand was resting.

"Tiffany," her father began, "you recall several months ago I helped Patterson begin the search for a computer company to work on the new contracts we have coming into the firm? Not to mention the plans for Heritage itself."

Heritage…computers…contracts….months. Tiffany felt sick. Her head began to spin and her heart rate picked up its pace. It was one thing to decide to love a man whose occupation may jeopardize her father's, but to know that man had misled her was another. Or had she mislead herself? That was a question she didn't want to ponder now.

Looking back and forth between the two smiling men, the truth dawned on her simultaneously as her father spoke. The words amplified in her ears. "Mr. Lewis's company, Computer Bytes, has won the contract."

Trevor wasn't who he seemed. Not who he pretended to be. *Worse, he wasn't what she imagined him to be…or was he still hiding secrets?*

Trapped inside of a tunnel and needing to get out, Tiffany took a sustaining breath. She pulled every ounce of fortitude she could muster and pasted a mannequin smile on her face. "Congratulations, Mr. Lewis, I'm sure this has been what you've always wanted. Isn't it great when everything you've worked so hard toward for months turns out just how you planned?"

"Tiffany, I—"

She turned toward her father, not wanting to hear anything that might have come out of Trevor's mouth. *Anything* would have made this situation worse. "Well, Dad, I can see you're busy, and I have to run." Tiffany spoke fast, not wanting to stay in the room a moment longer.

"You don't have to run off, sweetheart. Was there a reason you stopped by?"

Tiffany cut a quick look at Trevor. The fake smile she held in place slipped at the corners. "No, Daddy, it was nothing important. Nothing important all."

Turning back to her father, she kissed him on the cheek, and then left the office.

§

Trevor felt like a first rate jerk. The hurt look in Tiffany's eyes when she discovered who he really was would be etched in his brain for a long time.

He was thankful. As far as he could tell, the governor hadn't picked up on anything. Moments after Tiffany left, his meeting ended. He rode the elevator to the main lobby.

I should have told her, he said to himself as he left the building.

When he reached his car, he pulled his cell phone out and called Tiffany's phone.

Just as he'd figured, she'd turned it off. He switched the number to her office.

"Hello, Occasionally Yours, this is Jaunice speaking," came a bubbly greeting.

"May I please speak with Ms. Hatcher?"

If she refused to speak to him, he would at least know she was at work. He could drive over there and try to convince her to talk to him. People were less likely to make a scene in a place of business.

"No, I'm sorry, sir. She will not be in today, but you can speak with Ms. Dailey."

"Thanks, I'll just try another time." Trevor disconnected the call.

He knew Josephine Dailey was Tiffany's best friend, but he didn't know if Tiffany had told her friend about their relationship. Josephine would be a possible consideration if he couldn't get in touch with Tiffany on his own.

He speed dialed Tiffany's house.

"Hello, you've reached the Hatcher residence. We are unable to come to the phone at this time. If you would leave your name and number, we'd be happy to return your call," Tiffany's recorded message came through the phone. *Beeeeep.*

"I doubt you'll be happy to return my call, Tiffany. I can understand why, but if you could just give me a chance to explain…*please?*" Trevor knew he was begging, but he couldn't help it. He was willing to crawl to Tiffany on his knees and grovel if that's what it took to get her to hear him out. He just wanted to explain. Then maybe she would give him another chance once he told her everything.

This wasn't how he had envisioned the truth coming out. He had made plans at a restaurant for that evening, specifically for the purpose of confessing. By the looks of things, those needed to be canceled.

When Tiffany had walked out of the governor's office, he'd known at that moment he might have lost the best thing that had ever happened to him.

"Man," Trevor berated himself. "I shouldn't have lied to her. I should have told her the truth a long time ago and trusted what we had together."

Trevor started his car, pulled out of the parking lot and into lunch hour traffic.

After the news he'd gotten from Tim Patterson, he should be celebrating. There was no way he could be excited when he didn't know if there would ever be a place for him in Tiffany's life.

Fourteen

T iffany, come in!"

A soft voiced greeted Tiffany. Her pastor's wife, Paula, had been a confidant since her mother's death.

"Hi, Mrs. Paula, I hope I'm not disturbing you." Tiffany entered the house and was enfolded in a warm hug by the other woman. It always astounded Tiffany that she could pull so much comfort from Paula, who was much shorter and petite.

"Never. I was just making a list of the things I need to pack for Pastor and my annual trip to Italy. We're headed to Venice this time."

Tiffany envied Paula's joy in her relationship.

"That's great," Tiffany followed her through the house.

"Your timing is perfect; the tea just finished boiling. Have a seat."

Tiffany sat quietly as she watched Paula putter around the kitchen, grabbing cups and saucers and dessert plates.

Paula joined Tiffany at the table and served them both tea and a slice of her famous pound cake.

Even with all of the emotions churning inside of her, Tiffany couldn't resist a bite of the cake.

"Hmm, that's good." Tiffany's eyes closed of their own volition as her mouth savored the bite.

"It always pleases me that you like it," Paula spoke softly. "Now tell me what's wrong."

Tiffany laid her fork down next to the plate, not wanting to ruin the cake by fidgeting with it. "I look that bad, huh?"

Paula placed a reassuring hand over Tiffany's. "No, you don't. But I can see you've been crying."

"I've been a fool."

"Oh, that's hard for me to believe. You've always made very sound choices."

Tiffany snickered. "I used to think I was capable of making wise decisions. Then…"

"Then what?"

Tiffany could no longer stop the tears from welling up in her eyes again. "Then I met a man who made me lose myself."

"Oh, honey, that's not always a bad thing." The minister's wife reached over and rubbed her shoulder. "Who is this man?"

Tiffany reached for a napkin off the table and wiped her eyes, then began to fidget with the edges of the napkin. Paula would only be the second person she had told about her marriage to Trevor.

Paula sat quietly at the table, waiting for Tiffany to speak.

Looking at the older woman, she said, "He's my husband, Mrs. Paula."

Tiffany waited for the censorship, but it never came.

"If you got married without Pastor performing the service, it must have been a spur of the moment decision."

"It was."

"Tell me about this man that swept you off your feet."

Tiffany gave a smile and a small laugh, thinking of Trevor always put a joyous feeling in her heart, even when she was mad at him. "Mrs. Paula, honestly, we got married in Vegas under a weird set of circumstances. It was attraction at first sight…but not love at all."

"Is it love, now?"

"Yes." Tiffany took a breath, reached for her tea and sipped.

"That's all that matters, Tiffany," Paula said firmly.

Rising from the table, Tiffany stood behind the chair, feeling too anxious to be still.

"Mrs. Paula, if you understood what he has done over the course of this *marriage*. You would probably be telling me to head for the hills far away from Trevor."

"Trevor. That's a strong name. I had a friend once who named her child that… if I remember correctly, it means prudent."

A burst of laughter erupted from Tiffany, too quick to stop. She sat back in the chair and reached for another napkin to wipe the tears of humor away.

"Trevor is anything but…"

Paula glanced at Tiffany with a soft smile and a slight tilt of her head. "You know most people hear the word prudent and think prude or someone that is moralistic." She reached her hand across the table to Tiffany's again, in a reassuring gesture. "It is the ability to govern and discipline oneself by the use of reason. Therefore, it's possible to an outsider that Trevor might have married you on a whim, or that he has been reckless in the handling of it. Just maybe this is all part of Trevor's plan."

"That's a scary thought," Tiffany mumbled. "With all this mess, I couldn't begin to figure out what his plan could be."

"Well, you'll never know what it entails until you talk to him," Paula said confidently.

Tiffany looked at her minister's wife and smiled. "I know better than to ask how you know I haven't spoken to him yet."

Paula answered Tiffany's smile with one of her own.

"Well, I have held you up long enough. So I'm going to finish my cake, then I'm out of your hair."

Paula's smile brightened. "I'll even send you home with a slice …or two."

§

Trevor slowly pulled his car along the curb in front of the fence incased executive mansion in Capitol Square. He allowed his car to sit idle as he looked through the gate at the house. The fact that he stared upon the oldest continuously occupied governor's residence in the United States didn't even cross his mind. There was no thought of being impressed with the past when he didn't know if there would be a future for him and Tiffany.

142

He was angry. Everything within him desired to walk up to the house and ask if Tiffany was there. Earlier, he'd gone by her house and knew she wasn't home.

She was avoiding him.

He'd hoped she would be with her father, even though it could mean possible disaster for his company and its newly won contract.

It would have been simple for him to turn his anger away from himself and toward Tiffany for not revealing their relationship to her father. But he couldn't do it. More than half of this problem was his.

He was the one who'd sought her out in the beginning.

Deep down, he was the one who didn't want to jeopardize his career by allowing the truth to come out.

Tap, tap, tap.

Trevor was jolted out of his musing by knuckles rapping against his passenger side window.

Damn. The last thing he needed was some estate guard hounding him about his presence in front of the property at night. With no one else out loitering the block, he was an easy target for harassment.

Exhaling slowly, Trevor pressed the button in the center console to roll the window halfway down.

"This is really pathetic," the man said as he stooped down to speak into the opening.

"Manning," Trevor growled.

His was the last face Trevor expected to appear above the half-massed glass.

"Trevor Lewis...you always seem to have a habit of being in places you don't belong." A smug smile spread across Manning's face.

Trevor desired to wipe it off.

"What brings you to *this* side of town...dreaming big again?" Manning laughed.

That laugh sent chills of remembrance shimmering down Trevor's spine.

Trevor quickly undid his seatbelt and leaped out the car. Standing in the door opening, looking across the hood, Trevor spoke to his old college rival, "You're the last person who needs to talk to me about my dreams."

Manning began to take steps around the trunk of Trevor's car. "But I know your dreams…"

Trevor stepped toward him. "You don't know a *damn* thing about me."

"Of course I do…. scholarship boy." Manning stopped.

Trevor counted the two feet it would take him to reach Manning.

"You always make sure I never forget it." Trevor could feel his jaw muscles flexing as he clinched his teeth.

Manning took one step too many, as he came face to face with Trevor. "You know, Trevor, there is no charity Pell Grant program that will get you into Tiffany Hatcher's panties. Stay the hell away from *my* woman."

Before Trevor realized what was happening, Manning threw a sucker punch. Trevor barely moved in time to keep from being clocked. He sidestepped, then slammed Manning against the side of his car. Trevor's sense of touch heightened as he wrapped his hands around his nemesis' throat.

Shock registered into his adversary's eyes. Manning had always been a coward.

"You know I could kill you." Trevor's hands squeezed a little tighter. "I could snuff your life out…without taking a breath to think about it."

Manning's body began to flail against the car as his hands gripped Trevor's in an attempt to remove them.

"Do you think anyone would miss you? How long do you think it would take for them to find your worthless body?"

"You'd…never…get away…with it," Manning croaked on raspy breaths.

"I wonder what my reward would be for ridding the world of a parasite like you." Trevor could taste the sweetness of revenge as anger permeated throughout his body. This is what he'd dreamed about. This was what he had always wanted.

"Jail—" Manning squawked.

"You think I care about that?"

Manning began to make choking sounds while frantically clawing at Trevor's hands.

"What I cared about, you took away. Do you even think about the life you stole carelessly? Does she haunt you at night?"

Manning's gasps continued.

Trevor looked at the man he held in his clutches. Christopher Manning, the spoiled rich kid. The person who could kill someone and walk away untainted. Manning took away one dream and one life and never paid. He was poison.

Poison. Trevor didn't consider himself poison. If he killed Manning, he wouldn't be any better than the man he despised. He would have willingly allowed the toxin into his blood like an eager junkie. Trevor wanted more than that. He wanted a future unencumbered by any more nightmares.

Trevor let go and stepped back and watched Manning's body crumble against the side of his car.

"You're not worth it."

Manning coughed and choked on the gulps of oxygen rapidly filling his greedy lungs.

Trevor turned and walked back toward his driver's side door that stood open, patiently awaiting his return. He slid into the car and was in the process of closing the door when he heard Manning's words.

"Rebecca was nothing but a high priced whore who could be bought for any frat party entertainment. No one even said her name a month after she—"

The force of Trevor's fist contacting with Manning's jaw ended his stream of words.

"I did." Trevor turned back to his vehicle, got in and drove off.

Manning's body lay unconscious in the street.

§

The sanctuary was dim. The church's lights were low, but it was a representation of how Trevor felt. He walked to the front of the church and sat down in the front pew. He chuckled sarcastically. He hadn't been in a church in years, and even then, he would have been fighting for the back row. Now that he was in serious need of solace, the front pew appeared very welcoming to him.

Trevor sat down, closed his eyes and waited. He didn't know what he was expecting, but he knew he needed help.

He knew he'd messed up with Tiffany and didn't know how to fix it.

A slight throbbing in his hand reminded him of his confrontation with Manning. Looking down at his hand as he flexed it, he reflected on his old mantra… *One day Christopher "Golden Boy" Manning, you'll lose something that you hold dear…I'll see to it personally.*

Trevor had always believed that when he began to serve Manning his just desserts, it would feel good. He would get chills of vindication running up and down his spine and he'd celebrate.

Tiffany's face came to his mind. He hadn't considered that he could hurt the people who were associated with Manning.

No, he didn't feel like celebrating.

"May I help you?"

Trevor opened his eyes and looked up to the ceiling when he heard the melodic male voice, expecting Gabriel, the messenger angel, to have appeared.

Shaking himself for the wayward thought, he turned around and located the man standing in the center of the aisle, a few rows back.

"I'm sorry if I'm trespassing. I just needed a place to think."

The man moved closer. "This is one place no one could ever trespass."

As the man stood next to the seat Trevor was in, he could see him more clearly. The man stood about a foot shorter than him and was casually dressed in jeans and a T-shirt with a wool Ascot cap in his hand. Trevor figured he was the custodian there to check up on the place during the week.

"Do you mind if I sit with you for a moment?"

Trevor slid down the bench a little further and turned back toward the front of the church. The other man sat down in the vacant space.

Both men sat in silence.

The press of guilt weighed on Trevor's shoulders, making it difficult for him to remain quiet. "I don't know if there is help for me," Trevor said as he thought back to the man's original question.

"Why do you think that?"

"Because as the old saying goes, 'I made my bed, and now I have to sleep in it'."

"I don't know where that saying comes from, but if the people actually began to sleep in messes of their making without a way out…the world would be a disgusting place." The other man made a sound as if he were exhaling a breath. "Good thing that for everything there is forgiveness."

Trevor turned and discovered the other man looking at him. "That's God, not people. I've hurt someone pretty badly."

Trevor faced front again and debated whether or not he wanted to reveal his sins toward Tiffany to the stranger with the Ascot cap. Then he decided he had come inside the church for something, and maybe sharing with this other man would help him find a little peace.

Humorously, Trevor began, "It's been too many years to count since my last confession…"

The other man's boisterous laughter caused Trevor to turn back toward him and smile.

Trevor's smile slipped from his mouth. "Out of revenge, I married a woman I didn't love and because I thought she was special to a man I considered my enemy. I plotted out the revenge. It doesn't matter that I thought it was the only way to avenge my friend; I hurt the woman I married."

"Did you tell the woman you married what was going on?"

"No."

"Are you still married to her?"

"Yes."

"How does the situation stand now?"

Trevor bowed his head. "Worse than if she had found out I was using her for revenge. Because she knows I've lied to her and pushed her to consider jeopardizing her father's career, just to accept me in her life. Because I wanted to be with her."

Just saying the words aloud made Trevor feel miserable. Hurting Tiffany had been the last thing he wanted to do. He had even planned to tell her the truth about everything that night at dinner so their relationship could begin untarnished by the past.

"The fact you're here with a colossal weight on your shoulder, instead of out clicking your heels together over the contract, tells me you have some very deep feelings for her."

Trevor eyed the large cross hanging over the pulpit. "You're correct. I never expected this. But I fell in a big way."

"Love will do that." The other man stood. "You need to tell her."

Trevor stood as well. "I've been trying to reach her all afternoon."

"Don't stop until she agrees to listen to you. If she feels the way you do about her, then it won't take long at all."

"Thanks." Trevor extended his hand toward the man. "I'll get out of your way. I've held you up long enough."

The man grasped Trevor's hand. "It's no problem. I thought I was only stopping by to pick up my sermon notes for Sunday, but I guess I was wrong."

"No, you were right," Trevor said with confidence, as they broke contact. "By the way, I'm, Trevor."

"Anthony," he said, smiling and leading the way to the front of the church.

Nothing more needed to be said as both men remained silent as they exited the church. Anthony paused to lock the door, and Trevor continued toward his car with more lift to his spirit than when he'd arrived.

Fifteen

D*oon, doon, doon…*

Tiffany heard the high and low tones of the door chimes and rose from the couch in the living room where she sat idly flipping through a magazine waiting for Trevor to arrive. Tossing it on the table, Tiffany's chest expanded as she inhaled a deep breath. She walked toward the door and exhaled the air from her lungs slowly, audibly. The metal handle of the door felt cool against her palm as she reached out and grabbed it. She squeezed and turned, feeling each muscle in her right hand tighten around the knob. Tiffany was amazed how awake and alive her senses had become just from the ringing of the doorbell, and she hadn't even opened the door yet.

She shouldn't have been shocked at her response. It was Trevor, and he always did that to her. Made her come alive.

She looked at Trevor from head to toe, knowing his body as intimately as she knew her own. "Who are you?" It was the first thing she needed to know before she let him in. She had opened her door and heart to him too many times under false pretenses.

"Hi. I'm Trevor Lewis, owner of Computer Bytes. Computer geek at your service." Though he sounded as rich and soft as cherished leather, she also heard a dejected tone. His posture held a nonchalant bearing as he lounged with one shoulder against the doorjamb.

Tiffany didn't know which to believe. He claimed feelings for her one moment, yet he never revealed who he truly was.

She didn't trust herself to say more, so she stepped back to allow him to enter the house. After he crossed the threshold, she closed the door with a snap and led the way.

Not a stripper. As she moved toward the living room, her mind was on the man who owned the echoing footsteps thumping behind her. He wore jeans like skin, snug, fitting and cleaving to every bulge and curve. Leaving nothing to the imagination. She didn't need imagination; she knew what was held in those pants. She knew it by size, feel and shape. She knew it by how deep it could thrust inside of her until her eyes rolled back and it felt like her very soul had left her body on a cry of pleasure.

Her sex pulsated. She yearned to be sitting so she would be able to squeeze her thighs together and calm its throb.

Trevor. Even the sound of his name in her mind made her nipples tighten. She crossed her arms over her chest to hide the evidence of the affect he had on her. Reaching the living room, she sat down on the first piece of furniture she reached. A chair. *Perfect.* It would give her the distance she needed. Distance to keep her head clear. *Distance,* Tiffany repeated it like a mantra.

Trevor chose the couch across from her. Sitting on the edge, he leaned forward with his elbows balanced on his knees.

Ooh, man! Tiffany thought as she realized the view she had down his shirt. Crisp and white, with three buttons undone at the collar. Corded muscles and rope like veins traveled along the side, making Tiffany want to place heated, open mouth kisses on them. She couldn't stop her eyes from dipping lower to catch a glimpse of his upper chest and pecks. Her tongue slid out of her mouth to glide across her lips as she remembered how each lick of his skin would taste.

She cleared her throat abruptly. *This is not the time,* she berated herself. *This may be Trevor, the man who took you into your first moments of pure ecstasy, but he was also the man who married, deceived and made you out to be a fool of the first degree.*

Her anger returned with full force. "Why?" she uttered past her tight lips.

§

Ah, hell. Trevor thought. *Time to come clean.* What he really wanted to do when Tiffany opened the door in her sweet lace trimmed camisole top and knee length skirt was lay her down in the foyer on the parquet floor and ply his tongue against her wet folds and capture her essence. Instant arousal hit him. He clenched his jaw to stifle the groan that rose in his throat. His manhood began to swell and extend, making his jeans feel two sizes too small. *Man, you are* not *here for this.*

He was silent as he followed her barefoot trek down the hall across the gleaming wood. Unable to keep his eyes from watching the sway of her hips as the flowing material of her skirt brushed across her firm, round bottom. Everything in him yearned to run his hands underneath her skirt, to re-familiarize himself with the hidden curves of her thighs and butt. To touch the welcoming supple heat of her inner thighs and travel up them until he reached the part of her that was wet and declared her level of excitement would have been heaven.

He was happy when Tiffany chose the first chair in the room and sat down. Giving him the time he needed to rein in his desire. The look on her face helped. She sat with her lips pursed with anger, her arms folded across her full breasts and her legs crossed. The pain and hurt that filled her eyes tore at his heart. He had put that there. Now, his omissions could be the cause of him losing the one person who meant everything to him.

Gazing into those brown eyes that would be his judge and jury, he said, "I'm sorry. I never meant things to turn out like this."

She dropped her arms to her lap. "I don't want to hear how damn sorry you are. I figured that out hours ago."

Ouch.

"What I want is the truth. *The unadulterated truth.* If you can unravel all of the lies you have given me and find it."

Trevor knew he had this coming. He owed Tiffany this time of anger. He just hoped before the night was over he would be able to convince her to give him a second chance. Taking another glance at the set look of her face, he lost his confidence.

"Where would you like me to start?" He opened his hands, and then clasped them together.

"The beginning would be great."

Trevor sighed, leaned back in the chair and rested his linked hands on his abdomen. "I'll tell you whatever you want to know. Before I start, I don't want you to have any doubt that when I told you I loved you, I meant it."

Tiffany opened her mouth to comment.

"I meant it," Trevor said emphatically, bringing to a halt any doubt she was going to voice.

There was a momentary thick silence before Trevor began to speak. "In order to start this off, I have to tell you that this entire situation involves Manning."

"Christopher? What does he have to do with this?" Curiosity painted her face like a mural.

"More than you could ever imagine." Trevor cast his gaze toward the ceiling briefly, then looked across the carpeted floor at her again. *Watch your words. Remember what Christopher means to her.*

"Manning and I went to undergrad together."

Tiffany started to speak, but Trevor raised his hand to cease it. He needed to get this out without interruptions. "Hear me first, Tiffany." He took a deep breath. "We played football together, which is how I could even afford to attend the school. I was recruited. Not to brag on myself, but I had been warding off scouts since I was a sophomore in high school. I could have gone anywhere, but Leslie, my aunt, always told me to choose wisely. 'You won't be playing football your whole life,' she'd say."

"The owner of Elite Entertainment," she stated more than asked.

Trevor noticed Tiffany's arms were starting to relax. He could almost hear the wheels turning in her head.

"Yes. Leslie has always been there to support me. So I went Ivy League. Drakner College in New Hampshire. They didn't rank even in the top ten schools for football, but that was okay because they were an

Ivy League College." Trevor stood and walked to the side of the couch. He was anxious, and he was just beginning with the story.

Respecting his request, Tiffany remained quiet.

"From the moment I got there, I knew I was out of my league. I couldn't fathom how I would ever be able to relate with students whose parents and grandparents were corporate attorneys, stockbrokers, heads of hospitals, senators and Supreme Court justices." Trevor looked at Tiffany. "How could I compete with that?My father was a longshoreman until he died, and my mother owned a small cleaning business, which went under after she died my freshman year. But I was going to stick it out because I was determined to make it."

Trevor sat down on the arm of the couch, and he looked down at his hands as they clinched in suppressed anger. "I think that's why Christopher hated me."

"Hate is a very strong word."

"But perfect." He glanced up at Tiffany. "I initially came under his radar being on the football team with him. I was good. As a freshman, I got the position of starting quarterback. I was the one who was going to take the school to victory. Christopher was second to me, and he didn't like it. That's when the pranks started." Trevor got up, walked over to the mantle over the fireplace and placed both his hands against it, keeping his back to Tiffany. "For three years, I took the itching powder, tainted food, ruined clothes, defaced property and public ridicule."

"Christopher dropped off the team in his sophomore year."

"That just made things worse." Trevor's eyes went vacant as his thoughts drifted back. "The night we won our homecoming game, we were in the locker room celebrating. Things got rough and rowdy. Next thing I knew, I had a dislocated shoulder. I could never prove who did it, but I'm positive it was some of Christopher's loyal buddies who were still on the team."

"What did you do?"

"Nothing." Trevor shrugged his shoulders in a matter of fact manner. "I was glad it was my right shoulder instead of my throwing arm. But that taught me quickly to watch my back."

"Why didn't you report them?" Tiffany's naïve faith caused Trevor to turn around.

"To whom?" Trevor shook his head. "Their fathers were on the alumni board. Besides, if I had shown any hint they were getting to me, then it would have been worse."

Tiffany stood and walked toward him. "Trevor, what's worse than what they did to you?"

"Death." The ominous tone heavily weighed Trevor's words. He could see the shock and disbelief registered on Tiffany's face as her forehead creased, eyes glazed over and her mouth dropped open giving her a daunted look.

"Oh, come now, Trevor. Aren't you being a bit melodramatic?"

The comment hit Trevor with the impact of a large rubber mallet. It stole his breath and rendered him speechless for a moment. Trevor's head hung low as he took a deep breath. He had to remember Tiffany didn't know the real Manning. "Rebecca Camille Samuelson."

Tiffany's face scrunched. "Who is that?"

"She was my best friend." Trevor tilted his head and made eye contact with her. "She died." Trevor could hear his own voice, thick and quivering with emotions tenuously restrained. "She was my rock. One of the few people who looked beyond my athletic ability and saw me."

Trevor noticed the slight tremors in Tiffany's hands as she fidgeted with the seam of her top. Her eyes darted around the room, touching everything but him.

"This girl meant a lot to you." She still refused to look at him. "What came between the two of you?" Her hands paused briefly. "Let me guess. This is why you hate Christopher so much. He slept with your girl?"

Flippant was the word that came to Trevor's mind to describe Tiffany's tone, but the manner in which she toyed with her shirt hem told a different story. Even though she tried to hide it, he could tell the extent of his relationship with Rebecca disturbed her.

"Manning didn't just sleep with her. They were dating, and when he'd had enough of her, he got her drunk and passed her among his friends. She endured months of harassment before—" He cut his own words off. He needed a moment before he continued. He hadn't spoken about her in years and only once to his aunt after the incident.

"Before? Before what?"

She sounded breathless, Trevor thought as he watched the slow rise and fall of Tiffany's chest. He allowed his eyes a gradual stroll up her body, not missing the quickening pulse at the base of her neck as he passed it to rest his gaze on her face. "A 1960 candy apple red, white couch leathered interior, mint condition Corvette. That's what."

Her eyes targeted him, and he watched them swell with recognition.

"Oh, my God. That's Christopher's car," she pronounced, her eyes stretched wide to the size of mini espresso saucers.

"Tell her what she wins!" he sarcastically mocked game show hosts.

"Talk to me, Trevor." Tiffany's hand reached toward him.

§

Trevor's whole body went on awareness as Tiffany touched him. It was a simple act, but he was connected to her on a level he'd never known with anyone else.

He took a steadying breath and focused on the far wall over Tiffany's shoulder. He had to look anywhere but at her. Or he would lose it.

"As they say in the movies, 'It was the big game.' My coach informed me at practice the night before that a minimum of four NFL scouts would be in the stands to watch me play. There was a rumor that at least two of them would most likely have the general manager on the line ready to set up a meeting to negotiate contracts. There were teams that wanted me bad. That was the main reason I had chosen Drakner; I wanted to stand out. I was considering whether to forgo entering the draft. I was well on my way."

He felt the squeeze of Tiffany's hand on his forearm. He looked down and watched her thumb stroke his arm before it dropped back down to her side.

"That night, Rebecca and I had gone to dinner at one of the restaurants off campus frequented by students. Everything was going great;

during our dinner the atmosphere was charged. People stopped by the table dressed in assorted costumes of green and white to offer the team and me their support. Shortly before we left, Christopher and his chums came in." Trevor felt the burn in his shoulders as the tension in his muscles consumed him. "I remember feeling fortunate they didn't say anything to us. Just stared but left us alone."

Trevor leaned a shoulder into the stone of the mantel and closed his eyes. "It was a nice night, and we had decided to walk so I could burn off some of the excited energy coursing through my veins and focus on the game ahead." Trevor opened his eyes and looked at Tiffany. Seeing the arched eyebrows, high cheekbones, caramel kissed skin, full lips and the softness of her face. "I will never forget the sound of screeching tires. It's the sound of death on wheels." Trevor shut his eyes again. "We saw the headlights. I immediately knew who it was by the antique shape of them. There were more lights behind him from his friends' cars. I could still hear his laughter as he barreled toward us at high speed." Trevor opened his eyes. Pain filled him as he looked off in the distance, still trapped in the memory. He relived the cool breeze of the night kissing his skin, and his hands started to shake.

"By his speed, I knew he would never be able to stop in time. I grabbed Rebecca and attempted to get us out of the way. However, at the same time, Christopher slammed on his brakes and the car fishtailed. I was sideswiped. The doctors told me my body automatically braced for impact because of years of football training. Rebecca wasn't so lucky."

Trevor pushed away from the mantle and began to pace between the furniture, clinching and unclenching his hands into fists. "She was caught by the tail-end of the car. The force of it propelled her body ten feet and head first onto the edge of the curve. She died instantly." He stopped and turned to Tiffany, finally seeing through the fog in his mind.

Tiffany stood frozen by the mantle. "Trevor, I'm sorry."

"I'm glad to know that you are because Manning never said or showed it."

"What? Didn't he have to make restitution? Wasn't there a trial?" The indignation of injustice colored Tiffany's speech.

The bark of Trevor's abrupt laughter echoed through the room and ended in the same manner.

"If I learned anything while lying in that damn hospital bed and undergoing months of rehabilitation, it was that the Mannings of the world can get away with anything. Even murder." He sat down on the couch, his body weak with emotions. "All of my medical bills were paid for by Senator Manning. Rebecca's death was ruled an accident. There was never an apology. Public or otherwise."

Tiffany walked toward him. "Did Christopher ever visit you while you were in the hospital?"

A sardonic smile graced Trevor's face. "Oh, I was honored with the presence of both him and his father. Two days after I came out of knee repair surgery." He reached down and rubbed the reconstructed knee. "At least they put it back together. The Mannings stopped by. It was a short meeting to inform me the entire situation was an *unfortunate accident*. A misunderstanding between Christopher and me. They had witnesses to testify Christopher didn't see us walking in the middle of the parking lot until it was too late. He attempted to swerve away from us both, but nevertheless it happened." Trevor's hands were vigorous as they rubbed over his face and baldhead. "After they left, I made a vow to Rebecca that one day I would get revenge."

§

Tiffany plopped down onto the cushion of her vacated chair. "That's where I come in." Confirmation. It was worse than she'd expected. "Nothing in Las Vegas between us happened by chance, did it?" She looked across the room at Trevor. She saw the pain and anger of the past still resident in his eyes.

"No."

One word and she had her answer. She felt sick to her stomach as she thought about how she had fallen hard for Trevor over the last few months. How she had given herself to him unrestrained. "How did you convince your aunt to allow you to pose as one of her dancers?"

"I was actually doing her a favor. Believe it or not, in the beginning I never planned for you to be my way of getting to Manning. I used to dance for Leslie every summer. That's how I paid for part of my school tuition. Dancing allowed me to save a decent nest egg, allowing me to start my business. Even though I stopped dancing for her after college, she would occasionally call me if she was in a jam. I owed it to her. Leslie has always been there for me. I recently told her my company was up for a major contract, and I couldn't dance for her any longer."

"Daddy's old business." Tiffany's voice was vacant. "Why did you do the Vegas party?" Tiffany needed answers; every revelation tore another piece of her heart.

"Because it was on the other side of the country." His gaze pierced her. "It was you. The woman Manning was expected to marry one day."

A large part of her wanted to cover her ears and avoid hearing the truth. The other part of her had to know. She would need the truth to go on without him. Her eyes burned, the urge to cry was heavy upon her. Instead, she focused on squeezing her fist tight, burying her nails into her palm.

"People shouldn't believe everything the news tells them." Her voice sounded hollow to her own ears. Tiffany glared at Trevor. "So before you left Virginia you had already conceived the plan to marry me." Her laugh was just as empty. "That's why you wouldn't give me a quiet divorce." Tiffany nodded her head, finally understanding as she looked anywhere but at him.

"No. I didn't plan to marry you…"

Trevor's deep voice drew her eyes to him.

"My plan was to get you naked, spread your legs wide and feast on your sweet sex until you became hoarse with ecstasy…" He leaned forward over his knees. "Then bury myself so deep inside you I could feel your heart beat."

Tiffany squeezed her thighs tight, feeling her womanhood begin to swell and pulse at his words. Her hands started to tremble, and a bead of sweat trickled between her breasts. Her body betrayed her, even though she knew he had plotted to have sex with her out of revenge. "The kitchen," was all she could say.

Trevor continued. "I was going to use you the way Manning had used Rebecca and tossed her aside. I was going to one up him by sleeping with his future wife and letting him know it."

"So I was going to become your victim? Your revenge? All because Manning slept with Rebecca and was responsible for her death? Well, you got just what you wanted and then some...but the joke's on you." Angry and frustrated, Tiffany stood up, then sat down again, then rose again and walked over to the window, snatched the curtain open and stared out into the night. She was confused and hurt, and tears began to run out of her eyes unchecked. Tiffany's throat tightened and her voice wavered. "I'm sorry she died. I'm sorry Christopher is a royal jackass. I'm sorry you lost your love. I'm sorry. I'm sorry. I'm *sorrrry*," Tiffany said weakly as her legs gave out. She'd wanted to hear it all and was miserable now that she had.

Instead of feeling the impact of the floor, Tiffany found herself cradled in Trevor's arms. He sat on the carpet embracing and rocking her. She didn't want comfort. She didn't want to fall prey to his hold. Succumb to his touch. Tiffany began slamming her fists into Trevor's chest and shoulders, not caring where her blows landed. She just wanted to hurt him. To make him experience the pain she felt, in any way.

"Tiffany, honey." Trevor grabbed her violating fist and held them tight. "Listen to me."

She jerked and attempted to snatch her hands from his grasp. "No," she growled, as she propelled her body away from him. "I've listened long enough."

Tiffany stood, with violence in her eyes, attempting to pierce Trevor to his very soul. "I'm tired, Trevor." She used the back of a hand to swipe the remainder of the tears from her eyes. *No more tears. No more crying. No more being stepped on by men.*

Trevor rose slowly from the floor. "Tiffany, I know—"

"You know *nothing*." Tiffany spoke through gritted teeth. "Damn it, I'm tired of all the well meaning men in my life. Treating me like I can't think for my damn self. Trying to control my life to suit *their* purpose." Tiffany's hands flailed around her body. "My dad. Christopher. Now you."

"Baby—"

Tiffany threw up her hands in his face to ward off anything Trevor wanted to say. "Don't you dare, baby, sweetie, sugar-pie or honey me," Tiffany barked out, as she backed away from him. The urge to strangle him or pick up a chair and bash him across the skull was too overpowering to resist.

"I love you. Doesn't that count for anything?"

"No." Tiffany continued to back away from him. "Not right now. The only thing I want from you now is for you to get out." She wanted to run, to escape the horrid nightmare that had somehow trapped her inside.

Trevor stalked after her.

"Don't." She held her hand firm and steady as she put her palm up to stop his progress.

"We need to talk," he pleaded.

She crossed her arms over her chest. "No, *we* don't. *I* don't want to talk to you right now. *I* don't want to see your face. *I* don't want to stand in the same room with you, let alone breathe the same air."

Trevor didn't move or speak. He just looked at her with his toffee colored brown eyes. Those eyes that even now jeopardized her anger, but she wasn't going to allow it. Tiffany used everything within her to shield herself and harden her heart. "Get out. Get out. Get out," Tiffany snapped. She charged toward him and slammed into his impermeable body.

He was like a wall, not to be budged.

Initially, he did nothing to stop her tirade. Then he grabbed her shoulders in a firm hold and looked at her, his face full of regret.

Tiffany's voice was rough. It crackled from overuse. "You made me believe you were different. Someone who was supposed to care about my happiness. About me." Twisting away from him, she pointed toward the door. "Get the hell out of my damn house, Trevor," she said, each word filled with hurt, pain, anger and disappointment.

He closed his eyes and hung his head for a moment. She saw his chest expand as he took a deep breath. Then with one last glance at her, he turned and walked out of the front door. Out of her house. Out of her life.

Tiffany wanted, needed to scream. But like she had told Trevor, she was tired and emotionally drained. She walked over to the door and double bolted it. Without stopping to turn off the lights, she walked up the stairs toward the darkness and her bed. Like Scarlet O'Hara, she would think about it all tomorrow.

Sixteen

Trevor closed the door behind himself and stood there. His breathing became laborious, and his chest tightened to the point of pain, as if a heart attack was pending. "I should be so lucky." Trevor closed his eyes for a moment. *Anything would be better than life without Tiffany.* He'd believed if he were able to sit and talk to her, he would be able to make her understand. But he had been wrong. Everything within him wanted to turn around, open the door and hold her until she forgave him. But he knew it was too late. It was over. "You've really messed things up, ole boy."

He did the inevitable and stepped away from the door.

Click, snap!

Trevor stopped. The sound of the dead bolt locking into place let him know loud and clear that any further discussion with Tiffany that night was out of the question. She'd barred him from her life. Trevor sent up a prayer that it wasn't a permanent position for him.

As if carrying twenty linebackers on his shoulders, he continued his progression to his car. Guilt. It was a terrible thing to experience. Even worse, to know your trial was just for the moral crime committed.

He got in his car, sat behind the wheel and stared at the house. Lifeless. He couldn't bring himself to start the engine. He knew if he drove away this might mark the last time he would be welcomed back.

Everything in him confirmed the truth; he'd lost Tiffany. Too many lies. Too many secrets. Trailed by a confession that came too late. Shaking himself out of his stupor, he made a decision about what he had to do. Make things right.

With a parting look at the house and toward Tiffany's darkened bedroom, he knew she was lying in there hurting. He started his car.

With a heavy heart of despair, he drove away. There would be no secret entry for him tonight.

§

"I need to speak with the governor," Trevor said to the butler at the Governor's Mansion.

"Do you know what time it is, sir?" The older, silver-haired, white gentleman's pasty peach skin flushed red with shock.

Trevor looked down at his watch. "Twelve thirty-one and eleven, twelve, thirteen seconds."

Trevor didn't know if being a smart aleck would help him gain access to the house, but at this point, there wasn't much more he could lose. He looked past the older man's shoulder and saw the plain clothed guard in black jeans and a button down shirt standing at the base of the steps with a gun ready and available on his hip.

"Your name, sir?"

"Trevor Lewis."

"One moment please, sir," the butler said, then closed the door firmly in his face.

The door was thick and soundless. Trevor could only guess what was happening on the other side.

He was amazed how calm and relaxed he felt even though his relationship and possibly his company would be ruined by the time the sun rose. After ten minutes of staring at the door, Trevor sat on the first step and looked out toward the street. His car was parked out front. A state trooper had already driven by twice. He was sure his license had been run, and if the governor didn't grant him entrance, he would likely be arrested for trespassing and his car towed.

"Mr. Lewis."

Trevor turned around at the sound of his name. Instead of the butler whom he expected, it was Wallace, Governor Hatcher's right hand man. Trevor stood and stepped up, bringing himself on a direct eye level with the formidable man.

Wallace had to be at least six-two, with shoulders that spanned six hands across. He was supposed to be the governor's aid, but he could easily pass for his personal bodyguard, or an undercover hit man. Trevor just hoped that, when everything came out, he wouldn't fall on Wallace's bad side.

"The governor will see you. He is in his office." The intense mountain stepped aside and allowed Trevor to enter. "I'll show you the way."

Trevor didn't comment, but he nodded and followed the other man through the house.

"This better be important, Lewis." The gravely tone of the governor's words signaled Trevor to his location in the room.

The governor wasn't behind his desk where Trevor expected him, but instead was seated in one of two wingback chairs positioned in front of the fireplace. The embers crackled in the hearth as the governor sat dressed in a thick burgundy robe, which covered his striped pajamas. His legs were crossed at the knee, and black house shoes graced his feet.

Trevor heard the sharp sound of the door closing behind him, sealing his fate. "It is, sir. Otherwise, I would've chosen a more appropriate time."

"Humph." Douglas Hatcher looked at him; one eyebrow held a slight arch, and his lips rolled inward as concern etched his features. "Have a seat, Trevor. I prefer not to have a crook in my neck tomorrow as well as being exhausted."

Taking the empty chair, Trevor rested his body on the comfortable cushions with a heavy sigh. He took a moment and focused on his own fingers, bridged across his abdomen. *This is it.*

"It must be heavy. You look like you're holding the weight of the world, or expecting your hands to walk away."

Trevor looked up and met his father-in-law's gaze. "I've been seeing your daughter behind your back."

Hatcher's eyebrows lifted high on his forehead, and his eyes filled with question. "Are you here to ask for her hand?" he asked sarcastically.

"No. It's a little late for that," Trevor admitted.

He caught the subtle flinch of the governor's shoulder.

"Is she pregnant?" asked the governor, like the calm before a deadly storm.

Trevor's body tensed up on full alert. He was no fool. The governor might appear to be taking the information in stride, but he was Mr. Hatcher first, with a daughter named Tiffany. Any given moment the governor could decide to pounce, pummeling him with his fist. And Trevor wouldn't fight back, not Tiffany's father.

"No. We were married months ago."

"What!" Hatcher roared, his raised foot hitting the floor. He looked ready to vault from his chair.

"Sir, you may want to hear the rest before Wallace comes tearing in here to throw me out." Trevor braced himself. "Or worse," he mumbled the last part under his breath.

Hatcher leaned forward, forearms resting on his knees. "I'm listening. You had better make it quick, Lewis. While you're talking, make sure you give me a good reason why I shouldn't risk jail by wrapping my hands around your throat and choking the hell out of you," Hatcher growled.

Suddenly, Trevor knew what it would be like for a zebra trapped in the sight of a hungry lion. He imagined the zebra would feel the cool chill of its last breath as it slid into its nostrils, moments before the lion pounced.

Trevor looked Hatcher straight in his eyes. "I love her."

That admittance seemed to calm the beast—slightly.

Hatcher leaned back in the chair and angled his head from one side to the other, as if attempting to crack it or release pent up tension.

"Tell me, Lewis. What do you know about love?"

Trevor looked at this man, his father in-law. "I can do better than that. I can tell you everything."

Hatcher held up a single finger. "Before you start, answer this. Did you submit your company's package, before or after you contacted my daughter?"

"Before."

"You won the contract." Tiffany's father eyed him for a moment. "Was Tiffany your back up plan?"

"No. I never intended to use my connections with her."

Trevor didn't know whether he convinced the older man or not. He took the nod Hatcher gave him as a sign for him to begin his explanation. Trevor took a deep breath and watched as Hatcher's face appeared set in stone, carved out with ire. Hatcher's eyebrows pinched in a frown as Trevor dissipated the pure image of Christopher Manning for the second time that night.

Hatcher released a heavy sigh. He rubbed his hands across his face and hair, brisk and hard. Dissatisfaction resounded in the room around the older man. "I'd heard some things about him, but nothing could ever be corroborated. Besides, Christopher has made it no secret that he wants to marry my daughter." Hatcher rose and walked over to the side bar.

He opened up a canister, began to dump several heaping spoonfuls of coffee in the filtered top and pushed the coffee makers ON button. He opened the bottom cabinet, leaned over and took out two mugs.

The machine began to hum. Rich and robust, the scent of fresh brewed coffee permeated the air within minutes.

Trevor leaned forward, placed his forearms on his knees and glanced across the carpeted floor at Tiffany's father.

"Is that what you want, for her to marry Manning?" Cautious, Trevor watched as if the tip of a blade hovered mere inches away from his heart, awaiting Hatcher's response in order to plunge forward.

"No. However, I still have a decision to make." His features were composed, revealing nothing.

"On what?" Trevor tried to stay calm, cool and collected, emulating the other man. But it was no use. What this man thought of him was important. Very important.

Hatcher didn't mince words. "The outcome of this."

Trevor nodded his understanding.

The coffee stopped percolating. Hatcher poured two cups and returned to the seating area and handed Trevor a cup.

Trevor grabbed the hot mug in his hand. Trevor sipped, and instantly his mouth rejected it. Hot, metallic and thick, like brewed dirt. He held it in his mouth, glanced around the room, with a thought of ridding himself of it by spitting it across the room.

"Bad isn't it?" Hatcher took mini sips of the coffee, accompanied by quakes of distaste shaking his whole body.

Before Trevor could think of a response, Hatcher continued, "My housekeeper usually makes it at about five forty-five. So when I start my day at six thirty it is all ready for me."

"Maybe if we added some cream and sugar to it." *Salvage the coffee,* Trevor thought, as he attempted to rise.

"Sit. Apparently nobody gets what he or she wants at," Hatcher glanced at his watch, "one thirty in the morning. Drink up. Now, tell me about your involvement with my daughter."

It all became apparent to Trevor that he had awakened the dragon, and now he would suffer.

Once again, Trevor sipped the dark brew and forced it down his throat. "I was out for revenge. I knew Christopher had plans of marrying Tiffany."

"Everyone knew this."

"But I plotted."

He watched as Hatcher sat in the chair, mug balanced on his crossed knee with one hand. The slight tug at the corners of Hatcher's eyes the only reaction evident.

"And waited. The perfect opportunity fell into my lap when my aunt needed a dancer for a bachelorette party out of town. I used to dance for her while I was in college for extra money."

"Tiffany went to Las Vegas two weeks before her friend Diane's wedding."

"Yup, and I was the main attraction." Trevor planned to be open and honest, but he chose his words carefully, refusing to be disrespectful. "I'm embarrassed and won't go into details about what my plans were—"

"I'm a man, Trevor. I know what actions would hit a man straight in his…pride." A slight smile pulled at the corners of Hatcher's mouth.

Trevor hoped his finding humor in his plan of action was a good sign.

"Well, I couldn't go through with it." Unconsciously, Trevor took a gulp of the liquid and instantly regretted it. He swallowed, frowned.

Hatcher emitted a sound resembling a laugh, but Trevor wasn't sure because the governor continued to sit stoic.

"The next time I saw Tiffany, I was drowning my sorrows. I'd drunk a little more than I should have and came up with the clichéd idea of getting married in Vegas." He drew his hand over his face. "Honestly, if you would have asked me then why I married her, I would have said it was for revenge, but from the first moment I saw her...I can't explain it. I honestly love your daughter. Who knows, maybe I was starting to fall even then."

"Why did my daughter agree?"

"She was drunk."

"Hmm, amazing. Drunk or not, I always believed my daughter held a strong mind and a will of her own."

Trevor didn't know how to take the comment, so he remained silent.

"Is it binding?"

"The marriage has been consummated. Willingly and soberly." Trevor cleared up any doubts Tiffany's father may have had about him taking Tiffany while she was drunk.

"Glad to hear it. So what now? What do you want from me?"

The pressure in his neck and shoulders began to ease. "Nothing. I just wanted you to hear the truth from me. I couldn't call myself a man unless I explained things to you face to face."

"I appreciate that. I would have appreciated it more at seven in the morning, but I can respect you're decision."

"I can understand if you want to call Mr. Patterson and have him cancel the contract."

Hatcher leaned back in the chair and stared into the fire with a serious expression on his face while his one index finger idly stroked his chin.

Trevor's mind began to race in the quiet room. *Maybe I didn't say enough. Did I convince him I wasn't trying to do Tiffany any harm? Hell, who am I kidding? She won't speak to me. Harm has without a doubt been done. He could still decide to kill me. It would take me out of my misery.* Needing something to do to keep his mind steady, Trevor lifted his cup and took small sips, glad his tongue had gone numb to the taste.

"If given the choice between keeping the contract *or* continuing this marriage with my daughter, which one would you choose?"

The question caught him off guard. Which limb do you want mutilated maybe. Never at any moment since coming there did he think he might receive a glimmer of hope of getting Tiffany back. Or at least a chance to talk to her again. Trevor set the cup beside the chair and looked directly at the other man. "Sir, if I had to chose between Tiffany and the contract, it would be her."

Nodding, Hatcher stood with mug in hand. "I'll take that mug." He pointed to Trevor's coffee sitting by the chair leg.

Trevor handed over the vile brew. He took a resigning breath and stood to leave. "Well, sir, I thank—"

"Sit," Hatcher commanded from the side bar where he placed the two cups.

Trevor sat.

"Wallace," Hatcher barked.

The quickness of the door opening didn't surprise Trevor. It just confirmed that Wallace had been standing as sentinel outside. Ready.

Trevor swallowed. He couldn't lie to himself. He was nervous to meet his fate. At any moment, he expected Wallace to grab him and drag him out of the house or into some secret padded chamber a previous governor had installed for moments such as these.

"Get my daughter," he told the human mountain standing in the open door.

Without a word, the door sealed again.

Hell, no. Trevor stood and walked over to Tiffany's father. "Sir, the last thing I need is Tiffany thinking that I came here with more plans and ideas to manipulate her life."

"Trevor, I know that's not the case. I understand why you came here." Hatcher reached out and placed a hand on Trevor's shoulder. "And I can respect a man who stands up, admits he's wrong and chooses to take whatever punishment that comes."

§

"Hello?" Tiffany's voice was gruff and her eyes were gritty and heavy, as if the sandman had thrown his entire bag inside of them.

"I apologize for waking you, sweetheart, but I need to see you."

Her heart began to race. Tiffany attempted to catch a hint of what might be going on, but her father spoke calmly and inconspicuously. "Is everything okay, Dad?"

"Don't worry. It's not an emergency, but it is important."

"Alright, I'll be there first thing in the morning. Good nigh—"

"No, Tiffany, I need to see you now."

She glanced over at her clock. *Four thirty-three. It's only been an hour since I went to sleep.* Tiffany exhaled. "Now?" Of its on volition, her mind flashed to the night her mother was taken to the hospital. She had spent the night at Josephine's house, and her father had called her. He used the same calm, adamant voice. Tiffany pulled her body to a seated position and snapped on her nightstand lamp. "Are you sure you're okay, Dad?"

She could hear him release a breath through the phone.

"Yes, my girl. I'm fine," he said, perceptive and understanding. "Wallace should be there in about an hour."

"If you sent Wallace on an hour and a half drive to get me, it must be *very* important." Tiffany stood up and stretched. "Call your loyal friend and tell him to turn around. I can be out of the house in fifteen minutes, saving us all some time."

"Tiffany, I don't want you driving alone at this time of night."

"My cell is fully charged. I will be okay."

"If you're sure, sweetheart?" he said, his reluctance clear.

"I love you, Dad." Tiffany didn't know what was happening at the Governor's Mansion tonight, but she didn't want to leave anything to chance. Still holding her cell phone, she headed for the shower.

"I love you, too. See you soon."

Seventeen

"Dad?" Tiffany pushed open the door and rushed into the mansion. Anxious, she scanned the room for her father.

"I'm here, sweetheart." Her father walked out of his office and closed the door behind him.

"What's going on?" She moved toward him.

He met her halfway, kissed her on her cheek. "Let's go into the living room."

She viewed the emotionless expression on his face as he turned and headed in the direction of the other room.

This can't be good. Tiffany followed silently behind him.

When they reached the room, her father directed her to sit on the couch, and then he took the seat beside her.

"You're scaring me, Dad. The last time you were this solemn, mother was sick."

Her father reached out and squeezed her hand. "It's not my intention. No one's ill. It's nothing so grave."

"Then tell me what it is." Tiffany looked into his eyes, pleading for understanding.

"Tell me about Trevor Lewis."

"What?" Her heart plummeted to the pit of her stomach. He couldn't have said what she thought. She must've misheard him.

"Trevor Lewis, Tiffany."

She had not. Tiffany dropped her face into her hands, took a deep breath, then glanced at her father. She now understood the look. It wasn't grave but pained. He was hurt. And she had done it to him.

"How did you find out? Let me guess; I was that obvious when I came by your office and saw you two together, wasn't I?" She could have faked ignorance but decided it wasn't worth it. Besides, she respected her father too much to attempt the farce.

He shook his head. "It's not as important how I discovered the truth as how you feel about him."

It was time to let the cat out of the bag. Tiffany sighed and leaned back against the cushions. "At first, I was confused. I felt things for Trevor I've never felt before. Emotions I didn't want to feel." It wasn't strange for Tiffany to sit and talk to her father about personal things. Over the years, he had been her father, mother and confidant.

"Daddy, I'm sorry." Tiffany slipped off her shoes, brought her knees up to her chest and wrapped her arms around them.

"Why, honey? Sometimes you have no control over your heart."

"Maybe not, Dad." She placed her chin onto her knees.

"It may help if you start from the beginning."

"The beginning, huh? I got drunk, woke up to find myself in a strange man's bed and married to him."

"Spontaneity?" His face held a wistful look. "You're more like your mother than even I realized. Not what I expected of you."

Tiffany lifted her head and looked at her father, trying to glimpse traces of disappointment, but found none. "It wasn't what I expected of myself. Even worse, I fell for him. Hard."

He leaned back beside her. "Are you ashamed of those feelings?"

She turned fully toward her father and placed her elbow on the back of the couch. "Tell me something first, Dad. Did he use our relationship to get in your good graces?"

"No, sweetie he didn't," he said with a very curt tone.

"Are you shocked?"

"I am." He frowned. "It's not often you find someone doing the honest and right thing instead of pressing every advantage to get what he wants."

Her hands sifted through her hair. "Well, it really doesn't matter because it's over between us."

"Why?"

"It would have never worked. I don't know if I can trust what he tells me. What's a marriage without trust?"

"None at all."

"Exactly." Tiffany pushed up from the couch.

Her father remained sitting on the couch. "Why didn't you get a divorce?"

She turned and faced him. "I didn't want to embarrass you."

Tiffany's father moved forward with his elbows on his knees. "You know, Tiffany. I have always known you to be a headstrong individual. Determined. When you want to do something, you find a way to do it and allow nothing to stand in your way. You've been like that since you were small."

She folded her arms across her chest. "Well, maybe I've changed, Dad. Lost my determination."

He stood and walked toward her. "You're right. You have changed." He grasped her shoulders. "Not in the way you think. A few months ago, I was very worried about you. I began to fear maybe my career had sucked the life from you."

"Dad, I enjoy working with you."

He squeezed her arms. "Tiffany, I have no doubt about it. But you need your own life."

"Dad—"

"Let me finish, sweetheart. When you and Josephine opened up the business, I was excited. I thought, here is the perfect chance for Tiffany to find herself outside of my job. Honestly." He dropped his hands and looked at her. "I felt a little trepidation about not having you by my side."

Tiffany missed his warmth. The security.

"But you never stepped away. I even reduced your schedule of events with me. Opting to go alone rather than have you accompany me. Finally, over the last few months, I began to notice you spending more time at your company, coming into your own. I believe Trevor was responsible for it."

Tiffany wanted to deny it. She wanted to blame Trevor for her hurt and confusion. Not reward him for pushing her to follow her own dreams and desire. But that's why she loved him. He had made her find herself. He made her press through all the clutter of people and things smothering her life. Everything she thought made her who she was and made her discover the real Tiffany Hatcher. Tiffany's eyes began to burn. She knew tears were imminent.

"Daddy, what am I supposed to do?" The first tear fell. "He's lied to me so many times, about so many things. Half-truths and schemes."

"Tiffany, it's not my place to answer for him. Trevor is the only one who can do that."

More tears tumbled out unchecked.

He pulled her into an embrace. "Do you love him, Tiffany?"

"Yes, Daddy. But I don't know what to do." Her words sounded hoarse and desperate to her own ears.

Still holding her, her father stroked the back of her head. "Sweetheart, I'm so sorry we lost her. I'm sorry that all you've had is your old dad. You haven't been able to witness what fully comes with a relationship between a husband and wife."

Tiffany pulled back, giving her father a watery gaze. "I do remember, Dad. I remember how much you loved her and cared for her."

He chuckled. "Yeah, I did, sweetheart. But we also hid things in our attempt to protect the other. Mostly, I did. Especially in this job. Then your mother would find out the truth, and we'd argue and make up. But we stayed…until the end." Cupping the sides of her face, he said, "There hasn't been a day that has gone by that I don't wish she were here for one more argument. One more chance to make up. One more time to hold her."

Understanding dawned on Tiffany as she recognized the glassy wetness in her father's eyes. "Is that why you never married again?"

"I couldn't. Companionship is fine, but there will never be another Elaine." He brushed his thumbs underneath her eyes and wiped the tears. "I can't tell you if Trevor is your soul mate. The one who will complete you, but I urge you to find out. Be honest with yourself. You don't want to miss it. No matter how long it may last, I figure, if he found his way into your heart, then he can't be all bad. Do you love him?"

"Yes." Tiffany paused. "I love him."

"Then tell him."

"You're right, Dad." Tiffany took a cleansing breath. "It's time I faced this situation head on." Tiffany stepped back with her newfound resolve. "This afternoon I'll call him and—"

"Why wait? He's in my office."

"What?!"

§

Trevor heard the anxiety in Tiffany's voice and the deep, rumbling baritone of the governor's as he greeted her at the door. Their voices had faded over an hour ago when Trevor heard the soft squeak of the door as it opened.

Sitting in the chair the governor had occupied earlier by the fire, Trevor had a clear view of Tiffany as she stood silent in the doorway, clad in dark blue fitted jeans, a bulky sweatshirt and her hair pulled away from her face in a loose ponytail. Fresh faced and void of make-up. An expert, she kept her features schooled, showing none of her internal emotions. At that moment, he recognized how much she was like her father.

Slowly, Trevor stood.

"Good morning, Tiffany." He stood rooted to the spot in front of the chair.

"It would have been better if I'd gotten more than an hour of sleep." She closed the door and moved into the room, standing behind the other chair.

"I'm sorry." Trevor inhaled. Sweet and intoxicating, he could smell her scent across the room. Fresh and clean. She smelled like heaven to him.

The movement of Tiffany gripping the back of the soft leather chair drew his eyes. Hands that in the past had touched and embraced him. *Will they again?*

"Why did you come here, Trevor?" she quietly asked.

"I needed to come clean."

"I need to be able to trust you."

Trevor slid his hands in his back pockets, bowed his head and took a deep breath. "I don't want to mess this up again with you, Tiffany." He raised his head to look at her.

§

The sincere look in his light brown eyes pierced Tiffany in her heart. He reminded her of a puppy in a shop looking for a home. Everything within her yearned to be that place. Yet she remained scared and hurt.

Tiffany shrugged her shoulders. "I don't know what you expect me to say, Trevor."

Removing his hands, he took a step toward her. "Nothing, baby." Trevor ran a hand down his bald head, gripping the back of his neck. "I respect how you feel."

Her heart rate picked up with his nearness. "What makes you think you know what I'm feeling?"

"I'm no fool. I know I hurt you. Hell, I knew it would hurt, but I foolishly thought if I spoke to you I could make you understand."

"Trevor, I could never understand why you used me to get back at someone you hate." She didn't want anything between them, especially not Christopher's name.

He began to speak, but she raised her hand to stop him. She didn't want to argue. "But I've known you for a while now. You're not heartless, Trevor. Otherwise, you could have taken several opportunities to tell someone else about our marriage. The press even. You didn't." Tiffany ran her hands across the smooth furniture, wanting to reach out and touch him. She fought against it, knowing they needed to clear the air first.

Trevor shook his head and stepped forward until his shins were against the seat of the chair. "I should've left you alone. Been smart enough to leave the entire idea of revenge alone. Then I would've never conceived of doing the act in Vegas."

Tiffany reached across the chair and touched his cheek. "I don't condone your methods, but if you hadn't been so drastic in your revenge scheme, we would never have met."

Trevor's eyes opened wide with shock. "Yes, we would have," he said with confidence as he rubbed his face against the palm of her hand.

"How?"

"Because without the knowledge of our relationship, my company won the Heritage contract. We worked hard, and we deserved to win the contract. So on this Saturday when they have the celebration party, we would have met."

Tiffany's hand dropped away and her heart plummeted. "Sure." Tiffany's eyes made a quick arch toward the ceiling. "Without your revenge there would have been no interest in me."

"Are you kidding me?" One of Trevor's knees sank into the seat cushion, he leaned in, bringing himself against the chair. "I tried to fool myself in believing the only reason I wanted you was because of payback. But it wasn't. It was just you. When I stood in that kitchen touching and holding you, the only thing I thought of and wanted was you."

Tiffany closed her eyes, experiencing the warmth of his hands on her face. He smelled male, a sexy blend of musk and spice. Tiffany's heart rate accelerated, and her breathing became labored. Her lips became sensitive from the light brush of his thumb across them.

She opened her eyes. His position in the chair placed them on an eye level, but Trevor's eyes appeared mesmerized by her lips. Tiffany was excited to see the evidence of his attraction.

His eyes lifted and connected with hers. "What about you, Tiffany? What were you thinking about as I held you? Touched you?"

"You." She was breathless, unable to supply her racing heart with the oxygen it needed. Her head was spinning with excitement, and her insides bubbled with joy.

Trevor's hands captured her head, embedding his fingers in her hair. He moved in but kept his lips a breath away. His eyes darkened. "I'm sorry for hurting you, baby. I promise to do my damnedest never to hurt you again." His gaze searched her eyes. "I need to know you forgive me."

Tiffany rested her hands on his forearms. "I forgive you."

Capturing her mouth, he slid his tongue over her lips. Tiffany's mouth tingled as she relaxed and gave him access. He continued to tease her, alternating between nips of her full bottom lip and licking it.

Tiffany didn't know how much more she could take. She felt starved. She needed Trevor inside her, in more ways than one. "Trev—"

Answering her request, he tilted his head and sealed their mouths together. Tiffany feasted as his tongue entered her. Tongues twisted and dueled in and out of one another's mouths.

His arms wrapped around her, warm, comforting and strong. In one swift movement, he lifted her and slid her across the back of the chair. Her hips pressed against the top of the chair.

Their lips broke apart, and the sound of their heavy breathing filled the room.

"Come home with me," he requested.

Her body was on fire. She panted with need. Her feet dangled above the floor as the top of the chair dug into her midsection. "I don't think I can wait that long."

The question in Trevor's eyes was evident as she pushed away from him and off the chair. Stepping backwards, she never broke eye contact with him as she reached the door and locked it.

Trevor stood up out of the chair. "Are you sure?"

Tiffany's eyes dropped to the significant bulge at the crotch of his vintage jeans, her nether lips began to pulse with expectation. "I think we both are."

"Come here," Trevor commanded.

Tiffany obeyed eagerly. She moved forward, grabbed a fistful of her sweatshirt and yanked it over her head, tossing it on the back of the chair.

§

Hot, damn! His knees went weak, his mouth salivated and his body began to tremble. The sight of the sheer pink bra cupping Tiffany's breasts almost undid him. Her chocolate kiss nipples fought against the restraining material, begging for release.

Snap. Tiffany stood before him, opening the button of her jeans.

Trevor's eyes traveled down the supple flesh of her belly and followed her zipper as her hand orchestrated the release of each metal tooth. He dropped to his knees in front of her and pulled off her shoes. As the denim slid down her legs, he tugged them the remainder of the way until she was able to step out of them. *Beautiful and sexy.* He touched her calves, then glided his hand up the silky smooth skin of her legs. He grasped her hips, moved her body forward, placing a kiss on her lower abdomen above the top seam of her matching panties.

Tangy, moist heat. Trevor inhaled Tiffany's arousal. "I'm starving for you, baby." His hard shaft flexed against the constraints of his belt. He physically adjusted, shifting his manhood to a more comfortable position.

He dragged his tongue across the edge of the scant material, tasting her flesh from hip to hip. "Ahh…" Trevor could feel Tiffany's body begin to tremble against his tongue. Backtracking his path, he circled her navel, then dipped inside it and removed her underwear from her body and discarded them on the floor.

"Trevor, I need you," she said shakily.

Leaning back, he looked at her face. Her lips were slightly parted. The sound of her breathing, soft, rhythmic, matched the rise and fall of her chest.

"You're going to get me." Trevor gave her a slight push, causing her body to land in the plush leather chair.

Her eyes opened wide with surprise. A broad smile of anticipation played on her lips. Kiss swollen lips, full and sexy.

Trevor looked at Tiffany, capturing her gaze as he approached the chair. He grabbed her by the waist sliding her bottom close to the edge of the seat. Moving his hands down her thighs, he parted them. Still staring deep into her eyes and smiling seductively, he lifted her legs to the arms of the chair.

No longer denying himself, Trevor feasted his eyes on the vision of Tiffany's glistening sex. Like a piece of ripe fruit, Tiffany was ready to be eaten. His heart raced with excitement, and his engorged shaft stretched to an almost painful length.

He used his thumbs to open the swollen lips at the apex of her thighs. "Hmm, I want to indulge myself in you. Like my own personal Chai latte. Rich and spicy with lots of cream."

She gasped. Tiffany asked between strained breaths, "Who could think of coffee at a time like this?"

Leaning in, he tasted the spicy nectar of her desire. "Ah-ha…slippery wet silk." Excitement overtook him as his tongue flicked, stroked and glided through the cream of her arousal. Masterfully, he slid it around the inside crease, circling the aching bud, purposely not touching it.

Tiffany's hips undulated toward his attentive tongue, as shudders of pleasure caused her thighs and belly to flinch.

"Trevor, pl*eeease*…," she said like a stage whisper in an erotic play: husky, low and sexy.

Answering her request, he captured her firm nub in his mouth, pulling it between his lips and suckling it.

He recognized the fierce bouncing of Tiffany's legs. Her moans were raspy and muffled, as if something kept it from coming out clearly.

Trevor refused to look up, nothing was more important than Tiffany reaching her peak.

He knew what to do to take her there. Inserting two fingers inside her warm center, Trevor tilted them at just the right angle to touch her G-spot. The precise movement of his fingers accompanied by a few twirls and flecks of his tongue catapulted Tiffany into an orgasm.

"Hmm, sweet honey."

Tiffany snatched the sweatshirt down form the top of the chair. Stifled cries came out as her body shook when her climax engulfed her.

As the final quakes erupted from Tiffany's body, Trevor freed his member, sliding his jeans to mid-thigh. One last sample of her sweetness, then Trevor looked up and pulled the sweatshirt away from Tiffany's face.

Wasting no time, he leaned back onto the floor. He gave way to the weakness in his legs and hauled Tiffany down to straddle his lap.

"Ride me, baby."

Tiffany gripped his throbbing erection with her soft hand. The plush carpet was rough in comparison as it crushed under the weight of his bare buttocks.

Feeling her stroke him from base to tip, Trevor blew out a forceful breath trying to keep himself from getting lost in the thrill.

Tiffany slid the tip of his shaft over her wet core. Trevor groaned.

She guided his manhood to her hot center, and with one swift plunge, Trevor found himself embedded deep in Tiffany's tight, moist heat. His neck arched and his toes curled in his shoes.

"Oh, baby." Breathless and rough, Trevor didn't recognize his own voice.

He squeezed her hips as she began to raise and lower herself on his hard member. He found himself mesmerized by the bounce and sway of her firm breasts. Gliding his hands up her back, he leaned her forward, capturing one of her taut nipples in his mouth. Refusing to lose the deep penetration, Trevor bent his knees and lifted his hips, driving himself into the snug seat of Tiffany's desire.

His beautiful wife dipped her back and tipped her hips in the air, availing them both to the ultimate stimulation.

Their scent permeated the air. Breathing became ragged. They moved in unison, pushing and bucking against each other, moving toward the goal of completion.

His mouth released her breasts, allowing her to sit up and take command of their speed.

Tiffany rode him hard.

Sweet ecstasy, Trevor thought as he observed the lovely sight of his wife. "Touch yourself, baby." Trevor's request came out on panting breaths. He was moving with a building force toward his own orgasm.

Without question, Tiffany moved her hand between her legs.

Trevor delighted in the view of his wife pleasing herself. Her eyes slid closed, lips parted in a perfect 'O', and her rhythm became choppy as her progress headed for her second climax. *Captivating*. His wife's hand continued to manipulate her own enjoyment, her finger coated and glistening with her own juices.

Unable to take much more, Trevor gripped her hips. Rotating and gyrating, he drove his shaft into Tiffany.

When Tiffany's body convulsed and squeezed him into passion's grip, Trevor was powerless to stop his own release.

§

Tiffany lay prone on top of his chest while his hands caressed her back as the air cooled the light sheen of sweat on their bodies.

Her heart beat in rhythm with his, slowing down to its normal pace.

"Your father probably needs to use his office some time today."

"Possibly." Tiffany rested her elbow on his chest, propping her chin in her hand. "You think they heard us?" The beginnings of a coy smile twitched at the corner of her mouth.

Beaming a confident smile at her, his hand toyed with the wayward strands of hair that had come loose during their interlude. "Not me…but I'm sure they heard you the second time you climaxed."

With no blush or shame, Tiffany playfully smacked his bare arm. "Ha-ha, very funny."

"It's true. Now we need to get dressed and move this party to my house." Trevor swatted her on the butt.

"Ouch." Tiffany laughed. She ground her pelvis against his stirring manhood. "I'll agree, since I know you're *up* to the task."

Trevor lifted her away from him, before he was tempted to go for another round. The governor would never get his office back if they started again. "That I am."

He kissed her soundly on the mouth and stepped away from her. It took him a few deep breaths and several adjustments to get his pants zipped over his hardening shaft. While Tiffany made quick work of putting on her scattered clothes, he cracked open one of the windows and allowed the crisp breeze to air out the office, removing the subtle scent of their coupling.

Trevor walked over to her, holding his hand out. "Ready?"

"Yup." Tiffany took it and smiled.

Trevor squeezed her hand and led the way out of the office.

Wallace was the first person they saw, seated on the steps beside the office with a legal size yellow tablet on his lap.

As if nothing was suspect about them locked behind closed doors for over an hour, Tiffany said, "Hello, Wallace."

"Mrs. Lewis. Mr. Lewis," he replied without pausing, inclining his head to both of them.

Guess the right hand has been briefed, Trevor thought.

"Where's my father?"

Wallace stood with tablet and pen in hand. "He went to bed over an hour ago. I'll wake him in another hour. Anything I can assist you two with?"

"No. Just tell my dad I'll call him later." She never broke eye contact with Trevor. "Make that, late this evening."

"Will do."

Looking over Tiffany's shoulder, Trevor was impressed at Wallace's constant poker face. Looking directly into Wallace's eyes, so he understood his meaning, Trevor said, "Thanks."

Wallace gave one single nod of confirmation. "You're welcome."

As he and Tiffany left, Trevor had no doubt Wallace understood his gratitude for standing guard at the office door, making sure he and Tiffany remained undisturbed. Trevor wondered if the governor had put him up to it.

Eighteen

Tiffany moved away from her vanity, having added the last touch to her make-up, a chocolate tinted nude lip-gloss. She was ready for Heritage's celebration party to welcome Computer Bytes. Today, she tolerated the spa staff as they buffed, plucked, polished, scented and brazilianized her all for this moment. Walking over to her cheval mirror by her closet, she checked the finished product.

Trevor's a computer whiz and business owner. The thought still caused little flutters of excitement and awe to float around her stomach.

Looking at herself in the mirror, Tiffany was delighted. The new black cocktail dress looked incredible on her, just like the saleswoman had proclaimed. The fitted bodice with horizontal sections of material hugged her stomach and hips, enhancing her curves. The halter-topped dress tied behind her neck and dipped into a V between her breasts, doing a fabulous job of accentuating them. A drop-waist, full chiffon skirt with handkerchief hemline ending above her knees, finished it off.

It was the end of fall. The slight chill of winter's approach nipped in the air, but Tiffany braved the night with bare legs and a pair of open-toe, black sandal heels with straps that went up her calves. Roman style. She had bought them on a whim six months ago, never bold enough to wear them. They didn't "fit" in her father's world, but they did in her and Trevor's.

A small black Piquet handbag completed her ensemble. Inside, it contained her car keys, slim two-fold wallet, a tube of lipstick and a pair of underwear. Just in case they went to Trevor's condominium instead of her house.

Nodding in approval, spiral curls swung and bounced around her head. She'd spent half of her Saturday at the spa and beauty salon, allowing herself to be pampered for the night's events.

"I look good," giving herself accolades, she grabbed a wrap and headed out the door.

§

"Trevor!" Tim Patterson greeted him at the entrance with a handshake and a brisk pat on the back. "Welcome and congratulations once again."

Trevor took a quick look around at the thirty or so people scattered throughout the hotel ballroom Heritage had booked for the celebration. There was no sight of Tiffany or her father yet. Giving Patterson his full attention, Trevor smiled and returned the handshake. "Thank you."

Trevor and Tim made rounds through the party, making introductions between the Computer Bytes crew and the Heritage staff.

After about forty minutes of mingling and cocktails, the band began to play more upbeat music, and people started migrating to the dance floor. Trevor finally had a lull in his evening and took the time to scan the room with single-minded determination—to find Tiffany.

He spotted her coming from the coatroom. She looked sensational. Her dress was purely erotic. The uneven hem around her knees gave flirtatious peeps of her thighs as she walked. Sassy curls surrounded her head, keeping her hair off her shoulders, allowing a clear view of her back. Trevor held vivid thoughts of Tiffany and the dress for later that night. His fantasy included her leaving her shoes on.

"Yeah, erotic as hell," Trevor mumbled to himself.

Her father walked in behind her. Seeing Tim, the Governor spoke briefly to Tiffany then kissed her on the cheek and walked away to his long time friend.

Perfect, Trevor thought as he approached her. It had only been hours since he'd crawled from between the sheets with her, and he wanted her again.

"Hello," Trevor said in a suave way that used to make a room full of women scream.

Tiffany pivoted toward him, the smile on her face breathtaking. "Hi, ba—"

"I don't think we've been properly introduced, but my name is Trevor Lewis," Trevor cut in.

Her eyes lit up with understanding of the game. "I'm Tiffany Hatcher. It's nice to meet you, Mr. Lewis." Extending her hand to him, she gave him a sweet smile, the one she gave the loyal party voters.

Trevor's grasp of it was gentle. "Trevor. I know who you are, Ms. Hatcher. I've admired you many times in the news standing proudly beside your father."

Tiffany was subtle as she slipped her hand from his, continuing her role. "Tiffany. That's very kind of you, Trevor."

"Tiffany," he paused allowing her name to settle on his tongue, "may I ask you a question?"

"Maybe." She tilted her head, curls dangling. "It depends." She paused for effect, adding, "Trevor."

"On what may I ask?"

"Whether it's personal or not."

A low chuckle slipped past his lips. "Only slightly. Working with your father so diligently, do you ever get any time for yourself?"

A coy smile played on her lips. "Yes, Mr. Lew—"

"Trevor."

"Trevor." She paused again for impact, licking her lips.

Heat spread into the crotch of his pants. Trevor watched her chest rise and fall as she inhaled.

"I do," she finished.

"Could I be lucky enough that this is one of those times?" Trevor dropped his voice, allowing his words to touch her like a caress. "Tiffany."

"You're in luck," she said breathlessly.

"Then may I have this dance?" He held his hand out once again to her.

Tiffany placed her hand in his and allowed him to lead her as Jamie Foxx's *Unpredictable* invited them to the dance floor.

Trevor found them a space among the other celebrators. He was impressed with Tiffany, who moved fluidly.

Her hips swayed, arms swung, shoulders shimmied, legs shuffled and feet stepped. Tiffany didn't miss a beat of the music. Just like in the bedroom, her moves accompanied his well.

Trevor danced alongside her, executing a few moves that allowed him to whisper in her ear. "You can invite a sister to the White House, but you can't take the *sistah* out of her."

Eyes bright, her smile widened on her face, Tiffany tossed her head back and laughed.

§

"Hi, sweetheart." The governor kissed Tiffany on the cheek when she and Trevor approached him at the end of the night. "So did you enjoy yourself, Trevor?"

Between work and being with Trevor, she hadn't had time to speak privately with her father all week. After their conversation earlier in the week, she had no reason to think he had a problem with them, but she wanted to be sure. Tiffany watched her father. This was the first time he had witnessed her and Trevor together as a couple.

"Immensely, sir. My team and I are excited about the contract, and by the end of the month, we'll have assessed Heritage's system and business structure and be ready to roll."

Trevor wrapped his arm around her waist, and she turned her body into his. She was no longer afraid to show the world how she felt about him.

"That's great." Her father gave them a smile of approval. "I'm glad to see the two of you have worked things out."

She looked at the man she loved, pride radiating in her smile. "So am I, Daddy."

"Are the two of you heading out?"

"Yes, sir. Looks like a good time; things seem to be winding down."

"We'll see you on Sunday for dinner, Dad." Tiffany stepped out of her cocoon with Trevor and embraced her father. "Thanks, Dad." She placed a kiss on his cheek

Her father gave her a bear hug, like he had when she was younger and needed his support. "You're welcome, Tiff-bug."

Warm heat spread across her cheeks at hearing her childhood nickname. Her father's final mark of approval.

"Good night, Daddy." Tiffany stepped back and grabbed Trevor's hand.

"Good night, you two."

Hand in hand, she and Trevor headed to the coatroom.

§

"What's your fantasy, Trevor?" Tiffany stood in the doorway of the bathroom in Trevor's condo bedroom. Her only apparel—the Roman style strappy black sandals.

Trevor turned at the sound of Tiffany's approach, facing her in the process of unbuckling his black slacks, prepared to drop them to the floor. Her heart rate sped up as she witnessed his hands clutch the sides of his gaping pants' waistband.

Allowing her eyes to roam down his body, she smiled at his toes peeping out from underneath the hem. Tiffany admired the view. Trevor was an exceptional man, in many ways.

Her vision devoured all of his physical attributes. Being around him, she knew he worked out an hour and a half every day, faithfully, except on Sunday. His devotion showed in broad shoulders, strong ripcord arms with bulging biceps and a set of pecks that pulled her like a magnet toward him to touch. *A chocolate dream.*

Stepping forward, she placed her hands on his warm chest. Her hands moved of their own accord, kneading the firm muscles, her body close enough to feel the energy and heat generating between them. Her nipples became taut in response.

Leaning in, Tiffany kissed him. Tiffany took the initiative and mastered his mouth. Tracing his sexy lips until they parted, she angled her head to the side and delved her tongue inside, sealing them together.

189

Trevor's tongue joined hers in the oral love play as the chase continued in and out of each other's mouths.

Breathing laboriously, they stood staring at each other, taking needed gulps of air.

The first to move, she slid her hands down the rippling muscles of his tightly packed abs. Tiffany looked into his light brown eyes and saw his pupils constricted. Still winded, Tiffany whispered, "I don't believe you answered my question, Trevor."

"True Lies." His speech was grated and labored.

Her forehead pinched into a frown. "Not quite the answer I expected."

Eye contact was lost as Trevor's gaze moved across her body in a caress. When he locked his sight on the seat of her womanhood, each breath she took became strenuous to execute.

Not deterred by her shock, Trevor continued, speaking deep and husky. "You know the part in the movie where Jamie Lee Curtis is at the hotel posing as a call girl. Arnold Schwarzenegger is the client sitting in the chair asking her to dance for him?"

"Yes," Tiffany said breathlessly. She'd never considered the movie sexually stimulating, but with Trevor's eyes still holding the intimate part of her body captive, it was near erotic. Her sex swelled and pulsed.

"He just sat there in the shadows and watched her as she moved in the light alone." Trevor looked intently at her as their eyes reconnected. "Men are voyeurs by nature." He shrugged a single shoulder. "To me, the thought of the woman I love pleasuring herself as I watch…hmm."

Wet. Tiffany's own heated wetness pooled at the apex of her thighs when Trevor's words painted a mental vision of his fantasy in her mind.

"We'll have to see what we can do about that fantasy one day, but right now I have a fantasy of my own to live out." Tiffany grabbed his pants from him, letting them slither down his legs to the floor; his boxer briefs followed quickly behind them. "Lay down, Trevor."

Without question, Trevor obeyed, centering himself in the middle of the bed.

Wasting no time, she crawled onto the bed beside him, seating herself beside his legs. Reacquainting her hands with his body, Tiffany glided them all over his upper torso, feeling the light sheen of perspiration on his body as her fingers waltzed down his stomach, pausing only a moment to circle his navel before moving on.

Tiffany heard the catch in Trevor's breathing as she placed her hand on his engorged, steel member.

"I guess I'm not the only one your little story awakened."

"I've been aroused since you walked into the party."

As she began to massage his staff from base to the top, his voice broke. When she squeezed the tip, he groaned. She enjoyed her power over him.

Trevor's chest heaved. "Too much of that and you're going to find yourself in trouble."

"Let's see how far I can go before I push my limit." Tiffany bent at the waist and glided her tongue around his swollen head. She dragged the back of her tongue across its opening, licking his essence. Drawing the crown between her lips, she gave it the attention of her mouth while her hand gripped and stroked his length.

"Tiffany…baa-by…" Trevor's body arched and trembled.

Taking his mumbling pants as a request for more, Tiffany widened her jaw and lowered herself, taking as much of his thick shaft as she could into the moist recesses of her mouth. Trevor's fingers clutched the sheets as she caressed and suckled him. Tiffany reveled in the enjoyment of giving him pleasure.

§

"Grrrgh…." Trevor growled through clenched teeth. Everything in him wanted to explode. He couldn't take another moment of the fierce pleasure of her mouth. He wanted to bury himself between her legs. Needed his entire length buried deep inside of her. Grabbing Tiffany by the shoulders, he pulled her away from his sensitive member and tossed her onto her back. Wasting no time in spreading her legs wide and pulling her knees over his shoulders, he mounted her.

Tiffany let out a passionate scream and arched her hips to meet him.

Fire and Desire

One, two, three thrusts, Trevor slammed into her tight wetness. He squeezed his eyes shut, overwhelmed by the building pleasure as it blinded him. He was trapped in the pure blackness of ecstasy. He knew he was near his breaking point. Tiffany had become an astute pupil in the last few weeks. Her talented mouth had him hovering on the edge. Knowing he was being rough but refusing to be insensitive, Trevor began to slow his pace.

"Harder…don't stop," she pleaded.

Trevor opened his eyes and gazed down at Tiffany who was caught in the throes of sexual bliss, arms stretched over her head, hands flattened against his footboard, held ensnared as deeply as himself.

Giving into her demands, he leaned forward, pressing his chest against the back of her thighs for the ultimate advantage to drive deep inside of her.

Bearing down, Trevor warred with his patience and his need to release. Sweat rolled down his back, his body tensed as every muscle quaked with the desire to climax.

Balanced on the summit of completion, he felt Tiffany's body shudder and seize his manhood in a pulsating vise grip as she reached her peak. Trevor let go; restrained ecstasy caused pain-filled pleasure to slam into his abdomen as he tumbled over the edge.

§

"So Mrs. Lewis, how long do you want to continue with this date-like relationship?" Eyes closed, he rested naked on his back. Tiffany's body was nestled alongside his on her stomach. The plush softness of her breasts lay cushioned against the inside of his bicep. His arm wrapped down around her waist as his fingers drew lazy circles across her bare bottom cheeks.

Trevor loved the after sex moment when the entire world was quiet, and all that mattered was him and Tiffany.

She stretched out on her stomach, legs bent at the knee, ankles crossed and heels pointing toward the ceiling, with her chin propped in her palm as a single finger lightly traced his jaw line.

192

"Are you bored, Mr. Lewis?" she teased.

Trevor could feel the slight rocking of the bed as Tiffany continued to swing her elevated feet through the air.

Trevor's sleepy grin spread across his face. "Never that. Just wanted to know when you'd be willing to wear my ring."

"What ring?" Tiffany's legs stopped mid swing.

Trevor used his free hand to draw the velvet box from under the pillow, placing it on his chest. "This one." Looking at her, he saw her eyes were round as saucers, mouth gaped, speechless. Trevor's heart began to sink. *Maybe she isn't ready to go public yet.* "Are you going to open it?"

Her hands trembled as she reached out and lifted the lid. She drew in a deep breath as her gaze rested on the two-carat emerald cut diamond with baguettes down the sides, accompanied by his and her wedding bands.

Her eyes shone as they filled with moisture. "Trevor…" she whispered.

"Tiffany, for my Tiffany." Trevor swallowed down the lump of emotion in his throat so he could speak without croaking. "Marry me, Tiffany."

"We already are."

"For real, officially and sober. In front of God, family and friends."

Tears spilled from her eyes and the pattern of her words wavered. "Yes. Yes. When?"

Trevor brought her face down to his and rewarded her reply with a kiss. "How about we set the date for after the elections?"

"That's almost a year away," Tiffany shrieked.

Trevor stroked her hair. "I know, but we've been keeping the secret this long. A little longer won't matter as long as we are together. Besides, just like you, I don't want anything to overshadow your father's chances at the Senate seat. I'm a registered voter, you know? I have to look out for my party's interest."

"You're wonderful is what you are." Tiffany leaned toward him, preparing to show him what she thought of his considerate nature.

Nineteen

W e've got problems." Her father met them at the door of the Governor's Mansion Sunday night.

"What kind of problems?" Tiffany stepped into the house, kissing her father on the cheek.

Trevor and the governor gave each other a manly embrace, starting with a handshake and ending with a fierce pat on the back. It amazed her how close the two had become in such a short time.

"Let's go into the office." Her father led the way.

The last time they had been in her father's office was over two weeks ago, but all she could think about as they walked was the heated interlude. Trevor winked, obviously remembering their making up, causing heat to rise in her cheeks.

Tiffany barely noticed Wallace standing over by the window as a silent sentinel.

"Have a seat." Her father directed them to the two standard office chairs on the other side of his desk. He slid into his leather bond captain's chair behind the desk, and then held up an envelope. "We have a problem on our hands," he said, flat and void of emotion.

Tiffany couldn't help feeling a little nervous. Her heartbeat began to accelerate. Whatever was in that envelope had to involve her and Trevor; her thoughts began to race. She looked past the object in her father's hand at him. "How bad is it? Did someone get a picture of Trevor and me at the celebration party?"

Without comment, he tilted the envelope across the table. Trevor took it and pulled out the contents from the opening. Pictures and a white sheet of paper came sliding out.

Tiffany gasped.

"Aww, hell!" Trevor shouted in disbelief.

Tiffany sat beside Trevor, unmoving, unwilling to touch the pictures. Where she sat next to him, she could clearly see each shot as the photographer had captured her and Trevor's drunken marriage at the "Eternal Bliss" wedding chapel. She looked liquor happy as she smiled and wrapped her arms around Trevor as if he were her final lifeline. No dragging, kicking or screaming photos; she was there willingly.

"One hundred fifty thousand dollars in one week, or the pictures go to print. *Governor covers up daughter's drunken wedding.*" Trevor blew out air in a whistle after he finished reading the computer-generated note.

Tiffany shook her head in dismay. "I'm sorry, Daddy. Exactly what I didn't want to happen did."

Her father raised his hand up. "I'm just glad I knew about this before I got these pictures."

Tiffany had to remember to thank Trevor because, while she was trying to keep the relationship under wraps and attempted to end it, he had done the honorable thing and told her father.

"When was the envelope sent to you? Do you know who's responsible for them?" Trevor placed the pictures and note on the desk.

"Yes. We call him Eddie the Weasel. He is a sleazy reporter who freelances between several tabloids; whichever will pay him the most will get the story. When the messenger dropped it off, he said it was a gift from 'The Weasel.'"

"So what's our plan of action?" Trevor took a hold of her hand and squeezed it.

A united front. It warmed her heart to have him next to her in this fight.

"That was my question to you two. Where does your relationship stand?" Her father glanced down briefly at their linked hands.

Tiffany spoke first. "We'd planned to get married. Rather renew our vows after the elections. We were going to start dating publicly now to give everyone a chance to adjust to seeing us together." Tiffany's free hand idly played with the engagement ring tucked underneath her blouse on a gold chain.

"That would have been a great idea. A few people already commented on the two of you at the celebration party, believing it was the first time you had met. But now that the pictures confirm otherwise, it could get ugly."

"So what do you deem to be our best option?" Trevor asked. "I'm sure there's been a few ideas running through your mind since you received this packet."

Trevor's thumb began to make steady circles on the back of her hand. Glancing up at his face, she could see the slight creases in his forehead, an indication to her that his mind was considering possibilities of its own.

Her father's chair squeaked as he leaned back. "I've dealt with The Weasel before, so I'll handle him. But just in case he's working with someone else, or is double dipping his hand, we're going to need to act quickly."

"In what way?" Tiffany sat forward in her chair.

"You and Trevor need to announce your marriage. Soon."

Tiffany grinned and squeezed Trevor's hand. "Great. Trevor and I already have rings. We'll throw a dinner party—"

"More public than that." Her father cut her off. "A press conference."

"Is a press conference really necessary?" Trevor asked.

"Yes, it is," Wallace, the silent mountain, spoke up.

Three sets of eyes turned to him over by the window.

He continued, "You need something public. In a big way."

"Hit the media before he does," her father confirmed. "Even tell the press that you ran off to Vegas to get married on the spur of the moment."

"The ultimate romantic gesture," Trevor finished.

"Exactly." Wallace moved forward and stood behind her father.

Trevor sat silent, looking down toward the floor, tapping his leg. Tiffany and the others in the room watched him. She wondered what was going through his mind. *It is a little late for second thoughts. That train has already left the station.*

Her father was the first to question him. "Trevor, do you have a problem with my solution to this situation?" Her father's tone was heavy.

Glancing up, Trevor looked directly at her father. "No, sir. I realize this is a mess I got myself and you all into, and we have to do what we can to solve the problem." Trevor emitted a heavy sigh. "Since the press release comes out early next week about Heritage and Computer Bytes, that would be a great excuse for why we kept it a secret. We didn't want that knowledge to sway the board at Heritage since you and Patterson are friends."

"That's great." Her father slapped his hand down on the desk and chuckled. "The last thing we need is them using that angle and thinking something shady may have been going on. Quick thinking, son."

Tiffany saw the glimmer of light that appeared in Trevor's eyes at the endearment her father tagged onto the end of his declaration. *Son.* That word meant something to Trevor. She knew he'd lost both of his parents by the time he'd graduated college. Neither of them had lived to witness his success. There was his aunt, but it was something about the approval of a parent that just couldn't be replaced.

"Thanks." Trevor's voice sounded thick and strained.

The issue resolved for the time being, her father rose from his desk. "Now, let's go have that dinner."

As they exited the office, Tiffany hung back. When her father and Wallace turned the corner to the dining room, she grabbed Trevor's hand.

"What's up, honey?"

"Trevor, I didn't want to say anything to my dad. But I think Christopher might be behind this reporter."

"Why?" Trevor's eyes were dark, intense, and he took on an ominous tone.

"During my father's annual barbecue, Christopher and I got into a…" Tiffany searched her mental thesaurus for the perfect word, "…verbal altercation, shall we say. He made a few threats I thought were empty. But in light of what is going on now. I think he may have some-thing to do with it."

"Did he touch you?" Trevor stepped to her, his shoulders drawn up tight, tension evident in the clenching of his jaw.

Territorial, protective, echoed in Tiffany's head. A warm sensation spread over her body. "No."

Trevor looked at her, his eyes searching, as if he were attempting to discover if she concealed the truth from him. Satisfied, he leaned forward, embraced her and placed a quick kiss on the side of her forehead. "I'll take care of it."

"Trevor—"

"Don't worry; it's my job to look out for your welfare." Wrapping his arm around her, he nudged her forward. "Now, let's get in the dining room before your father sends Wallace after us."

Tiffany laughed. "We definitely don't want that."

§

Everything was set and planned. At the end of the week, Wallace would notify specific members of the press and inform them that there would be an impromptu announcement by the governor and his family. They would be contacted at the last moment so as not to tip off Eddie the Weasel.

Trevor had confidence that the governor and Wallace would orchestrate the conference exactly the way they wanted it to go, but it was his job to take care of Manning.

It was time for him and Manning to have a man-to-man talk.

"You've really sunk to a new low, Lewis," Manning said when he walked into the underground parking garage and spotted Trevor leaning against his own car, with his feet crossed on the broad yellow line that separated their cars. "Stalking, is that your profession now?"

"Ferreting out rodents, more like it." Trevor didn't change his nonchalant pose. The muscles in his shoulders burned with restrained tension, and his hands itched with the urge to wrap themselves around Manning's throat.

Manning's nostrils flared. "Well, I wish I had time to quibble with you, but I'm a busy man. Nothing you would know anything about." Manning headed for his driver's side door.

Trevor blocked his entrance. "I'll be out of your way in a moment. I have a few things to discuss with you, first."

Manning stopped dead in his tracks. "Don't take me for a sucker, Lewis. Last time you got in a lucky punch. I've beaten guys bigger than you at the boxing club for play."

Straightening his posture, Trevor stood facing Manning. "Give me another reason. Any reason to beat you until you have to find a new hole to breathe through," Trevor barked at the other man.

Trevor could hear the grinding of Manning's teeth and witnessed his eyes pulling in at the corners as the other man gave him a fierce assessing look.

"Back off," Manning spit out.

"You got it wrong, buddy boy. It's you and your lackey that are going to back off." Trevor jabbed his finger into Manning's sternum. He drew a small bit of pleasure from seeing the other man wince. Not as much as he would had he hit him.

"You don't know what you're talking about." Manning tried to get around him. "Playing on dangerous ground, Lewis. Watch your back. Because you're headed for a rude awakening."

Bucking toward Manning, Trevor saw him flinch regardless of his verbal bravado. Trevor still remembered the joy from the last time he and Manning had an encounter, and he'd punched and laid him flat. But it was times like this he had to restrain himself and be the bigger man.

Shoving Manning against his Corvette, Trevor walked past him. Out of the corner of his eye, Trevor caught sight of a pink piece of paper as it fluttered from Manning's suit jacket pocket. With a bit of prestidigitation, Trevor reached out, scissoring it between two fingers and palmed it. Feeling the prickle of the slip of paper as it stabbed at the inside of his palm, Trevor glanced down.

In the blink of an eye, Trevor looked down at the mini sized note. "North West, now" was the only thing written in block style angry strokes.

In that same blink, he expertly flipped it over to the plain back to make sure he wasn't missing anything else.

Pivoting around, Trevor held the slip out to Manning. "You dropped—"

Manning turned from his car and snatched the paper from Trevor as anger flushed his face, practically turning his yellow complexion burgundy. "Stay out of my *damn* business!" he roared.

Lifting both palms up in a "no harm, no foul" gesture, Trevor leaned back against his own car. He folded his arms across his chest to hide the clenching of his fists because he would have liked nothing better than to beat the man to a pulp, but in situations like this, restraint always worked best.

Trevor said, in a low deadly tone, "Stay away from Tiffany, and that includes your secret pet, too. You *lost* Manning; stand up and take it like a man for once."

Manning's face pinched in a sneer. Opening his car door he yelled, "Tiffany made a mistake by getting involved with the likes of you, Lewis. But I'm going to be the one who bails her out of it. Then her and her father's debt of gratitude will be owed to me for cleansing them from the likes of you."

Trevor scrunched his brow, tilting his head in confusion. He never understood people who held onto something that wanted to be free. "Why would you go through so much trouble to attain maliciously someone, who doesn't want you?"

"It's little people like you, Lewis, who will never truly understand politics. It's all part of the game."

"One day it will bite you in the end."

Ignoring him, Manning got into his car and slammed the door, revving his engine. He backed out of his parking spot with squealing tires against the painted garage floor and pulled off.

Trevor quickly got into his car and cranked his engine. "I don't know why you'd be in a hurry to meet someone on the North West side of D.C., but I'm about to find out." Trevor reversed his vehicle, shifted into drive and guided his car toward the exit ramp.

Twenty

Trevor reached the exit of the garage, perplexed with indecision about which direction to go until he spotted Christopher's vintage Corvette headed up the road where the street numbers became larger.

"You've got guts. I'll give you that, Manning." It was dusk out, and soon it would be dark. Not many D.C. natives were brave enough to head to the North West side after the streetlights came on. People who lived and worked in the area were the exception to the rule.

Trevor continued his clandestine pursuit, keeping a block's distance, so as not to tip off Manning. He followed him up and down streets tagged by alphabets and numbers, until Manning turned into the parking lot of a pool hall located on 14th and K.

"Who do you possibly know in this district? Why are you here, Manning?" Trevor mumbled.

Trevor traveled up the street, slowing his car, staring into his rearview mirror, making sure Manning entered the building. He was surprised to see Manning without his jacket and tie. Manning was no fool. His Bill Blasé suit would have stuck out like a sore thumb. On a brother in this neighborhood; it shouted money.

Once Manning was inside, Trevor backtracked and parked two stores away. He secured his car and checked around him. It wasn't dark yet but getting close. Jeans and a button-down shirt helped him to blend in better than Manning's apparel. Rolling his shoulders back, his gait was brisk but confident. He only hoped whatever business Manning conducted wouldn't be long enough to get the cars stolen before they left.

A few pedestrians hustled by him to their destinations, not pausing as they passed him. He walked past a vintage record store before reaching the door where Manning had entered. Eight Ball was the name of the establishment etched on the glass window. He strolled by with nonchalance. On the side of the building he searched for a side door or an employees back entrance. He'd prefer not to be spotted by Manning or whomever he was meeting.

Trying a side door and finding it locked, Trevor moved on toward the back alley.

"What in the hell do you think you're doing calling me at work?"

The sound of Manning speaking in a grated voice stopped Trevor inches away from the back corner of the pool hall. Taking a risk, Trevor flushed his back against the rough brick wall. A dumpster sat right at the back corner of the building, a barrier between him and the mystery meeting. Slipping his hand into the back pocket of his jeans, he pulled out his flip-top cell phone. Opening it, he placed the ringer on silence, and then switched it to camera mode. Easing it around the corner, Trevor prayed the black cased phone wouldn't be spotted in the dark.

"You're not the only one taking a chance," the other man pointed out.

"It's a greater threat for me," Manning barked.

Trevor held the phone out just far enough to see who was around the corner. At first, when Trevor looked into the mini screen he could only see the back of Manning as he stood in the shadows beside the backdoor, until a short stocky man stepped closer to him directly underneath the overhead lamp.

"Yeah, but I'm the only one who will go to jail."

Who is he? Trevor wondered.

"Tough," Manning said impatiently, crossing his arms over his chest. "I don't have all night. What's your news?"

Selecting the button on his phone, Trevor turned off the flash and selected the capture choice. Pulling it close to him, he closed it and returned the cell phone to his pocket. Not wanting to chance either man seeing it.

"Did you hear something?" The short man sounded nervous.

"Yeah, your time running out," Manning whispered.

Trevor strained to hear, doing his best to decipher the men's low tones.

"Something's going down."

Trevor could almost feel the anxiety of the short man.

"Like…what?" Manning asked, sounding broken and rough, as if he were speaking through gritted teeth.

"I was at the mansion working on Sunday, and Miss Hatcher and Trevor came over."

"Tiffany always has Sunday dinner with her father."

Manning had planted a spy. The mystery man worked at the mansion? Trevor ran a few faces through his mind, trying to place him, but came up blank. He was glad he'd taken the picture and hoped it came out clear enough for the governor and Wallace to recognize the man. He almost felt sorry for him. Almost.

The shorter man must not have gotten a reaction from Manning because he emphasized the next word. "Together. Embracing."

"Is that what you brought me here for?" Manning sighed more than said.

He knew. Somehow Manning found out about Tiffany and me. Either the word had already gotten out, or Manning was working with the reporter as Tiffany suspected.

Straining his ears to hear more, Trevor listened.

The short man remained silent for a moment longer. Trevor figured the short man had realized the same thing he now understood.

"No. They had a meeting in his office. I stood outside the window, trying to see, but that damn mountain blocked my view."

Trevor laughed silently, thankful to the "mountain."

"So you have nothing for me?" Disappointment laced Manning's words. "I'm out of here."

Loose gravel crunched under shoe soles headed in his direction. Glancing around at the few cars in the side parking lot, Trevor had nowhere to hide quickly without someone seeing him. His body braced with expectation of meeting Manning. Prepared to back away, he froze when he heard Manning's next words.

"Don't touch me," Manning snapped.

The short man must have grabbed Manning.

Surprised, Trevor had never heard Manning speak without using his self-assured politician voice. Like Tiffany, he was learning more and more about his fellow alum every day.

"Some guy named The Weasel had a package delivered. By the look on Wallace's face, it wasn't a 'Thinking of You' card."

"Are you sure?" For the first time that night, Manning didn't sound so confident.

"Yes." Excitement permeated the short man's tone. "Earl...Andy...Eric."

Trevor heard a slapping sound, like flesh against flesh. He figured the short man palming his forehead trying to remember.

"Eddie. Damn it. That bastard's burning both ends."

Trevor's mind began to race. *Had Eddie tried to extort money from Manning as well, or was he taking Manning's money for the info, then reselling it?* Trevor continued to listen.

"You know him?"

"Every government official worth their salt knows of him." There was a small pause, then Manning finished. "You leave him to me."

"Whatever you say. What do you want from me?"

"Nothing. I need you to lay low for a while. People are on to you." Manning directed. "And *you* lead to *me*...we can't have that. It's time for you to find a new place of employment."

"No problem. I had a few days off anyway. I won't even be missed. It's perfect timing."

"Great. Don't call me. I'll contact you."

"You sure you don't need my assistance?"

"No. I know just how to muzzle this dog."

At that moment, the side door opened and a gaunt older man came out stumbling and singing to himself. Trevor made a quick pivot, grabbed the side door, slipped inside and pulled the door shut behind him.

twenty-one

S o do I get an exclusive scoop or what?" Liza Wilkerson asked eagerly, phone obviously pressed firmly to her ear. She was the editor for the society and entertainment section of the *D.C. Chronicle*.

"Who am I speaking with?" Tiffany bluffed, hoping she could buy herself some time or think of a quick idea to put the editor off.

"It's me, Tiffany darling. Liza Wilkerson." Liza's country drawled, syrupy sweet, singsong voice came clearly through the receiver.

"I'm not quite sure I know what you're talking about, Ms. Wilkerson." Tiffany sat down on the corner of her desk. She had been on her way to Josephine's office to go over some of the end of the quarter stats when she answered the phone.

"Don't you Ms. Wilkerson me, Tiffany dear. I've known you since your fifth birthday and your father was running for Congress."

Only if known was another word for track and report. "Liza, what can I do for you?"

"Like I was saying, Tiffany. I want the scoop. Who is the gorgeous guy you have been seen around with over the last couple of weeks?"

Tiffany could almost hear her panting with excitement on the phone.

"Tiff, are we still—" Josephine came walking into her office.

A single raised finger stopped her friend's words.

Josephine lifted an apologetic hand to her mouth, silencing herself.

"There's nothing to tell." Tiffany waved Josephine forward.

Her friend sat in the chair next to where Tiffany was propped against her desk.

"Tiffany, *please*. Don't think I'm going to believe that for one moment."

"Liza—" Tiffany started.

Fire and Desire

"Darling…" Liza went on as if Tiffany hadn't spoken. "I'm saying linked arm in arm."

At least she and Trevor knew that their plan to become more public with the relationship was working.

Tiffany sighed. Liza Wilkerson was at the top of the game of society gossip. She should have known if Liza was calling personally, then she had a reliable source. Or more than likely the story was big enough since she wanted her hands in it. Tiffany decided it was best to be honest, especially since her father was planning a press conference some time soon. Having Liza on their side would do wonders to counteract anything The Weasel divulged. "Liza, I'm going to trust you…" Tiffany allowed the weight of her words to saturate the atmosphere, "…and tell you that there is a relationship between myself and this man. But I won't go into any further details. If you trust me and not print or reveal anything, then within the week you will have all you need for your article."

"Most reporters wouldn't be able to say this, but I believe from my years of being in this business I have earned a lot of people's confidence. We have a deal. Your news within the week for my silence."

"Thanks, Liza." A weight rose off her shoulders.

"Can I get an exclusive?"

Tiffany laughed. Liza hadn't made it as head of her division for nothing. "I'm not crazy enough to promise you that."

Chuckling along with her, Liza finished by saying, "A journalist has to try."

"Yes, she does."

After farewells, both women hung up.

With a hard and long burst, Tiffany exhaled air from her lungs.

"That bad, huh," Josephine said from her quiet position in the chair.

Tiffany looked at her and smiled. "Honestly, I will be glad when it's over, Jo."

"When is the press conference?" Cross-legged, Josephine continued to lean back in the chair, the picture of relaxation.

Placing her hands flat against the desk, Tiffany slid herself across the desk until the back of her knees bumped the edge. "Dad is supposed to let us know."

"I've said it a million times before, Tiff, but I will never envy your position. Living in the limelight…" Josephine shook her head.

"I wouldn't wish it on anyone either."

They shared a grin of understanding.

"How are you and Trevor?" Josephine wiggled her eyebrows at her.

An instant chortle bubbled out of Tiffany's mouth. "A lot better than you and Ruben since I haven't heard any wedding plans."

Josephine dropped her head in the palm of one of her hands and groaned. "I know. I know." She raised her head; a wisp of a smile graced her mouth. "Things are going well and we've had the discussion, but I'm dragging my feet for the time being."

"Why?"

"Because the business is doing great. Now that you're able to come on board practically full time, I'm moving toward being agreeable to the offer."

"Jo, I'm sorry. I know everything for this company has leaned heavily on your shoulders in the past. If I haven't said it enough, thank you."

"You would have done it, too, if the situation were reversed."

Tiffany had never felt more blessed for their friendship than she did at that moment.

"You know, Jo, Trevor and I were planning a real wedding before this entire Weasel stuff started. Now we're just going to have to come out with the marriage. But I want you to know, I was going to ask you to be my maid of honor."

Jo stood with one hand on her hip and the other wagging a finger at Tiffany, her gestures full of faux indignation. "Of course you were going to ask me. Who else could take that honored position? I've been your best friend since kindergarten, and if you think for one moment you're getting away with not having me by your side because some slimy no good for nothing reporter is out to make some cash…" Jo paused, folding her arms and rolling her eyes at Tiffany, "…you better think again, sister."

Holding up both of her hands to ward off chastisement, Tiffany laughed until tears streamed down her cheeks. "Okay, Okay...I get it." Placing a hand on her chest, Tiffany released a calming breath. "So what am I supposed to do to make it up?"

Smiling, Josephine folded her arms across her chest. "Well, allowing me to throw you and Trevor a wedding party is one way. Of course, I'll give the toast so there is no doubt about my position at the function."

"You got it." Tiffany launched herself off the table and hugged her best friend.

§

"Hi, honey," Tiffany propped her cell phone between her ear and shoulder as she continued to pack up her briefcase. Excited to hear Trevor's voice, her heart raced and her knees turned to jelly with thoughts of the evening to come. "How is your day going?"

"I'm on my way. How long until you finish up at work?"

"I'm getting my things together now. Want to meet at my place or yours?" Tiffany zipped up her brown, three-compartment leather Samsonite case and held it beside her leg. She was ready.

"You're closer to home at your office. We'll meet at your place."

Tiffany heard the distinct sound of cars and horns blaring in the background. Even at this time of night, people were rushing to get somewhere.

"Sounds great. Are you hungry?"

Trevor's groan came loud and clear through the phone. "You bet I am."

Tiffany snickered, and then said seductively, "Well, I'll see if I can find something to satisfy you."

"Baby, don't do this to me. I'm sure it's hazardous to drive in my condition." Trevor blew out air slowly, as if attempting to calm himself.

Loving the affect she had on him, Tiffany smiled secretly. "I want you to get to me safely, so I'll see you soon."

"I love you."

The sound of those words always made her heart stop for a moment, sent warm tingling sensations racing down her arms and curled her toes.

"I love you, too." Tiffany said softly.

The conversation ended and she cradled the receiver and proceeded out the door. She took a page out of Jaunice's book and went to the stairs instead of using the elevator. She felt high and exuberant. At lunch, she had gone to an international boutique and picked up another sexy nightgown to add to her collection. The midnight blue creation was made of pure schappe silk. The gentle frayed material had tickled her skin when she tried it on. *This will start the night off just right.*

Leaving that boutique, Tiffany had darted down the street until she located the next store. There she'd picked up her main outfit of the night…something that would remind Trevor of how they'd met.

A coy smile played across her lips as she anticipated Trevor's reaction when he saw her in it.

Giddy, she removed her cell phone from her purse, called a local restaurant that was on the way to her house and placed an order for pickup.

§

"Honey, I'm home."

Tiffany heard Trevor call out from the front of the house; her heart rate accelerated, and her cheeks pulled her lips into an excited grin. *My husband is home.* Mentally or verbally, the word husband sent a frisson of heat racing across her spine.

"I'm in the kitchen, babe." Tiffany finished pulling the food from the carryout bag, then turned to the cabinet to get plates to serve it on.

"Sweetheart, I need to talk—"

She knew the instant Trevor walked into the kitchen, from his audible intake of breath.

"Tif-fany…" her name came out on a breathless whisper of adoration.

Glancing over her shoulder, Tiffany's body began to tremble at the intense look Trevor was giving her bare skin. The floor length peignoir was sleeveless and conservative in the front to the point of lying against her collarbone. But the back was an entirely different matter. It opened, revealing the full length of her spine, stopping underneath her love dimples at the base.

"Do you like what you see, Mr. Lewis?" Tiffany began to turn toward him.

"Don't move."

Heavy, sexy and smooth as French silk, Trevor's voice trailed over her skin as if he'd touched her. Tiffany found it hard to fill her lungs with oxygen. Her chest rose and fell with each laborious breath. She watched Trevor saunter closer to her in a slow and purposeful stride.

The dishes made a clatter, as they slipped from her hands to the countertop in front of her. Tiffany didn't even consider whether they had become damaged or not. Her focus was on Trevor. Trevor alone.

She watched his pace, anxiously considering how many steps before she would feel his hands on her skin.

Four steps away. Her sex became full between her legs, pulsing and responding as if stroked there. She squeezed her thighs to stifle its yearning.

A noise came from Trevor, as if he were conscious of her action and the cause, the sound was substantial, guttural and deep, the force of it resonated around the kitchen as if pushed through clenched teeth. She bit her lip to keep from crying out in response. Two steps from her.

A cloak, the heat of his body draped around her, causing her knees to become weak. She leaned forward against the marble, placed both palms flat on its cold top and took a breath. A cleansing breath to regain control of her senses, but Trevor was there, standing behind her. His nearness caused her lungs to seize the air when his lips captured the curve of her neck in a kiss.

Her legs wobbled. She would have crumbled to the tile floor if Trevor's arms weren't wrapped around her stomach, pulling her backwards, aligning her with the front of his body. Evident in the hard strength of his manhood pressed firmly against her hips, no illusions.

"This better be your idea of a seduction…"

"How you would react to this gown has been on my mind all afternoon." Tiffany could smell the musk scent of Trevor's cologne, combined with the ethnic seasonings of the Thai food lying on the island, her mouth watered, not for cuisine, but for the nourishment of the only thing in the room that could satisfy her. Trevor.

He ground his pelvis into her cheeks, causing the gown to rub her naked skin underneath, tingling and tantalizing it.

"This is what this stunt is getting you…"

Tiffany reached back, palming his jean clad rear-end, holding him in place. "Good, because it's what I want…" She licked her lips as titillation through expectation of what was to come stitched in and out of her words.

Mouth to skin, Trevor adorned her back with hot open mouth kisses until he reached the material where it lay on her bottom. The hand on the front of her body moved up, capturing her breasts and kneading them. He kissed each silk covered cheek, before he retraced his path with his wet tongue, swirling patterns along her spine. When he slid up the back of her neck and detoured to trail over her shoulder, she was in full pant. Her hands squeezed the forearm of the hand toying with her pebbled nipples through her gown, silently begging. Praying he got the message, she had to have him now; she was on the verge of losing her mind. Searching behind her, she fumbled around in an attempt to locate and undo his pants.

"I need you too, baby," he whispered.

Tiffany, too caught up to speak, her laughter of relief bubbled inside of her when one of Trevor's hands joined hers at his fastenings, freeing him from the restraint of his jeans.

A button unsnapped and metal teeth released as his other hand became busy dragging her gown up her legs to reveal her hips.

"Just like I like it, all natural…" Approval laced Trevor's voice as the cool air caressed her bare bottom.

They were the last coherent words Tiffany heard, for a red haze filled her mind as Trevor's fingers stroked her, discovering the wetness.

"Sweet, mercy—" He gripped her thighs, lifted her leg and slid her knee on the edge of the counter and plunged forward.

She was open, splayed wide for easy access. It was a sexy feeling, and the position aroused her on a higher level. The seat of her desire throbbed with excitement and expectation while his first thrust lifted her onto her toes. She held onto him for balance.

Each gyration caused her hips to arch deeper into his. In and out, her core was on fire and alive. She began to cry out with each breath as he continued to propel himself to the hilt, grinding against her. Her sex squeezed him, attempting to hold him buried inside her. She was on edge, and her only thought was on satisfaction. Tiffany didn't care which one of Trevor's hands held her, or which one now twirled around her clitoris. It was all magnificent.

The thick rod of his sex didn't stop sliding in and out of her slick center as his fingers continued to strum her, both sensations pushed her closer to the brink. She was losing control. Her cries became louder, her head fell forward, and she leaned her forehead on the front panel of the cabinet as one of her hands slapped the polished wood above her head.

Lowering himself, Trevor heightened the level of his penetration until her body quaked between him and the counter, and she shattered in glorious ecstasy, screaming her release.

The vigorous pounding of his hips confirmed he was seconds behind her. Then his body stiffened and roared, joining her in sweet completion.

They were still, hearts pounding, breaths ragged, waiting for the return of sanity. With a feather kiss on her shoulder, Trevor withdrew. Shaking, he brought her leg back down. He staggered away and collapsed on the side of the island.

On shaky legs, she turned toward him, as the skirt of her peignoir drifted down her legs and pooled around her feet.

He lounged on the middle counter, jeans halfway down his hips and his member still thick, laying on his abdomen, pulsing. She caught the cocky smile and wicked wink Trevor gave her. Grabbing the kitchen towel beside her, she hurled it at him.

He began to advance toward her.

"Tiffany…Trevor…?" Her father's voice coming from somewhere on the other side of the kitchen door paralyzed them.

Trevor was quick to action. Grabbing a paper towel, he cleaned, readjusted himself and pitched it in the trash. He stepped to the sink and washed his hands. "No sweat. Everything looks normal. Answer him."

"Normal?" Tiffany questioned in a stage whisper, and then swung around reminding Trevor how low the gown dipped in the back. "How long do you think he's been here?"

"Have no fear. We're married." He kissed her on the lips when she turned toward him. "Besides, your dad used to change your diaper. He's seen your cute, little tushy before," Trevor spoke in baby talk.

Squinting her eyes, Tiffany gave him a cross look. "You know what—"

"Governor, we're in the kitchen," Trevor yelled over her retort. "Go get cleaned up, I'll entertain your father."

"I still have to walk past—"

"Good evening, you two." Governor Hatcher walked into the kitchen at that moment, smiling.

"Hi, Dad, we're just getting ready to have dinner, want some?" Tiffany advanced toward her father to greet him. She was grateful that the skirt was so long it required her to pick it up to walk. Grabbing the skirt of her peignoir and pulling it up high, helped the material gather at the small of her back. *Still revealing, but I get to keep my dignity.*

Her father received the kiss on his cheek. "No thank you, I already ate. Besides, at my age all that exotic food doesn't agree with me."

"Well, Dad, I'm going upstairs for a moment. I'll be right down in a minute."

"Not a problem. Trevor and I will be fine until you return."

Maybe he didn't hear us, Tiffany thought until she caught a flicker of humor in her father's eyes. *Dignity has left the building.* Holding her nose in the air, she exited the kitchen. Hearty male laughter trailed behind her.

Twenty-two

B oy, it's good to know this kitchen will be holding stories from a second generation." The governor walked up to the stool on the other side of the island and sat down.

"Glad to add to the family memories." Trevor felt good bonding with Tiffany's father. Deciding to fix their plates, Trevor cleansed his hands, and then used the dishcloth to wipe off the counter. Reaching behind him, he picked up the two forgotten plates and began to dish out food from the restaurant containers to fill them both. He covered one with a napkin and pushed it to the center. "I know it's your house, but can I get you something to drink, sir?"

"Yes, if there is any tea, I would love some."

"That makes two of us. Your housekeeper makes the best I've ever tasted." Trevor walked to the refrigerator, retrieved the pitcher, moved around the kitchen to get tall glasses and served three drinks.

"You look comfortable, Trevor. At home." His father in-law drank his tea, observing him over the glass.

"I feel comfortable."

Trevor couldn't read the older man's thoughts. As always, the governor was an expert at keeping his feelings guarded until he wanted someone to know what he was thinking.

Prolonged silence filled the room. Trevor began to eat while the governor nursed his tea.

Trevor became alert to everything in those moments, the ticking of the clock on the wall, the hum of the refrigerator and even the night birds calling lovers outside.

"Trevor, I wanted to speak to you and Tiffany together, but since I have you here, I wondered what your plans were for living arrangements.

I know you guys are moving between your place and here until after this mess with Weasel is resolved."

Weasel. Christopher and the short mystery man. Damn, he'd forgotten about the evening's events once he'd spotted Tiffany.

"We've looked around at a couple of houses but have yet to find any that fit."

Trevor watched the governor's chest expand as he took a deep breath, pausing before he spoke.

"Talk it over with Tiffany, but I would be grateful if you two decided to live here."

His mouth dropped and gaped open. Trevor was speechless for a moment. "Are you sure, sir? One day you'll be done with politics and want to retire and have a little peace. By then Tiffany and I may have started having children. Positive you want to be bothered with the noise?"

"Absolutely. One of Elaine and my only regrets is that we didn't have more children before the years of the cancer battles." A momentary hint of melancholy entered his voice. "If you're worried about your privacy, it's understandable. You two being newlyweds and all." He made a loud production of clearing his throat.

Trevor chuckled, getting his point.

"My rooms are on the other side of the house, with a private entrance I can use if necessary. Or I can have a small father in-law house built in the backyard."

"Neither of those options will even be necessary. I'll talk it over with Tiffany, but I don't have a problem with it." Trevor scraped the scraps of food from his plate into the sink disposal, rinsed it and placed it in the sink. "Actually sir, Tiffany has lived here all her life. I was worried she might have problems leaving it. I think it's a great idea. Since I will be doing most of my time at Heritage now anyway, it's very convenient."

"I think she would've adjusted and overcome. But for my own selfish reasons, I'd love it."

"Then we'll let you know." Trevor slipped his phone out of his pocket. "Sir, I'm glad you stopped by tonight. I have something I need to talk to you about."

"I'm listening."

Trevor pushed the buttons on his cellular until he located the photo album. "Look at this picture and tell me if you know this guy." He slid the phone across the marble top.

Capturing the phone, the governor held it up. His face scrunched as he pondered the picture. "He looks familiar for some reason, but I can't place him."

"Well, he works on your staff in some capacity because he has access to what has been going on."

"What?" he snapped. "As in what type of things?"

Tiffany chose that moment to enter the kitchen, wearing flip-flops, jeans and a camisole top. "What's going on?"

"Trevor says that this man works for me and has some information." He tilted the mini screen toward Tiffany. "I recognize him, but—"

"That's Dan," Tiffany interjected.

"Dan?" Both men's gazes snapped toward her.

"He started during your annual barbeque. Todd said he had hired him and a couple other men for the function. Maybe he kept him on after."

"I need to call Wallace. What do you know about this man, Trevor?"

Trevor looked at Tiffany, then returned his gaze to the governor. "I went to talk to Manning, man to man about leaving Tiffany alone. Even though you all have been family friends for years, Tiffany was beginning to feel uncomfortable around him."

"Is this true, sweetheart? Has Christopher been harassing you?"

Placing a hand on her father's shoulder, Tiffany's eyes seemed to plead with him to stay calm. "Yes, Dad, but nothing has happened as of yet. It was just the way he spoke to me after we'd gotten into a disagreement about our future together." Bewildered, Tiffany shook her head. "I don't know who he is now, or if we ever truly knew Christopher in the first place. But I told Trevor I thought he may have something to do with the pictures." She sighed. "I must have been wearing blinders before not to realize how obsessed he was over the public image of *us*."

Her father appeared to relax a little when he glanced across the island top at Trevor. "So what did you find out?"

Leaning forward on his elbows with his hands clasped together in front of him, Trevor repeated what had transpired from the events of the parking garage to the meeting between Manning and Dan.

"So is Christopher behind all this?" the governor asked.

"I don't think so. I got the impression that Dan's job is to follow Tiffany and snoop around the mansion for information that Manning can use to get you to persuade her to marry him."

Trevor eyed the flexing of the governor's jaw. He didn't know if the governor was upset or disappointed. The Hatcher and Manning friendship was ending after a lifetime of births, weddings, barbeques and funerals.

"Dan knew about the packet from The Weasel. He was somewhere around when the courier dropped it off. The little bug even tried to peep in your office window when we all met, but apparently Wallace's broad shoulders kept him from observing anything."

"Good," Tiffany chimed in.

She hadn't said much, and Trevor wondered how she was taking the information about Manning having her followed. He'd ask her later when they were alone.

"At least Christopher wasn't having her followed in Vegas and isn't involved in the photos."

"True, he wasn't involved in the taking of them or sending them to you. But he does know about them and has seen them," Trevor relayed. "I believe he's being blackmailed with them as well. He made a comment about The Weasel 'burning the candle at both ends.' Apparently, this reporter is trying to double dip. Manning told Dan to lay low for a while, and he would handle things."

"The Maggot." Slamming the side of his fist on the island top, Hatcher stood. "I'm going to my study, I need to call Wallace." He turned and held Tiffany by the shoulders. "Don't worry, honey, I'll take care of this mess." He kissed Tiffany on the cheek then headed out the door, pausing, he turned. "The press conference is set in two days. Wednesday morning meet at my office."

"We'll be there," Tiffany and Trevor said in unison.

Rounding the counter, Trevor pulled Tiffany in his arms. "Are you okay with all this?"

"No woman likes to find out she's being followed." Sliding her arms around his neck, she leaned into his embrace fully. "But with you, my father and Wallace looking out for me, what could go wrong? I'm the safest girl in the world." Tiffany smiled.

Her full supple lips drew him. Leaning forward, he kissed her deeply. Tiffany responded to him without hesitation, running her hands up the back of his head. That touch was almost his undoing. Trevor pulled away. "The power you have over me, girl." Taking a breath, Trevor refocused. "Before I get carried away again, how do you feel about living in this house and raising a family here?"

Tiffany's eyes opened wide and her mouth dropped open. "Honestly, Trevor?" A wisp of air came out, light words spoken as Tiffany's eyes searched his.

He chuckled. His wife looked like a little girl given the keys to her favorite candy store. "Yes, sweetheart."

Tiffany encircled his neck with her arms and squeezed. "I'll talk to Dad after the press conference."

Trevor stepped away, so he could have a clear view of her face. "Your father and I have already spoken about it. He actually brought it up. He even volunteered to build a small house in the backyard so we could have our *newlywed* privacy."

Tiffany blushed.

"Yeah," Trevor said, "I'm sure he was here for part of our before dinner activities."

As Tiffany's color deepened, Trevor kissed her on each warm cheek and laughed. *My beautiful wife.* "Sweetheart, I've watched how you acted when we've visited houses and how you walk in with so much hope and leave dismayed. You love this place."

"I do, Trevor. But understand this; any place I am with you will be perfect. I love my father and our family house, but *you're* my husband. Without you, I have no home at all."

Trevor was speechless. He'd given Tiffany himself, filled with pain and revenge, and she replaced it with a real, untainted love.

"Now, Mr. Lewis. If you'll follow me upstairs, I'll show you what I had planned for the rest of our evening."

"I can do better than that." He lifted her in his arms, exited the kitchen and led to her bedroom. *Let the governor worry about the state of the union tonight. I'm going to make love to my wife.*

Twenty-three

"T revor."

His pulse leaped at the sound of Tiffany calling his name, beckoning him into the room. She had stopped him at the door when they arrived upstairs, telling him she needed a few minutes to change.

Now, she was ready, and so was he. Turning the knob, he entered the room. The glow of candlelight softly radiated around the bedroom. The music, ambience and the subtle scent of Tiffany's perfume were all seductions meant to lure him.

He froze. Anticipation rose in his body as he spotted Tiffany.

"What's the matter, Mr. Lewis, or is it, Mr. Fireman? Cat got your tongue…?" Tiffany's words exuded sex appeal.

The sight before him made him speechless.

Sexy, sassy and wrapped in leather. The flickering candle lights danced across Tiffany's body as she lounged in the middle of the bed. One leg draped over the side and the other digging into the mattress anchored by a stiletto heel, lifting her hips into an alluring arch.

Her position caused the fragile hold he had on his desire to boil close to its breaking point, but the cat mask that covered half of her face brought a smile to his lips.

Man, am I in for it tonight.

His eyes followed one of her hands as it drew invisible designs from her breasts to her navel and back again with the tail of her costume.

Words stuck in his throat as he watched the swinging that Tiffany's raised leg had begun.

"See something you like, Trevor?" Her lips arched into a beguiling smile.

He gave himself an internal shake, took a step back and casually propped himself on the doorjamb. He was hot and hard, and she hadn't even touched him yet.

Clearing his throat, he said, "Yes, and I wish there were words to describe you. Sexy as hell just doesn't seem to be enough."

Tiffany bowed her head, but not before Trevor caught a glimpse of the blush on her face.

Ahh, there's my Tiffany. As much as they had both done with and to each other, her natural innocence always moved him.

Back into her role, she rose from the bed and executed a catwalk that turned him inside out. A trembling started inside of him. Trevor clinched his fists to keep his hands from shaking with evidence. *Damn, I'm not going to make it.*

"Well, Trevor, as you can see, I've been a busy little kitty."

"Yes, you have," he replied, his breathing husky and labored, as if he had just finished running a race.

"You're not the only one with hidden talents." She stopped in front of him. "I have a lot of plans for you tonight." Reaching out, she ran the tip of the cat tail across his chest to his abdomen. "All night." She straightened and removed the tail.

Trevor leaned forward as if to give chase, closing the gap between them further, but not bringing their bodies into the contact he desired. Just near enough to allow the warm heat from his mouth to tickle the shell of her ear. "You have my full cooperation."

He smiled; her breath hitched, revealing she was just as affected as he was by their nearness.

Tiffany directed him where to go with a fan movement of her fingers.

He followed.

She pushed forward one of the overstuffed reading chairs into the middle of the floor. "Sit," Tiffany said, her words laced with promise.

Trevor obeyed.

Tiffany moved away and walked over to the stereo, once again demonstrating her sleek catwalk for him.

Damn, that walk is rapidly driving me to the breaking point. As he watched her hips sway, he could imagine being deep inside of her as that rhythmic oscillation guided him toward a blissful end.

Tiffany was nervous, not with fear, but excitement. Her heart held a steady rapid beat, her breasts were heavy and full, and her sex tingled like she'd spent hours in a mint bath. She wanted everything to go right. Her plan was to affect Trevor with desire and wanting, the way he had done the very first day they had met. When he'd danced, turned her on, then brought her to a level of awareness she'd never experienced before while they were in the kitchen.

Yes, tonight is the night, she thought with a smile.

She reached the CD player and selected the music.

When the intro tunes of Ruben Studdard's "After the Candles Burn" began, Tiffany took a deep calming breath, turned and moved toward Trevor, with the saunter she'd perfected as if it were her signature. She blew out the candles in the room, leaving only the two on the nightstands. By the time she reached Trevor, the room held a deep, intimate glow.

She stood before him silently; legs spread wide, not wanting to say anything that would break the tension in the room. She could tell by the swollen bulge in his pants that the remaining candlelight flickering across the black leather suit had the desired effect.

The soulful sounds of the artist permeated the room, her signal to begin.

Trevor watched as Tiffany began to rotate her hips from left to right with the beat of the music. At that moment, he realized the full extent of what Tiffany planned for him. The lighting was subdued to perfection, each flicker of remaining candlelight against her leather costume made him want to beg to see all of her secret places hidden inside.

His eyes followed Tiffany's hands as they started to glide over the exterior of the black suit, touching thighs, hips and waist repeatedly. All the elements of an erotic dance were present, and he knew he was in trouble.

Tiffany's hands moved to her breasts, around her neck and into her hair, which was hanging loose down her back, as she turned and gave him her profile. One of her hands found her breasts, while the other slid down her abdomen, disappeared between her thighs and played. Tiffany's eyes closed as she bit down on her lip. She had the look of euphoria, as if she were enjoying herself alone in a room. Trevor's breath caught in his throat, and his heart beat forcefully in his chest as he watched Tiffany act out his personal fantasy before him. The dim lighting aided and intensified the vision. Up and down, her hand went as her wrist flexed.

Then she opened her eyes and gave him a brazen look.

However, unlike his dream, this was not a solo dance for her pleasure, but one intended to end in a partnership.

…I'd rather see your silhouette once the candles lit…

Tiffany squatted and his world tilted. Holding her hair at the crown of her head, she brought her body up right with slow gyrations. Then down again she went, this time coming up with the aid of one hand touching various places. Tiffany never took her eyes off him. The third time she went down, she released her hair, placed her hands on her stomach, rocked her hips and gradually rose as both hands slid down to the part of her body Trevor wanted most. Trevor could feel the head of his manhood swell and throb. He unbuttoned the top of his jeans for relief. He hadn't felt close to going off in his pants from visual stimulation since he'd hit puberty. But he was damn near close now.

…hold me, baby…keep it coming, baby…'til after the candles burn…

Once Tiffany's body was erect, eye contact was lost as her hips executed several twists until she revealed the full expansion of her back to him. Seized by the desire to remove the outfit and run his tongue down the curve of her naked spine, Trevor stared at the arch in her back. He trembled with excitement when he heard the metal teeth of the zipper and saw the top become loose around her shoulders.

Fire and Desire

Tiffany's hips continued to move sensually, rocking back and forth as she undressed. Trevor watched her with expectation. *Sweet heaven.* Trevor moved his hand down to his crotch and adjusted the demanding bulge in his pants in an attempt to ease the tight fit. She relaxed her arms behind her back. Her shoulders danced a shimmy until the garment slid off her arms and dropped to the carpet. Trevor's breath came out ragged as the head of his manhood swelled even more, something he would have believed to be impossible.

She gave him a saucy smile over her shoulder.

Snap, snap, snap, snap, swoosh! That was the only warning Trevor received before he was staring at Tiffany's bare legs after she removed her pants—quickly. Trevor was impressed at his wife's ability to execute a move that took a couple of months for professional strippers to learn. Tiffany's hips continued to undulate as she stood before him in her knee-high boots and a sexy black thong.

Trevor wasn't sure if his legs would hold him, with all of his blood having raced to his crotch in anticipation, but he rose and began walking toward the object of his affection.

Tiffany saw him coming and turned toward him. Trevor's steps faltered. The soft sway of her bare breasts caught his eye. He was still mesmerized as she lifted her arms above her head, brought her body in contact with his and rolled her hips against his.

Trevor took a deep breath, trying to calm his heated body. He looked at his wife's half-masked face, captured her hips and lifted her. Instinctively, Tiffany wrapped her legs around his hips as he moved toward the bed.

"Why, Mr. Lewis, wouldn't you like to see the rest of the dance I've worked so hard to purr-fect?"

Trevor reached the bed, placed a knee down, and said, "Definitely. I'm just moving your stage and adding a partner." He laid her onto the bed, stood and undressed without ceremony. He heard the intake of Tiffany's breath as he revealed the extent of his erection.

He returned to the bed, opened her legs, advanced up her body, and rested his hips in the juncture of hers.

§

Tiffany didn't have to concentrate on the words of the song, or what she was doing. Being with Trevor had become as natural as breathing. Her back arched as he touched her breasts, kneading and squeezing them until her nipples stood up and begged for attention.

He granted it. Tiffany moved her hands to his head as the heat of his mouth surrounded her engorged peaks. He suckled, flicked, and circled each one. When she didn't think she could take anymore, he proved her wrong.

"Trevor..." Tiffany felt the lips of her sex swell and the moistness increase with every action of Trevor's mouth.

Trevor raised his head, his pupils had constricted with desire and the intense look in his eyes ensnared hers. "Yes, call my name."

He tilted his head and captured her lips in a searing kiss. Tiffany dueled with Trevor's tongue as it slid into her mouth. The taste of him was rich and full. He ran his tongue under the inside of her lips and sent chills down her spine.

Giving her a parting nip, Trevor lowered, alternating between kissing and love bites down her body. He paused briefly, circled her navel with his tongue and sent waves of spasms through her body.

Trevor placed his hands underneath her thighs and took a firm hold on her hips. Her legs splayed wide, Trevor licked one thigh, then the other. Looking up at her, he said, "Now, show me those moves."

Tiffany listened to the music of the next song and gave herself over to it. Her thoughts were on nothing but obeying Trevor's request and pleasing him.

§

Trevor watched Tiffany's hips begin to sway to the music. He looked at the snug material as it outlined the part of her body he yearned to taste. He leaned forward and used his tongue to trace the edges of the garment. Trevor could smell the sweet musk. It was the scent of his woman.

Shifting aside the black cloth, he saw her swollen, glistening folds, then sampled the nectar of her womanhood.

Fire and Desire

Tiffany's breath became labored as his mouth feasted on her. Trevor licked, nibbled and she moaned. He suckled, and her hands grabbed at the headboard. He flicked and she grasped the sheets. Trevor played with her clit, and she cried out. He desired to drive her wild as she had done to him with her enthralling dance.

The sheets pulled as Tiffany began to dig her stilettos into the mattress and bow her back off the bed. Trevor could see she was on the verge of an orgasm as her breath became erratic and her belly trembled. He gave her swollen nether lips one last parting lick. He wanted to have his member buried deep inside of her the first time she went over the edge tonight. He smiled with the thought of how many ways he planned to stimulate her until she reached her peak.

After he repositioned himself on top of her heated body, he placed one of Tiffany's hands on his engorged sex. He gritted his teeth against the pleasure her hands caused as she gripped and massaged him.

Trevor placed his mouth next to her ear and asked, "What do you want?"

She lifted her hips and allowed the lips of her womanhood to give him the first kiss of love. "You, Trevor. You inside me."

Trevor gave her the response she wanted and drove his shaft deep inside of her. Buried to the hilt, as Tiffany arched her neck, cried out and clenched the tight wet walls of her sex around him.

Hot. His manhood was wrapped in an inferno of sensations. He could feel every contraction she made around him. His wife's body was smooth as silk where it touched and surrounded him.

Trevor looked down where they joined and connected. He was amazed to see Tiffany's clit once again swollen and ready for another climax. A smile creased his face and excitement bubbled inside of him at the sight of his wife's desire.

As he ground his hips, pressing himself against her stiff bud, Tiffany's breath hitched, and her body gripped his shaft, confirming his belief.

Tiffany opened her eyes and looked at him, as her lips gave him a soft smile.

"That feels good, Trevor." Her hands moved down his chest, and her thumbs brushed his nipples as they passed.

Exhaling a breath, he bit on his lip to keep himself in check as her body adjusted to his length. Spicy sweet. The scent of their bodies combining was an aphrodisiac to his senses, driving him wild. She was his wife and he craved to be inside of her like his lungs yearned air.

Feeling his wife's body relax and her hips begin to undulate, Trevor started his task of taking them both over the edge. Tiffany wrapped her legs around his waist and eagerly met each thrust and grind of his pelvis. Their groans and moans of passion saturated the atmosphere. They were in harmony.

Her muscles quivered around him. Joining her was his aim. He lifted Tiffany's legs to the top of his shoulders. The position granted them both maximum stimulations as he drove deep inside of her to reach his completion.

Tiffany cried out as she broke through the wall of pleasure. Multiple quakes of her body around his shaft caused Trevor to erupt into ecstasy.

The music ended, and long moments passed before Tiffany's legs slid down his side, and he had the strength to raise himself on his elbows.

He removed the mask from her face and wiped sweat away from her eyes. He smiled down at the woman who accepted him, including his faults. She had taken away the revenge that filled his soul and replaced it with her love. "I love you," he said, still a little breathless.

Tiffany returned his gaze, placed her hand against his cheek, and brushed her thumb across his lips. "I love you."

"Honey, you may want to warn a brotha the next time you're going to do a teasing act like that."

"Why? Didn't you enjoy this?" Tiffany offered a broad smile.

"Yes." Trevor placed a kiss in the center of her forehead. "But the next time, it may kill me."

Tiffany's burst of laughter filled the room.

Twenty-four

"Hi, baby, how's your day been so far?" Trevor spoke into his earpiece as he drove through traffic.

"It's going well. How's Heritage coming along?"

Tiffany's soft voice caused his heart to expand. He'd never known love like what he felt for her. He would be glad when he was able to tell the world she was his, not just dating him, but his for life. "Awesome. All the guys from CB are having a ball creating and designing the systems for Heritage. It's a worthy project."

"I'm glad to hear it."

Trevor imagined her smiling on the other end. He shook himself. He had a task to do and needed a clear head to accomplish it. "Well, I called to let you know I'll meet you at the house, but I'll be a little late. I have something to check on." Trevor attempted to keep his voice light and his words vague. He didn't want Tiffany to worry.

"That's fine. It'll give me a chance to cook. I'll see you later. I love you."

"I love you, baby. When I'm on my way, I'll call you."

"All right. Trevor…" Tiffany hesitated.

Trevor gripped the small phone. "Yeah, sweetie?"

"Be careful," Tiffany responded softly.

"I will." Trevor closed his cell phone with a snap. To tell him to be careful, Tiffany must have noticed something in his voice.

Finally arriving at his destination, Trevor turned into the residential parking section and pulled into a spot that was two rows away from Eddie "The Weasel" Sherman's house but faced his front door. Manning wasn't the only one with connections on the police force. Trevor took a chance that someone with Weasel's reputation for shady activities might have a record. This morning, he had made a call to a friend he used to dance with at EE. Rob had called him just after lunch with the information.

Trevor looked at the townhouse. Three sixteen was his number, but the six had broken away from the top nail, making it appear to be three nineteen. He assumed the number was like that from Weasel's laziness, or purposely done by him. It probably worked in the reporter's favor, bringing him time if someone were looking for him, and depending who lived in the real three nineteen, Trevor was sure it gave The Weasel a greedy opportunity to get a peep at his neighbor's mail on occasion.

Trevor hoped for a chance to lay eyes on The Weasel. He knew the governor and Wallace were taking care of it; he had no plans of messing that up. But it was daunting to know someone was out dumpster diving and taking pictures of him and Tiffany.

Trevor got out of his car, walked to a metal newspaper stand on the corner, dropped in the specified change and retrieved a paper. When he returned to the car, he got in the passenger side, so if anyone saw him, he'd look like he was waiting for the driver of the car to come back.

After an hour, the sun faded and evening set in, and Trevor's luck paid off. A sun bleached red 1998 Toyota Corolla pulled into three sixteen's parking spot. A shaggy brown haired, lanky guy of medium height got out. With his T-shirt and blue jeans, he would have faded into the scenery. *Great for his profession.* Evident in the large camera bag he carried on his shoulder and the two black, kitchen-size trash bags he held in his hand.

"Out fishing for food tonight, I see," Trevor mumbled aloud.

He watched as Weasel's beady eyes scanned the surrounding area before he put his key in his door and entered the dark residence.

"In your line of work, you *better* watch your back." Trevor saw the light in one window come on. He could see a tall rectangular shape and what appeared to be the square frame of the back of a chair. He figured it was the kitchen area. Next, a light came on in an upstairs room.

It was too tempting to knock on the door and confront the sleazy reporter. After about twenty minutes, with no other movement in the house, Trevor prepared to leave.

Before he could get out and switch seats, he saw Manning arrive and park a row away from him. Manning backed his car into the spot, then stepped out of his car and with purposeful strides walked up to Weasel's door.

"Well, what do you know, Mr. 'Soon to be Congressman.' You are very comfortable in the most unlikely places. Instead of sending another one of your flunkies, you decided to handle it yourself. Less witnesses." Trevor chuckled and observed the situation, grateful that Manning had been too preoccupied to notice his car.

Manning knocked on the door three times, made a quick glance over his shoulder and checked the doorknob. Trevor was surprised it was open. Manning quickly stepped in and closed the door.

Is he expecting you?

Trevor used that opportunity to slide over to the driver's side. Fifteen minutes later, Manning came storming out of the house, suit coat and tie skewed. He pulled the door behind him, as if a ghost was inside and hot on his heels in pursuit.

Not watching where he was going, Manning almost stepped on a Teacup Terrier an older woman was walking. The woman snatched the dog up into her arms, giving it a consoling stroke as she gave Manning an affronted look.

Manning stopped, snatched his coat and tie in place. Trevor witnessed the swift expansion of Manning's chest as he attempted to catch his breath. In an instant, a change in the politician's demeanor happened.

Manning gave the woman one of his infamous baby-wooing smiles and apologized to her and the dog, stopping short of reaching out and petting the pooch. Instead, he bowed his head gallantly and continued with his escape.

In a flash, Manning was in his car and gone. Too fast for Trevor to consider trailing, which he'd had no plans of doing.

What in the hell was going on? Trevor pondered the question. If he were a betting man, he would have expected to see The Weasel come storming out of the apartment behind Manning. But nothing.

By the way Manning had looked, he had no doubt a fight or some type of scuffle had broken out.

A foreboding feeling was nagging at his gut. *Something's just not right.*

How far would Manning go to secure his seat in Congress and force Tiffany and her father's hand?

Trevor shook his head. Manning could have had any woman in society, but his propensity to always win and have his way consumed him now just as it had when they were in college. Five years ago, it hadn't stopped until Rebecca had died. *Whose life would it cost this time?*

Curiosity was nipping at his mind. Trevor reached over and grabbed a piece of paper from his center console. On one side, it held a copy of a tester page from a program he was installing at Heritage, and the other side held the information he had jotted down about The Weasel when Rob called. He had gotten the address and phone number of the reporter. When he wrote it earlier, there was no intention of calling The Weasel, but circumstances had changed.

Trevor opened his cell phone and began to punch in the numbers. Halfway through the seven digits, he stopped. If something had happened to The Weasel, his cell number would be in the reporter's phone record.

Instead of blocking the call, he drove to the shopping center a block away from the reporter's residence and used the payphone on the side of a convenient store to make a quick anonymous call to the police, telling the operator a fight had broken out and he was concerned that someone may be hurt. He gave them the residence and hung up the phone after the woman confirmed she would send a patrol car out.

More than enough for one night. Trevor returned to his car and headed toward home.

Twenty-five

When Tiffany awakened the next morning in bed, she was surprised to see Trevor awake and staring at her.

"Good morning, sleepy head." He leaned down and kissed her on the tip of her nose.

Tiffany snuggled her body against his. "You're awful bright eyed. What time is it?" Smiling, she walked her fingers down the center of his naked chest, a purposeful destination. When she reached his navel, she swirled a finger inside.

Trevor's stomach contracted.

Tiffany gave him a surprised look, then touched the warm flesh of his hard shaft. "Well, Mr. Lewis…you are standing quite tall this morning." Wrapping her fingers around him, she began to massage him.

Trevor's breathing increased, and his eyes closed for a moment. "Don't start something we can't finish."

"We have time for anything our hearts desire." Her stroking increased.

He groaned, "We're…press…late…conference…going to be."

Tiffany laughed as the urgency in Trevor built, causing all of his blood flow to descend from his brain, removing his ability to provide literate conversation. "Trevor, it's only…" Glancing over his broad shoulder, she looked at the clock. "Get up. We're going to be late." Tiffany released him, threw back the covers and vaulted from the bed. "We have twenty minutes to get dressed and be on the road to Richmond. Why didn't you tell me?"

Trevor lay in the middle of the bed. "I tried—" He pointed to his firm upright member. "But look what you started."

Tiffany gave him an apologetic look as she headed into the bathroom. "I'm sorry, Trevor. I'll take care of you later, I promise." She turned on the shower and tested it for warmth. "We really need to shower and go."

"You're damn right we need to shower, but you're going to take care of this now." Trevor got up from the bed and followed her into the bathroom.

Tiffany shrieked with delight when Trevor stepped into the shower behind her.

"What are you doing? We don't have time for this." Tiffany wiggled around, grabbed her puff and added gel.

"Of course we do. It will only take a minute." Trevor pulled her into his arms.

Tiffany gave him an affronted look as he worked the soap into a foamy lather. "A minute…?"

The smell of vanilla and apples permeated the area.

Trevor smiled at her evident frustration. "Yeah, don't worry…*I'll take care of you later,*" Trevor added in a mimicking singsong voice as he planted kisses on the swells of her breasts, pulling her body closer to his aroused one.

Tiffany pretended to be shocked but couldn't hold the expression and laughed. "Well, if you're set on doing this, we're going to have to come to some type of compromise."

"Just leave it to me."

And she did.

§

Trevor picked up the shampoo gel bottle and put it in her hand. "Hold this." He lifted Tiffany. "Wrap your legs around me."

As she obeyed him, Trevor leaned her back against the wall of the shower. She arched her back and screeched, "Cold!"

Trevor winked at her, propped his foot on the side creating a seat for her, then held his hand out for gel. After it was filled he began lathering and arousing her simultaneously. He suckled her nipples while he glided his cleansing hands over her back and arms.

Their breath became heavier, audible.

Fire and Desire

Pulling away from her breast, he moved onto her stomach and breasts. As he washed her swollen peaks and taut belly, he kissed her. Thoroughly loving her mouth, he continued to bring them both to readiness.

Moving away from her succulent mouth, Trevor got more gel from Tiffany. He noticed the glassy look in her eyes, saw the rise and fall of her breasts and could feel the purposeful undulation of her hips, her desire in full force.

Taking her even higher, placing his shaft against her heated opening, he started rubbing the soap into her thighs, hips and bottom as he plunged forward. Tiffany's legs tightened around his waist as her hot core clamped around him. He leaned into her and flushed her body against the wall.

As Tiffany met each of his thrusts with arching hips, the water cascaded down their slick forms and danced with scented bubbles at Trevor's feet. Her body squeezed and pumped him like a fist. His bubbly hands moved down her legs to her feet. Grabbing her ankles, he held on as the increasing sexual tension drove him to madness. Deep, hard, quick thrusts took them into oblivion. Tiffany cried out her release as he exploded inside of her.

For a moment, they stayed there as the water beat against the porcelain flooring, slowly recovering. Unlocking her legs, Trevor stepped back and allowed Tiffany's slick body to slide down his as his hands found the last stop needing washing. His hand went between her legs. He gently massaged and bathed her pulsing sex. Tiffany climaxed again.

Trevor placed his lips against her ear and whispered, "You're two to my one…You're right baby…you will take care of me later."

Tiffany bent down and launched her soggy puff at him.

It smacked Trevor in the chest as his laughter erupted into the steam-filled room.

§

"Sorry, we're late, Dad." Tiffany walked into her father's office and embraced him.

Squeezing her tight, her father said, "Don't worry, honey. I already had Helen arrange to have it moved down an hour after what happened last night." Stepping back, he eyed her up and down, verifying to himself that she was okay. "I told Trevor last night. Didn't he tell you?"

Tiffany swung around and caught sight of her husband's mischievous smile. She'd known Trevor had told her father about Dan's lurking, but he'd failed to mention the time change. Lifting her brow at him, she conveyed the message she would get even with him. "It must have slipped his mind."

Trevor stepped forward and shook hands with her father. "Morning, sir. She was sleeping so well I didn't want to disturb her."

"You're so thoughtful, Trevor." Tiffany batted her eyelashes playfully at him.

Trevor grinned broadly.

"Well, I had no doubts she was in good hands." Pulling her attention back to him, her father asked, "Are you all right, sweetheart? If you're not up to this...we can cancel it all together."

"No need to cancel. I'm fine, Dad." Tiffany smoothed her hands down the front of her salmon and cream pinstripe suit jacket. The final image in her mirror said confident and secure. "I'm more than ready to tell the world I'm happily married to this wonderful man."

Her father nodded toward Wallace, who stood beside the door in silence. He opened the door. They all prepared to walk out the door when Helen, a middle-aged black woman with a salt and pepper short natural, walked into the room.

Speech anxious, Helen said, "Governor, forgive me for the interruption. I know you all need to get to the pressroom, but you need to see the newsbreak." Helen rushed to the wall unit, grabbed the remote and turned the television on. "I don't know if you all saw it, but during this morning's report they were talking about that reporter who was found dead in his apartment last night..." She quickly found the local news channel and turned the sound up.

The door clicked shut as they all did an about face and moved to the center of the room and gathered around the screen.

235

"…apparently, Bob, Congressional candidate Christopher Manning was seen at the reporter's house around his time of death." The slender man's straight, brown hair waved in the soft breeze as he spoke into his handheld microphone to the anchorman sitting in a small corner box, answering his questions relayed through his earpiece.

"Dave, this isn't the first time a political figure has been brought in for questioning. I'm sure Senator Manning and his family's law team will have all of this straightened out soon. Any information on what the connection may have been between 'Golden Boy' Manning and the tabloid reporter? Seems like a bizarre association."

"You're correct, Bob, a strange match indeed. The word is that an eyewitness places Manning coming out of the house minutes after the time of death. Furthermore, Dan McRyan, a retired D.C. police officer, came forward moments ago with some new information about Christopher Manning. "

"Well, however this turns out, it will definitely be interesting. Thanks, Dave."

Helen pushed a button on the remote, causing the screen to go black. The room fell silent, for a long moment the only sound heard was the humming of the ceiling lights.

"Helen, please let the press know we will be with them momentarily," Governor Hatcher said, turning away from the wall unit and walking toward his desk.

Helen set the slender black controller down and exited the room.

"Christopher being questioned about a murder." Tiffany was awestruck, looking at her father, she asked, "I'm sorry to say, Dad, Christopher's not the man we thought him to be."

Trevor spoke up as he stepped up to her and placed his arm around her waist. Christopher Manning's life was in the hands of the police now. They had more important things to deal with. "So what's our plan of action for the press conference now?"

"Nothing different. I'm pretty clear about what we should tell them."

"Dad, is that because you think the police have the pictures in evidence and will come out soon?" Tiffany asked, feeling a bit uneasy about the new revelation involving Christopher.

"No. That hasn't been an issue since the day following the arrival of the package."

Tiffany and Trevor's eyes observed the silent mountain as he walked past them to the door. She glanced at Trevor who looked at her, a single eyebrow lifted a confirmation to her thoughts that possibly Wallace was somehow the one responsible for retrieving the pictures and negatives.

"Why do I have a feeling this conference is not what we originally discussed?" Trevor said as he followed Tiffany and her father out of the office.

"You're right, but patience is a virtue, Trevor." The governor led the way to the pressroom, trailed by Tiffany, then Trevor as Wallace brought up the rear.

"A daily practice for me, Governor."

Tiffany could feel his hand squeeze her shoulder, as he continued, "A daily practice."

She wrinkled her nose at his sarcasm as they entered the elevator. With a quick decision, Tiffany slid her rings from her left hand, giving Trevor her band and placing her engagement ring back on her finger. Just that morning, she had removed the ring from the gold chain she wore under her clothes and placed it on her hand, and Trevor had given her the band with a kiss before they left the house. His earlier words echoed in her thoughts. *It's not the way I had planned to give it to you, but I love you and that's most important.*

Now, because of the death of a reporter, they were being given a second chance to do things right.

As the elevator descended, her father said, "When we get in here, I'll begin the conference. You two just stand beside Wallace and follow my lead."

Before either of them could answer, the doors slid open, and they exited across the hall from the entrance of the pressroom. Her father stepped up to the podium among flashing lights exploding through the room from several cameras as Wallace directed her and Trevor to stand along the side out of the lens range. Pretend spectators.

"Good evening, ladies and gentlemen of the press. It's good to see friendly faces in a crowd. My staff and I selected each of you specifically because most of you have been loyal and faithful constituents. I could always count on you to be both objective and trustworthy."

Tiffany noted the warm responses her father's words invoked over the group of anxiously waiting reports. A few nodded and others smiled. As always, Governor Hatcher had a way of making everyone in his presence feel appreciated.

"Thanks for your kind words, Governor. Lester Neil with *Eye on Washington*. Like everyone else in the room, I'm eager to know what this ninth hour call is about. There's speculation that it has something to do with your candidacy for Senator."

Tiffany watched her father give Lester and the other reporters a broad smile as laughter danced in his eyes.

"A smart group of people, you all are." He paused as his gaze traveled the room, connecting with each person of the press. They sat on the edge of their seats, pens poised on mini tablets. "I have decided not to run for the office of Senator of Virginia."

Shock reverberated throughout the room. Tiffany pasted a smile on her face and schooled her features. *No need to let the press on to the fact I didn't know anything about this announcement.*

As a conductor orchestrates musicians, her father selected each reporter, maintaining control over the firing squad of multiple questions. He let them know that after his term of office ended, he would be looking at going back into the engineering business.

Tiffany admired his skills as she wondered to herself why her father would keep his plans from her. They always discussed his plans for his career. A part of her tried to understand his possible reasoning, but the other half of her admitted she was hurt.

"Governor Hatcher, Liza Wilkerson with the *D.C. Chronicle*."

Acknowledging her, her father said, "Yes, Ms. Wilkerson."

Liza, an older woman with frosted blonde hair, stood. "Governor Hatcher, like most have already said, I will be sad to see you go. My question is directed to your daughter." Never one to let a scoop on a story drop, Liza Wilkerson called the attention to her.

Her father grinned and directed Tiffany to stand beside him on the podium. Tiffany walked the few steps to the front of the room with assurance while she ran through her mind a list of possible questions Liza would ask. She knew this was her opening to discuss her and Trevor's relationship.

"Your question, Ms. Wilkerson?"

"Ms. Hatcher, I've been following you most of your life as you've stood by your father in his career; no need to stand on formalities, call me Liza."

"Liza." Tiffany beamed a smile at the older woman.

Murmurs of laughter fluttered in the room.

"Tiffany, for years the public has been awaiting an announcement about a Hatcher Manning wedding. Can you tell us why that never came?"

She had dreaded these questions. After the breaking report this morning, she knew the topic would come up.

"My relationship with Christopher Manning, beyond our friendship, has never been up for discussion and will not be today. But I will say, don't believe everything you read and hear in the news."

Amusement erupted among the reporters.

When the noise level returned to a normal hum, Liza asked, "Do you believe he's guilty?"

Bulbs flashed as Tiffany leaned toward the microphone to reply. "My father and I have been protected by the men and women on the police force for years, and we have the fullest confidence in the law enforcement agency. I *believe* justice will be served, however this plays out in the end."

"Point well made, Tiffany. My last questions are about this new man in your life," Liza stated.

Other reporters chuckled at the plural ending to the word question.

Tiffany made brief eye contact with Trevor who stood proudly along the side. She saw his brief nod and smile. She took a deep breath and reminded herself that Wallace had taken care of The Weasel, so there were no pictures. "I believe, Liza, you're speaking of Trevor Lewis, my fiancé."

"Isn't he the person you were standing beside a moment ago?" Liza was a seasoned professional, her question performed its intent as all cameras swung toward Trevor vying for a good shot of him. "I must add that's quite an impressive piece of jewelry you have on your hand. Have you set a date?"

Camera personnel snapped pictures of her folded hands, motionless at the upper rise at the top of the podium.

Out of the corner of her eye, she saw Trevor incline his head toward her. They had spoken about having a wedding, but the blackmail pictures had put a halt to those plans. *Now the pictures were no more.*

Enthusiastically, Tiffany forged ahead. "Yes, he is and, yes, we have. But forgive us. It's only open to family and close friends."

Performing for the cameras, Trevor blew a kiss at her. Tiffany couldn't stop the heat that spread into her cheeks.

Liza continued, saying, "My research tells me..."

Tiffany's heart plunged. This was the decisive moment. The instant where she would discover whether or not other reporters had been privy to the Vegas incident.

"...that he is the owner of Computer Bytes, and his company is handling a recent contract to develop a network for the governor's old company, Heritage. Is this correct?"

Tiffany could feel cool tingles drift across her spine as she relaxed. "Yes, it is."

"Donald Woodson, Governor, from the *Minute Report.*"

Tiffany stepped to the side as her father stepped back to the podium.

"Mr. Woodson," her father recognized the reporter.

"I'm not sure you would tell us if it did, but did the relationship between your daughter and Mr. Lewis have any influence on your decision to hire his company."

Her father stepped to the side of the podium and casually leaned on his elbow. It was his let's-speak-as-friends pose.

"Now, Mr. Woodson, what kind of *man* would I be if it did? I didn't find out about the relationship until after I'd made my decision. I would have picked his company regardless. By Mr. Lewis being the astute and professional businessman, he made sure his company won the contract without there being a conflict of interest."

"Will you be going back to Heritage, Governor?" A male reporter, standing beside a man holding a camcorder labeled *Washington Sentinel* threw out.

"That and a lot of other things remain to be seen. Thank you everyone for coming, good day." Her father raised a hand, signaling the meeting had concluded.

When the four of them were once again secured inside her father's office, Tiffany approached her father.

"Dad, why didn't you tell me you had decided not to run for Senator?"

Grasping her hands, her father said, "Tiffany, forgive me. I've been very concerned about you. Until recently, I didn't know how you would fare not being constantly by my side. Not because I didn't have confidence in you." He reached up and touched her chin. "You didn't have a lot of confidence in yourself."

Her father's words hurt, but she couldn't deny she had lived in his shadow for years out of comfort.

"You mean, you would have continued in politics for me?" She was flattered by her father's admission.

"Yes, but thank the good Lord, I didn't have to. You and Josephine have built a very successful business, and I'm proud of you."

Leaning forward, she kissed her father on the cheek. "Thanks, Dad. Now for the exclusive scoop…" She held her hand in front of him as if a microphone was in it. "Will you be returning to Heritage in the future?"

Continuing with the play, her father placed his lips above her closed fist, saying, "The discussions are on the table but will not be approached fully for some months when my governor responsibilities have been satisfied."

The four of them enjoyed a laugh as he pulled her into his arms and hugged her.

Epilogue

It had been two months since the press conference, and Trevor had counted every day until Tiffany would be his. No pretense, no lies and no secrets. Today, he and Tiffany would begin their life as man and wife.

He stood at the altar next to Pastor Anthony McKinley, the man he had met the day he went to the church for guidance. He turned out to be the Hatcher family minister. He had come to have a deep respect for the man and his wife, Paula, during his and Tiffany's six sessions of marital counseling. At that time, he and Tiffany had been honest with them about their original vows spoken. Without judging or condemning, the ministerial couple agreed to conduct the ceremony to renew their vows.

Trevor looked to his left and glanced at the mountain standing next to him. His best man. Over the years, he'd worked hard to make his business a success at the sacrifice of developing friendships. Even though he was close to the men he worked with, he had never allowed himself to bond with any of them outside of the office.

He was grateful that while he and Tiffany made the wedding plans and arrangements, his relationship with Wallace had moved to another level. They had become friends and confidants. Wallace had availed himself to Trevor, assisting him at times in his "groom's duties." Trevor had learned over the weeks that, like himself, Wallace had lost both of his parents. Their deaths occurred during his first year of internship with Congressman Hatcher, explaining the bond between Wallace and the Governor.

Trevor smiled at his Aunt Leslie who sat in the front row, as Josephine, Tiffany's maid of honor, and the last of her five friends came down the aisle.

He heard the beginning notes of Jim Brickman's song "Beautiful," the cue for the two ushers who had closed the double doors to re-open them for Tiffany's entrance.

The first sight of her standing in the archway in her wedding gown, holding onto her father's arm, astounded him. He understood how the prince felt awaiting Cinderella. Tiffany was beautiful.

Trevor's chest swelled with pride. Peace settled around him. Their day had finally arrived.

Tiffany advanced toward him in a slow fluid walk as the skirt of her white suit trailed behind her. His eyes never left the transparent material of the veil draping over her face.

Though I've never seen anything as beautiful as you…

Wayne Brady's lyrics echoed the emotions filling Trevor's heart as Tiffany approached him. He was speechless.

She stopped in front of him, close enough for him to reach out and touch her, but he remained in his place.

As the music faded, Pastor McKinley asked, "Who gives this bride to this man?

Governor Hatcher said in a rich baritone, "I do." He kissed Tiffany's covered cheek, then placed Tiffany's hand in Trevor's awaiting one, squeezed them together, then stepped away.

Trevor didn't miss the glistening water in his father in-law's eyes.

He and Tiffany stood facing each other as the pastor began the ceremony. Trevor wasn't sure if it were his or his bride's hands trembling.

The pastor spoke briefly about the biblical purpose and sanctity of marriage. He and Tiffany had decided to forgo the question about anyone having a reason why they should not be joined together in holy matrimony. After all the obstacles they had hurdled to be together, they refused to let another thing or person stand in their way.

"Tiffany, you may give Trevor your personal vows," Pastor McKinley said.

Tiffany gave her bouquet to Josephine, retaking Trevor's hands. Her brown eyes gazed at him through the cloud of her veil. "All my life I've waited for someone I wouldn't have to question whether or not to give my heart to him," she said, voice quivering. "It would just happen as naturally as I breathe."

A tear dropped from beneath her veil onto his hand.

"You came along, Trevor, and changed the way I thought about myself. You stepped in, and I began living." Her voice broke. "I love you, as my friend, my lover and my husband."

"Now your personal vows to Tiffany, Trevor," Pastor McKinley instructed.

The emotions bubbling inside of him earlier squeezed at his throat. He had to swallow several times in order to speak. "I wasn't looking for a friend, but I got you. I didn't know I lacked light in my life, and then you smiled," he said shakily. He drew in a deep breath to regain control. "I never knew I was empty until you filled my life and my heart. I could see I was broken until you made me whole." He pulled their clasped hands against his heart; his throat was so tight, and his last words came out raspy. "With you I learned to trust and believe. You are my friend, my lover and my wife. I love you."

Pastor McKinley directed them through the traditional vows and the placing of the rings, and then said, "I now pronounce you husband and wife. You may kiss your bride."

Lifting the gauzy material to the top of her head, Trevor cradled her face in his hands. Gazing into her eyes, he said, "I love you." Then he wrapped his arms around her, pulled her into an embrace and kissed her passionately amongst the cheers and shouts of joy bestowed upon them by one hundred family and friends.

§

What would you do if you got caught in the revenge you set for someone else?

Fall in love.

Group Discussion Questions:

1. On a whim, Tiffany makes a decision to marry Trevor. Do you fault Tiffany for her drunken behavior?

2. As sweet as revenge is, does Trevor's plot against Manning make him more of a villain because he tried to steal another man's woman?

3. What prompted Trevor to go and see Governor Hatcher in the wee hours of the morning?

4. When Tiffany's father received the pictures from the reporter, why wasn't he upset?

5. If it had not been for Trevor, at what point in Tiffany's life do you think she would have finally broken away from her father's image?

6. Was Trevor wrong in his decision to use Tiffany to fulfill his revenge against Manning? Why or why not?

7. What significant event happened after the Dallas and Redskins game?

8. What traits do you think attracted Trevor and Tiffany to each other?

About the Author

Monique Lamont was born and raised in San Diego, CA, and now currently resides in Virginia with her loving husband and two wonderful children. She loves to travel, read and write. She holds degrees in both education and counseling. She has always enjoyed working with people. Currently, she is pursing her M.A. in English and Professional Writing. Fondly, she holds a membership with Chesapeake Romance Writers.

In her stories, she loves taking the impossible and making it possible, sensual and believable. She has been writing since sixteen and working toward perfecting her skills ever since. In 2003, she published her first novel, *Merger for Life*, while living in Europe. Since then, she has won the publisher's award for her second book, *Double Take*. She went on to publish *Healing Hearts* and *Freedom's Quest* (part of an anthology), and there are many more to come. Visit Monique at her website: http://www.romancingyou.com

She loves to hear from her readers: rmancn_u@yahoo.com

Parker Publishing, LLC

Celebrating Black
Love Life Literature

Mail or fax orders to:
12523 Limonite Avenue
Suite #220-438
Mira Loma, CA 91752
(866) 205-7902
(951) 685-8036 fax

or order from our Web site:
www.parker-publishing.com
orders@parker-publishing.com

Ship to:
Name: _____

Address: _____

_____

City: _____

State: _____ Zip:_____

Phone: _____

Qty	Title	Price	Total

Shipping and handling is $3.50, Priority Mail shipping is $6.00 **FREE standard shipping for orders over $30**		Add S&H	
Alaska, Hawaii, and international orders – call for rates		CA residents add 7.75% sales tax	
See Website for special discounts and promotions		Total	

Payment methods: We accept Visa, MasterCard, Discovery, or money orders. NO PERSONAL CHECKS.

Payment Method: (circle one):   VISA   MC   DISC   Money Order

Name on Card: _____

Card Number: _____ Exp Date: _____

Billing Address: _____

_____

City: _____

State: _____ Zip:_____